YENBO PALMS

A QUEST

by Edward Flaherty
The third novel in "The Landscape Architect" series

What do you think of when you read Yenbo?
Yenbo, the place.
Read and learn.

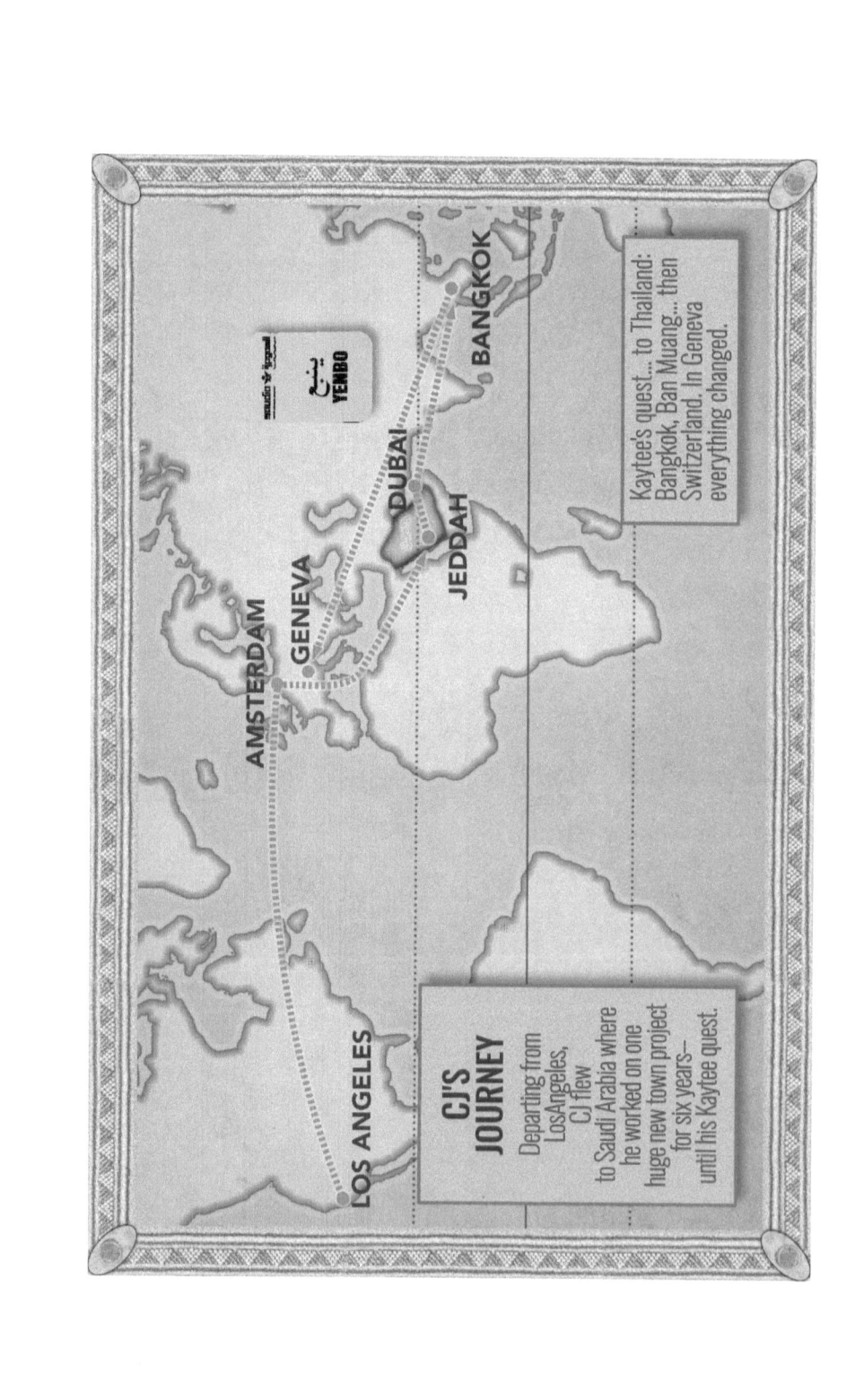

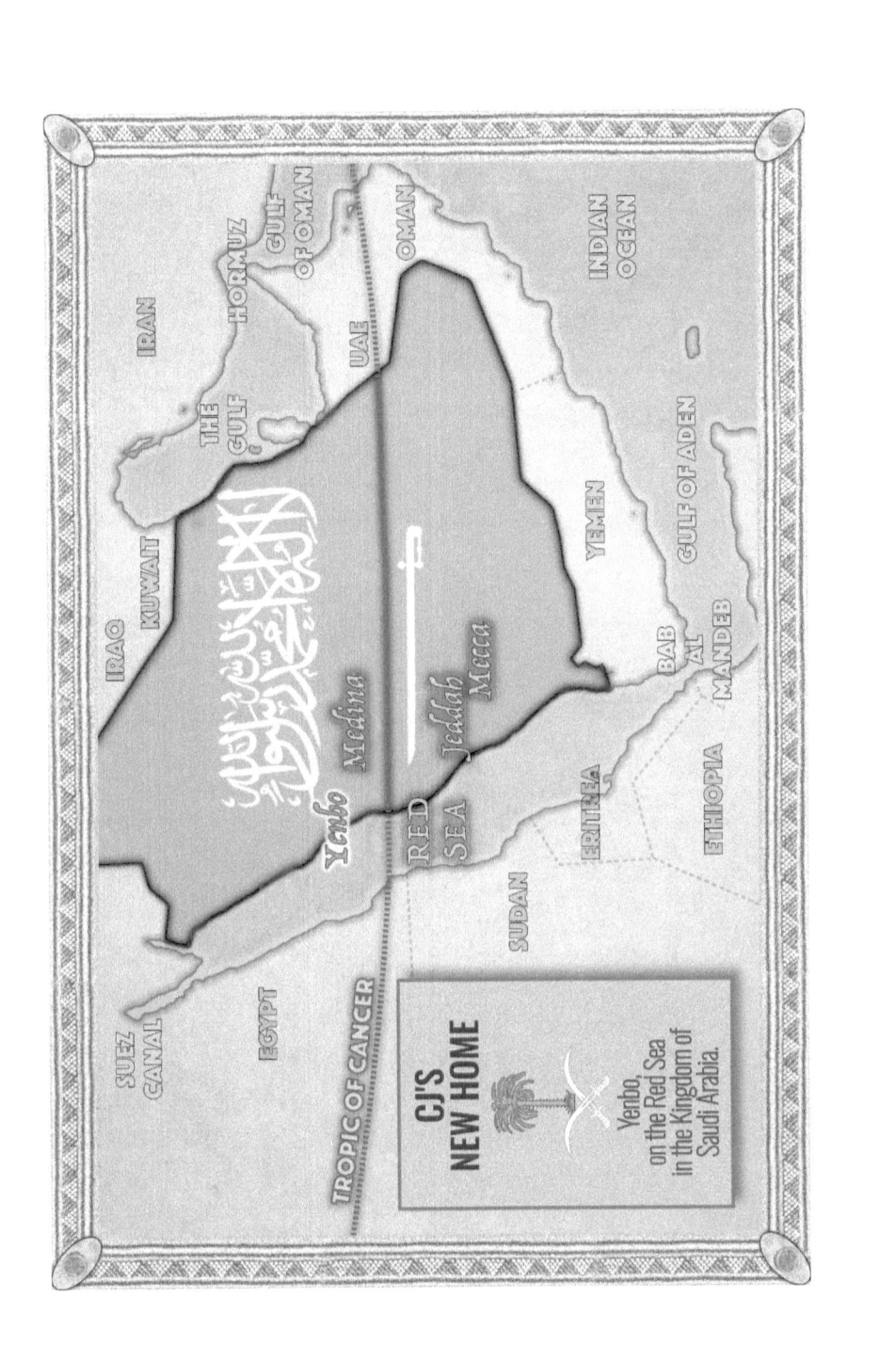

When Kurt, as CJ's executor, took possession of CJ's diaries and design journals, he found six years of diaries, a dozen of them, all handwritten; but the design journals, there were several in A4 size hardcover, looseleaf ring binders. They were filled with hard copy computer print-outs. Kurt found more--plastic sleeves holding memory cards and thumb drives with all of CJ's Saudi Arabian landscape photos.

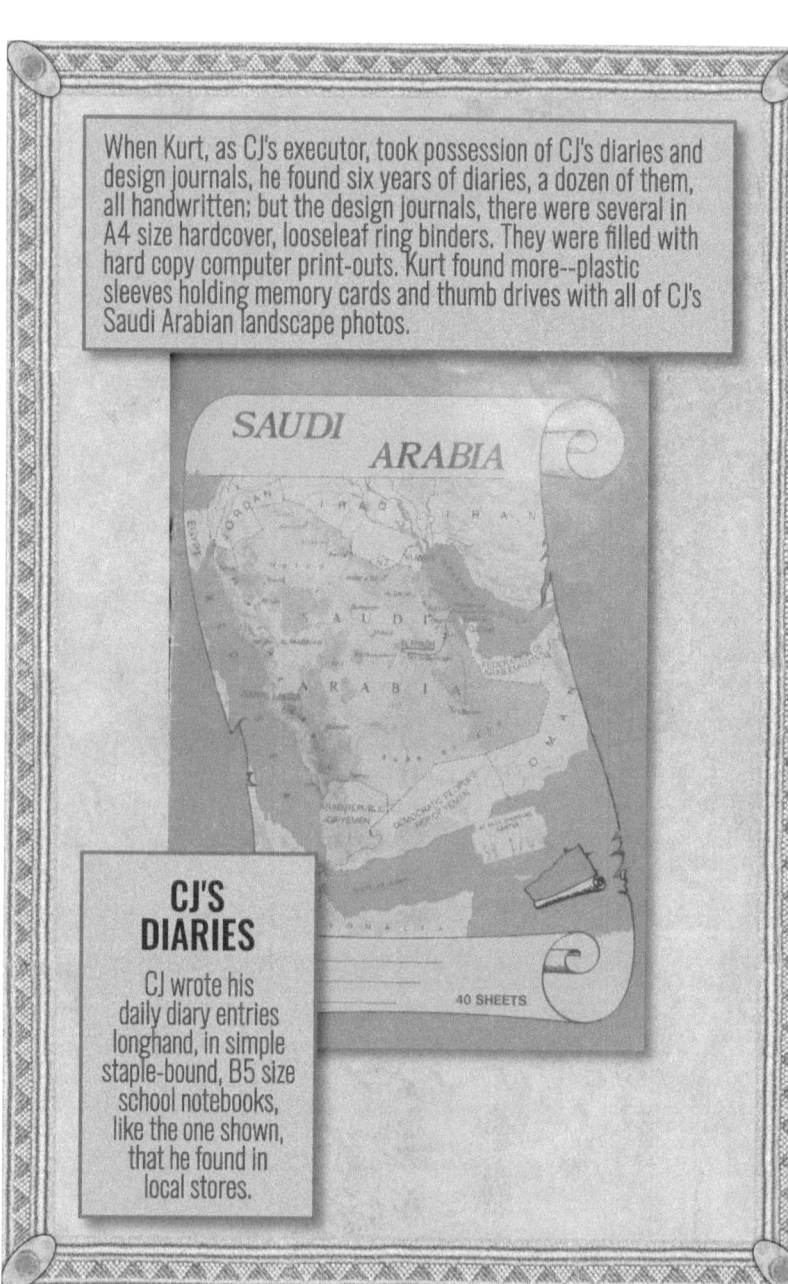

CJ'S DIARIES

CJ wrote his daily diary entries longhand, in simple staple-bound, B5 size school notebooks, like the one shown, that he found in local stores.

Preface

In the late 20th and early 21st centuries the Kingdom of Saudi Arabia made significant investments in its landscape and people. The Kingdom transformed resources from its vast sand and stone deserts. They turned their oil and gas products into energy and water to develop health, education and liveable cities for their people.

CJ, bringing water and gardens to Yenbo, must resolve their uniquely complex environmental, botanical and horticultural problems. In doing so, he buries himself in his work. Why and how did he get there? Had he planned it as a professional move?

After graduation from university, CJ built his landscape architecture career. It was not simple or usual. He returned to the New Mexico landscape where he had grown up; but life had other plans for him. Southern California and W Kurt Milligan re-entered his professional life. Then unplanned-on personal events prompted his move to the Arabian Peninsula. There he found the landscape was way more than his job, way more than he imagined—a most threatening combination: the Tropic of Cancer, the Red Sea and Araby's chimeric desert sands.

It wasn't the green new town or the arid, lifeless deserts that arrested CJ. It was a landscape unseen that beguiled him— mysteries from the past, hidden by the drifting sands.

I'll let California surfer and landscape architect, W Kurt Milligan, CJ's long-time colleague, friend and narrator, set in detail the *Yenbo Palms* context in his foreword.

Edward Flaherty

Foreword

Readers, try to get into this.

In my boutique Santa Monica, California Landscape Architecture office, CJ worked for me. First while he was a student doing his summer internship. Then years later, after he was a licensed and well-experienced professional landscape architect, he rejoined for five more years. We were colleagues for over a decade. We became friends. We had bonds. He was an awesome go-getter.

About seven years ago, when CJ, seeking much larger responsibilities, took on a new job in Saudi Arabia, I agreed to become his Executor.

Then in the last year, all hell broke loose. I received a Special Delivery letter notification that CJ had died in Cairo. Details were scant.

He was a guy, a friend I brought into the world of Los Angeles landscape architecture. Dead? Cairo? What the hell? I was incredulous. Something mysterious... strange aura. My life was about to change. Never figured on this.

Yenbo Palms? It's only the beginning.

Keep your stuff together,

Kurt

Contents

1-W.Kurt Milligan

LAX-Schiphol-LAX

...Kurt explains...

Me and CJ? Here's my take.

CJ left SoCal (Southern California), getting on to eight years ago, to begin his expatriate landscape architecture work. We had been buds—but lots of time had passed. I was busy with my office and he had become little more than a memory... except for his postcards. They were from the places he took vacations—mostly from the UK and the Netherlands.

Not too long ago, I was home in my beach bungalow on Pacific Coast Highway. My view was the Pacific Ocean west to the horizon. Non-stop waves rolling in. I heard them crashing. And, as far as I could see, the sun's rays sparkled and danced... sweet—my idea of heaven on Earth. I had just sat down on my terrace for lunch when my doorbell rang.

The postman had a registered Special D (Special Delivery) envelope for me. It came from Amsterdam. I had no idea what it was. I signed for it.

In the quiet of my bungalow, I opened it up. There were two documents from the legal department of an international Dutch bank headquartered in Amsterdam.

The cover letter was short and direct. It notified me that Christopher Janus was dead. Dead? I choked on my own saliva.

What?! I never dreamt this would happen. My lunchtime appetite disappeared. I sat down and looked at the front and back of each of the two documents. Was it a joke? Was someone

15

having me on? Pulling my leg?

Reality bites. Bitter, it tasted bitter. This reality shocked, stuck in some strange place that made everything else meaningless—took the air out of life. I read and re-read both documents. Sadness. I felt sadness. His landscape architecture career cut short? Unfinished, his career like him and me, unfinished.

The single attachment was a certified copy of the death certificate. CJ had been officially declared dead by unknown circumstances in Cairo—Cairo??—by joint simultaneous declarations from his employer and from both the Egyptian and the United States authorities. Unknown circumstances?? What does that mean, or what doesn't it mean?

I didn't want to believe what I was reading. It didn't seem right. He had been into a huge landscape architecture project in Saudi Arabia. He loved that challenge. That was the CJ I knew. Was I mistaken? I couldn't put any of it together.

I went to my desk drawer to review his most recent postcards. I needed a timeline. Cairo? I thought he was in Saudi Arabia.

He had regularly sent me postcards—but I didn't pay them much attention—threw them in the back of a drawer. Now, however, I was interested. I dug out the postcards. The most recent were strange. They were not his usual.

A year and a half ago, his last postcards came from Thailand and Switzerland. I didn't think too much about it then—just shoved them in the drawer. But now as I thought about it, he had never been to either of those places before. I was still in shock.

His very last postcard came from Switzerland about 18 months ago. So, I speculated CJ had worked approximately six years in Saudi Arabia. Then he, as best I could figure, probably went on some kind of walkabout gig—Thailand, Switzerland— likely ending up in Cairo a month after he left Saudi Arabia.

It was all guesswork, the best I could do under the circumstances. I was stunned. I wasn't really sure what to make of the whole thing.

The date on the cover letter was recent. The date on the death certificate was one month ago. The cover letter asked me to telephone the Dutch bank offices on the first working day after receiving this package.

I made the phone call. The telephone exchange was business-like and brief. My life was changing—faster than I realized.

As CJ's executor, I had to go to his bank in Amsterdam. The bankers verified my identity, then wired the tickets and funds to my account.

In less than a week I was on an international flight—not really my gig. From LAX, I flew direct to Amsterdam Schiphol. I never imagined all the Executor responsibilities on an international death.

CJ never gave me a copy of his will; but the bank did. After expenses, his assets were to go 80% to his mother and 20% to his father. I verified their names and contact details. The bank assured me they would take care of all the particulars. Surreal. Was this really happening?

The will named me as Executor and had further stipulated a generous sum for my use in accomplishing my duties. And as CJ had told me that LA night in Trader Vic's when I agreed to be his executor, his personal diaries and design journals had been bequeathed to me.

Yenbo Palms would begin later. That story was still the farthest thing from my mind. Hell, I had a landscape architecture business to run.

Amsterdam—the BIG thing I learned in Amsterdam—not only was the legal death by unknown circumstances, but CJ's body had not been found. No body was recovered. That threw me for another loop. I was already having difficulty believing he was dead. Now there were no clues or clarity on suicide, accident, murder or... off-the-grid. It wasn't just how and why. It was how, why and if he was actually dead. The confusion and lack of details overwhelmed me. But as Executor I had work to do.

From CJ's safety deposit box in the Amsterdam bank, I took possession of his diaries and design journals and prepared them as accompanied baggage in my return home. CJ's last bank account activity in Cairo was a $3,000 withdrawal seven months ago—nothing since.

But that wasn't all. CJ had a collection of solid gold bangles. The banker told me that it wasn't unusual for Western expatriates working in Saudi Arabia to buy 22-karat gold jewellery and send it home. They had it assayed and confirmed it was 22-karat. They suggested they could sell it locally and add the proceeds to his account for distribution. I agreed. CJ had no financial debts. He was always careful about staying out of the red. No issues in closing out his accounts.

In my three days in Amsterdam I had assisted the bankers in bequeath distribution to CJ's mother and father. CJ had never talked much about his parents. I knew he wasn't close with them. The bank's legal department contacted and handled everything with them. That suited me just fine.

The bankers shared with me contact details of the Cairo authorities and others who had certified CJ's death. And that was it. No additional details.

Before I knew it I was on a flight from Schiphol back to LAX. Finally, I had some time to think through the last two weeks. My emotions ruled. Wipeout—tumbled. I was tumbled and didn't know what to think. I felt the strangest mix of deep sadness with disbelief. Craziness sloshed through my head. Even the flight hurt. CJ—a friend—a loss—big time.

***

The Executor (Kurt)

...Kurt continues...

On the flight home, business class was only half full. I put my feet up, tried to put my sadness aside and review everything from the beginning. When and how did it actually begin? Was he really dead? What had actually happened? And Cairo? Why was CJ in Cairo? Eight years ago, I was just being a nice guy, a friend. Now I was knee deep in an international mystery I knew next to nothing about.

Let me take it from the top.

My name's Kurt, W Kurt Milligan, undergrad in Fine Arts at Berkeley and Masters in Landscape Architecture from Cal Poly Pomona. I'm born and bred Californian. Los Angelino. I love the year round, mild, sunny climate, my Harley, the Pacific Coast sunsets and the surf.

If I have all those every day, I'm happy. Single, getting on to middle age, I'm an old-time confirmed bachelor, dedicated surfer and I love my work. I make my career as a landscape architect and majority owner of a boutique landscape architecture firm in Santa Monica. I handle the books, all the legal stuff, and in my spare time, I oversee design for the firm.

If you can absorb all of that about me, I'd be surprised. It's pretty heavy.

Let me summarize. Berkeley? Left wing, arts. I got into Art Deco. I got into the mix of geometry and glitzy, sweet emotion. Cal Poly? Taught me practical landscape-based landscape architecture. I loved the lines of geographic units, latitudes and longitudes. Showed me how humans simplified the landscape to live on it.

And surfing? Hell, who doesn't like California beaches, the waves, the girls, the sunsets. I blended all those together while managing the design and all the regulatory office admin stuff. Anyhow, all of that was in place when CJ came into my life.

I first met Christopher Janus some 15 or so years ago. He was a student intern for one summer in our firm. The story is long. My memories hurt, so I'll stick to the main points.

CJ came to us first as an intern, I was his mentor. Then some years later he returned as a properly licensed landscape architect. Though he was from flyover country, he settled in pretty well to our SoCal (Southern California) lifestyle. We hired him to oversee project installation, but he also did project management.

Above it all was, I guess, the best way to say it... he had a penchant for design. He liked to call me practical, in a cynical way, until he saw me on my Harley. I told him don't be a stray cat. My Harley is practical out here in the beautiful 365 California sun.

Design had always been important to me. And LA has always been the hub, the nexus of the "latest thing" in architecture/movies/television/media influencers. I knew if I wanted life cycle success from my office, I had to do more than follow-the-leader. In LA competition is intense, fierce. I just wanted to surf, to get by. But I was enough of a business man to know if I slacked I would lose clients. CJ had given my business the design edge it needed. Style, he gave my firm its distinctive LA style.

So, who was this Christopher Janus? Here's how I knew him. After settling in, he became a Los Angeles guy. He had teeth, tan, blond hair. He was slender and cool—that quintessential look, George Hamilton, LA guy. He knew how to talk when he was on his game, but his hair was not quite perfect.

To me, he struggled with an inner noise. Everyone around him felt it. In particular, I could not take it when he pushed his design agenda. Pushed! That was the key offence.

He could always be found drinking Piña coladas at Trader

Vic's looking for design arguments, where he would, to quote Warren Zevon, "... rip your lungs out, Jim". He started things. He looked for trouble. He was a fighter, while also a good guy. But there was something inside him that pushed him to edges, on everything.

Together, we won a lot of SoCal design awards. I loved him for that. He kept my firm on the cutting edge. He knew how to keep his balance when it was important. I credited that to his original roots.

CJ didn't talk a lot about his past, but he had Midwest roots. His dad was born in Detroit when Detroit steel and Detroit autos were proud and strong symbols of American post-WWII success. Detroiters and the Midwesterners in general are known as flyover people; but they are hard-working and dependable. That was CJ's stock.

Los Angeles? That was his mainstream professional career and you can't get any better quality, finer finish or well-wrought craft than Los Angeles landscape architecture. He was all into that.

CJ and I both taught design in the UCLA Extension programs. And I chaired the regional SoCal Landscape Architecture Design Awards Committee.

I am not a traveller, not a tourist. Like I said, I like LA, its climate and my Harley at sunset on Pacific Coast Highway. I can't ask for more. But professional obligations sometimes make us suffer hardships.

My only time out of Southern California has been once a year when I have attended weeklong International Design Conferences in places like Kyoto, Geneva, Firenze. I go to those historic places like a tourist on a weeklong break. Last year I was in Dubai for that same conference, where I gave a talk on Landscape Architecture Design, SoCal Style.

On design, I thought design had become boring. CJ thought landscape architecture was missing the big picture, missing the force, missing its strength. But both of us agreed change was not coming from naïve university graduates.

And he didn't think our commercial work afforded the substantial design opportunities he sought. That's how I knew it. That's the basis of our professional landscape architecture relationship. It worked... until one day.

***

Executor?

...Kurt continues...

One day, CJ asked me to meet him after work at Trader Vic's in the Beverly Hilton, on Wilshire and Santa Monica, in Beverly Hills.

Trader Vic's is the kind of scene—hip, relaxed, in-crowd—that I dig, especially the relaxed bit. I suppose CJ figured he'd fit right in to the LA scene by being a regular there. And he did. He'd been a regular at Trader Vic's for the last five years.

On the evening, I looked around. He wasn't in the middle of the action. I found him at an out-of-the-way table, far from the TV, far from the pulsating entertainment. He was sitting quietly, nursing his Piña colada. I ordered the same. When the waitress came with my drink, he chugged his Piña colada and upgraded to a 151Punch. I questioned him with my eyes. He just sat there looking serious. I wasn't reading him at all.

After his 151Punch arrived, he took a sip and started, "Down deep something has been brewing."

"Bring it on," I said, expecting another tit-for-tat design fuss; but that wasn't the case.

"Kurt, listen. I have to get out of LA. Every discussion, every project anymore is like a broken record—can't find any new paths—feel like a hamster on an eternal wheel. Even my design squabbles with you, which I have often enjoyed—now, they're nothing but a symptom of my tedium—and that's just the surface."

CJ had it going.

"Design 'success', awards, have become meaningless. How many downtown plazas? How many suburban headquarters? How many residences in the Hollywood Hills? Exciting at first; but after five years—boring.

"I need challenges, but around LA, every office is doing the same projects. Not interested in government work. Can't even consider that. Politicians interfering with planning and design. The adage—good 'nuf for gov'm't work—no can do."

"So, c'mon, like what's up," I asked.

He paused for a moment, then began, "We've had our design quibbles, squabbles, out-and-out arguments over the years…"

"So? Old news."

"Seriously! All that led to you helping me get that teaching design gig at the UCLA Extension Program. That was great stuff—made me think through the automatic private practice design routine and turn it into a can-do series of logical steps for beginners. Loved that exercise. Thanks, big time."

"Get to the point, CJ. What's this all about?"

"I'm making a change and I need your help."

"What do you mean? Take it from the top."

"Long story short, I've taken a new job… in Saudi Arabia."

"Wha? Saudi Arabia? Dude, what? Why? This doesn't have anything to do with that time you left our place for six months with another company, does it?"

"No, no… not at all…"

"That always confused me—you wanted more money, bigger projects…"

"Yeah, but those guys had a design project in Saudi Arabia and they were just drafting circles on planting plans—they paid well but it was crap work—had no design or hort realities. That's why I came back."

"When you came back… those were the good days… CJ, when you helped set up that Landscape Soccer League—eight teams. You got our company to team up with Hooters to sponsor the league and each team was from landscape and hardscape firms who bid on our jobs."

"Yeah, that was fun—remind me."

"The league worked because each company had a slew of Mexicans and a handful of Americans. Hooters arranged the refs and cheerleaders. We arranged coolers and beers for each game. Everyone had a blast."

"Oh yeah!"

"We got more quality installations on all of our projects because of that and the Hooters girls—phew—too much—every Sunday afternoon. Good times had by all. What are you talking about Saudi Arabia—give up the Hooters?"

"Yeah, good times. But I have a chance for responsibility, and control of landscape planning, design, construction, operations and maintenance for a new town of 200,000 that is already under construction. I've been looking for bigger projects and this is it. Plus the pay is excellent."

"No kidding?!"

CJ wanted two things. He wanted a big project challenge. He also wanted me to be his Executor.

"Executor? Why?" I asked.

"I have no brothers or sisters. I have no longer any connections with my divorced parents."

"Is that it?"

"Well, frankly Kurt, I've been keeping personal diaries and design journals for years and I'd like to leave them to someone into landscape architecture, into design—someone like you... we've known each other since I did my internship here... so, I was thinking... should something happen to me while I'm out of the country, I'd turn them over to you."

I thought. My landscape architecture work and Manhattan Beach surfing kept me fully engaged. I didn't even think I might have to leave LA to execute the duties. And CJ? Well, I had enough of his way-out design arguments at our office. But, hell, sure, if something happened to him, I could take his landscape architecture design effects. That didn't mean I agreed to wade through his tedious search for design perfection, so....

"Sure, for sure CJ, I'd be glad to." I was thinking that CJ, knowing how much I depended on his design input, wanted me to have his innermost thoughts on design (daily diaries and design journal writings) for reference in my firm. He did have a thoughtful, helpful side to his personality. At least that was my thinking on the day.

"Wonderful," he said, "that's a load off my mind."

Little did I know then that in seven years, courtesy of CJ, I would become engulfed in the strangest international mystery.

In two months' time he up and left LA, after five years of award-winning projects with us. He left for the Kingdom of Saudi Arabia. His explanations didn't help; I never really understood.

Me? I didn't need to understand. I just strapped my surfboard to the side of my Harley, went out to the beach, and caught a couple waves. Surf, sunset and the Pacific Ocean air. My LA world. I was cool, totally cool.

***

I Had to Read

I summarize. CJ was approaching the sweet spot of his career, in his early 30s, and very successful. A landscape architecture design award winner in Los Angeles when, about eight years ago, he just pulled up stakes and left to work in Saudi Arabia.

CJ did have baggage. Despite his awards, many of which helped grow our office, his professional design insecurities often erupted in heated arguments with colleagues in the office. He had deep uncertainties that undermined his professional relationships—could never find the balance.

But after chewing on that a bit, I concluded, "So what?! Every designer has design arguments with other designers!"

He turned his back on his Los Angeles problems. Put that in a basket with his strange attraction to Araby. When he took the job in Saudi Arabia, he looked forward to larger design management responsibilities and the arid desert culture of the Arabian Peninsula. He called it a clean landscape, a new canvas. It's clear he was searching. Tell me he doesn't sound like TE Lawrence!

And there's more. CJ didn't carry on about his past; but from time to time after a long night at Trader Vic's, he would talk about his mother and father.

Listen to this, CJ had serious personal family problems related to his decision to go to Saudi Arabia—even further back—his parents had long been divorced. They both were overbearing. He disowned them. When CJ left LA for Saudi Arabia, it was the final straw. He became persona non grata to his mother and father.

But again, after consideration, I thought, "What was that? Wasn't as if he turned to a life of drugs or crime, joined a cult, or whatever. Was there something he didn't tell me?"

From outside, who can say what happens inside a family? It's popular for people to complain about dysfunctional families. I say a dysfunctional family is normal. Every family has unresolved weirdness somewhere—sometimes out front—sometimes in the closet. Bottom line though—CJ was in deep—deeply imbalanced—deep with insecurities.

And his journals? I had to read them. At first, I did a quick run through them. He seemed to use them like he used his work—a cocoon, a place of shelter—shelter from things that troubled him.

After six good years in Saudi Arabia, everything in CJ's new life came unravelled, setting in motion not just a quest, not just a pilgrimage, but a most unusual series of events.

He appeared to have it all together. He was a problem solver—he fixed things and with style; but his catch, paradoxically, was that the one problem he wouldn't, couldn't solve—his own existential problem—he wouldn't, couldn't touch it!

In his journals, he saw plants as central to landscape architecture. I already had seen this when I worked with him in SoCal. But in his journals he got into it—deep, very deep.

He saw the landscape and garden professions—horticulturists, gardeners, landscape architects, ethnobotanists—were chock full of people determined to make all things plants and humans complicated, way too complicated. In his own words, "people who couldn't tell the forest from the trees".

He was searching for something basic, simple, straightforward and clear. I thought CJ might be on that path.

Nobody had ever written a dummies' guide to plant, garden and landscape design—every book was like a never-ending whack-a-mole exercise.

CJ, despite his professional sparks, his family issues and existential uncertainties, was into something and he was

28

committed. He passed away. Couldn't have been suicide. Death by suicide? Can't be. He wasn't the type. He was 100% into design, landscape and landscape architecture.

**

How?

...*Kurt continues...*

I was smack in the middle of a mystery. CJ had disappeared in Cairo. He had not been heard from. He had not been found. I could do my Executor duties as if he was truly dead. But something inside me told me I should dig a little deeper.

I had put aside 10 days for my Amsterdam Executor work. I began re-reading his diaries and design journals—this time with care. I was able finally to work through the sadness of "losing" a close friend.

His diary entries were carefully dated. He was disciplined that way. But the entries were almost shorthand. They were hastily scribbled down details. He included descriptions of natural and social landscapes. He included events, happenings, settings. While his entries weren't daily, they were frequent. They always included the location, the date, the time of day, and the weather.

His design journals, that is what he called them, were another level altogether. They looked to be smoothly written stories. They filled several numerically sequenced workbook binders. The stories often incorporated his diary details. Sometimes his design journal stories were lucid. I thought perhaps he was building content for a future autobiography.

CJ wrote an introduction to his most recent design journal. He told his inner thoughts. I quote: "...little did I know that diaries and journals would be my way of life. They worked for my jobs and for my own analysis of design and understanding the strange events I encountered in my journeys in exotic landscapes. They became my portal to myself."

Some of CJ's design journal stories were like stubs. They were not fully worked out. He was questioning what he saw in the landscape and what he thought about it. What was clear were his uncertainties; but even his uncertainties gave me pause for design reflection. He did know how to tell a story. The more I read, the more I was intrigued; but clues and answers were not easily forthcoming. They reminded me how much I, my firm, missed his design presence.

I had to put some kind of timeline together. I tried to contact CJ's employer for details; but their Human Resources people refused to release any of his personal files. And his parents? I reached out to them. They were aggrieved but CJ had long ago stopped regularly communicating with them. They had fewer postcards than I. Dead end.

I had hoped to track what happened to CJ. Specifically, I was curious to understand in the period between when he was traveling the landscapes of Thailand and Switzerland and 18 months later at his administratively documented death in Cairo. His writings told me a lot; but I couldn't do it all. Cairo's information was thin.

The strangest thing about CJ's passing away was, in the notes made by the US Embassy personnel in Cairo, that they found no body. No other people were involved. I was amazed how little information I had about what happened to CJ in Cairo. When I tried to piece it all together, the most recent timeline still had curious gaps.

Following six years of cryptic diaries and richly veined design journal stories from Saudi Arabia, his documents continued with similar detail from both Thailand and Switzerland. That lined up well with the postcards I had received from him 18 months ago. That was all. Nothing after his last post card from Grindelwald, Switzerland and nothing at all from Cairo.

CJ, my colleague and friend, had mysteriously passed away in an exotic locale. I had to summarize what I knew. I had to timeline it. I counted back from the date of the death certificate.

1. Seven years and seven months ago, CJ left our firm in Los Angeles to work in Saudi Arabia. And he kept working in Saudi Arabia for six years.

2. In the last year and six months, I did not hear from him. Didn't think too much about it. His postcards were never more than "Hi, how are you". Besides, I was running a landscape architecture business. That kept me fully occupied. But this time I scrutinized his postcard dates. His last was from Grindelwald, Switzerland, 18 months before his death certificate. I had nothing later. So he worked in Saudi Arabia for six years, and did a road trip in Thailand and Switzerland for a month. That's all I knew before my trip to Amsterdam.

3. In Amsterdam I received slightly more details of the last 18 months as assembled by the Bank from CJ's employer, the Egyptian authorities and the American embassy staff. Those details follow.

a. Eighteen months ago, CJ did arrive in Cairo to begin his job. That jived with the date of his last postcard I received from Switzerland.

b. Twelve months after his Cairo arrival, CJ apparently "passed away" in an off-road automobile accident in Giza. It involved no other persons or cars. They did not find his body. Those were the only accident details. And I had no details at all about what CJ was up to during his twelve months in Cairo.

c. Then six months after the apparent accident, joint simultaneous administrative declarations from his employer and from both the Egyptian and the United States authorities, proclaimed CJ officially dead. It all sounded to me like administration just had to clear up outstanding paperwork. Administration? Paperwork? No details, no facts. But at least the timeline was making sense.

d. It took the Amsterdam "legal beagles" a month to clear all their admin hurdles before I received the Special D. And that was just two weeks ago, a year and seven months after CJ arrived in Cairo.

Well, I made my timeline but it didn't tell me anything, except what I didn't know—CJ's twelve months in Cairo were void of any details prior to the accident. And the accident itself? Next to nothing.

CJ's passing away seemed more likely a cover-up rather than a death. If it was an automobile accident, why no police details? Why no photos of his vehicle? Why no hospital reports? Things didn't add up. I needed more info. I needed to dig deeper. And that's how the idea for this story began.

I thought I might find in his diaries and design journals the clues to clear up the mystery of his death. I have taken primarily from his design journals. I have edited his stories to give a travelogue flow to CJ's rich natural and social landscape content. Not much editing was needed. Primarily, I pared down the volume to keep the flow quick and continuous.

CJ and I had never seen eye to eye on many things, especially design. But he had an energy. His energy and know-how contributed a great deal to our regular design awards for built projects. And his journals had that same energy.

Drawing upon CJ's diaries and design journals, I decided to let CJ tell his own story of Los Angeles, Saudi Arabia, Thailand and Switzerland. He was a design generator. For him, design was mysterious. He was searching, a lifelong design hunter; but at the same time he won design and built project awards. He grew our workload. Success overlapping uncertainty— that's how I remember him. Maybe I knew him... maybe not... but I had to get on with it. I had two quests—his death details and the results of his hunts—his design directions.

I figured the closer I looked at his writing, the closer I might come to understanding what happened. He always dropped breadcrumbs in his design.

So, let's get on with it.

2-Goodbye SoCal

Accident

...in CJ's own words...

After I graduated, I married my university girlfriend of six years, Sachy, to whom I gave my heart and soul. We stayed in the university town where, with a local one-man office landscape architect, I found my first professional work.

Those were tumultuous years, both at home and in the office. Tumultuous? Yes! I picked up something unspoken from my time in northwest Africa; and I still didn't understand what it was. Was it from the landscape? Was it a mental tentacle that had its roots in that landscape? I did a whole lot of speculation without certainty. The uncertainty and my daily real-world mentality made my personal and professional life hell.

Something had to be done, but what? As soon as I earned my professional license to practice landscape architecture, we moved to New Mexico, where I had grown up as a young boy and teenager. I figured, perhaps something in the landscape that had formed me, might heal me from my awkward imbalance.

Sachy and I moved to a suburb of Albuquerque. I would drive three days per week up to the Taos region where a Navajo Shaman worked to remove a "problem" from my hearing. To make it short but not so sweet—my hearing "problem" was some kind of "spell" that had lodged itself in me when I was doing my design study in Morocco.

After six months of the Navajo shaman "treatments", I felt a normalcy gradually reappear. Over the next five years, so many good things happened. Once Sachy and I re-stabilized our relationship, we started a family. She gave birth first to a son, then a year later to healthy twin girls.

Meanwhile, I became familiar with local New Mexican real estate development business, artisans, contractors, maintenance companies, engineers, architects and, of course, the multi-level governmental regulatory structures. I built a team, a loosely linked home office network of planning, design, construction, and maintenance. We were doing well. The kids were healthy, growing up; and Sachy home-schooled the three of them.

Twice a week Sachy took our kids for a picnic at the nature reserve—combining it with some science and math. She always texted me when she left home, when they were having lunch and when they got back home. Me, I was always on the go with landscape architecture projects.

I always kept the police band on the radio—good heads-up on traffic problems. On the day, I heard on the police radio about a traffic accident involving a refrigerator truck, a car, a lot of people, a huge fire and deaths on Coors Blvd, not far from the nature reserve.

Didn't think twice about it until I didn't get the lunchtime text from Sachy. When she didn't answer my text, I tried to call her—no signal from her phone.

Worry began. I was on a project site, south of town. The worry was building inside me; then I had an incoming call from the County Sheriff. I picked up immediately. Asked me if I was the owner of the vehicle with New Mexico license plate number "Lil Wing".

That was Sachy's car. Fear walked all over my worry. I couldn't hear anything on the phone. I drove immediately to the site of the accident. It took 25 minutes.

Those 25 minutes never existed. I finally arrived at a confusing chaotic mess. The accident had twisted her car into a ball, totally blackened by the now extinguished fire. Ambulances all over. Sirens and flashing lights all over. Police and EMS running everywhere.

A heavy truck and its trailer, full of illegal immigrants, had run a red light and t-boned her car at high speed—then rolled over on it. Both vehicles had exploded in flames. There were twenty or twenty-five illegal immigrants being loaded onto a police bus. That much I could see. I could not find Sachy or our kids.

Then I found the County Sheriff. He took me aside. Sachy was in serious condition and already taken to the nearest hospital. His face filled with grief when he next told me they had found my three children all dead on the scene.

I felt like someone shoved a fist down my throat, ripped out my heart and everything attached to it. I raced to the hospital with the only hope I had. They told me Sachy was in a coma, but I could sit next to her.

And then, as if my life hadn't already been shattered, she briefly opened her eyes. She recognized me and asked, "The kids?"

She saw my eyes. Her eyelids fluttered. Her eyes rolled back into her head. Grief descended on her and became her blanket of death. I couldn't breathe.

After that, I have no memories. For the rest of the week, I have no memories. I couldn't sleep in our bed. I couldn't use our kitchen. A horrific loss. I moved out of our house—it was unspeakable, the depth of hurt.

The guys I worked with did everything to help me through. But after six months, nine months, one year, I was still useless, still devastated. The car, everything in my life, reminded me of Sachy and the kids. Every day. I could not rise above it. Every day, I faced an emotional mountain to climb. Pain and emptiness reinforced everything I saw and did. Memories hurt my heart and suffocated my head.

In desperation, I called the West LA office in SoCal, where a couple of years ago I had done my internship. I explained to the owner that I needed a fresh start. He needed another landscape architect and welcomed me.

I sold the car and all our possessions. I took one suitcase with me on a Greyhound bus to Santa Monica. As soon as I arrived, I contacted the owner, W. Kurt Milligan, the landscape architect who mentored me when I was a student intern.

I couldn't talk about what had happened in Albuquerque—didn't want to be questioned—wanted to be free from the loss. Burying my head in a new job, I figured, would be the ticket. I hoped the change would, like a Pacific Ocean high tide, wash away all remaining hurt.

I hoped the new job, new people, new location would fill the emptiness in my life. And it did. At first.

***

Kurt Says

What the hell!? First I heard.

Accident? Deaths? Wife and kids killed? I had no words as I read this. Slack-jawed.

In SoCal, CJ never talked about his family or this episode. He carried this stuff inside.

Made me think—with this kind of hurt, this kind of pain— bottled up inside—maybe it was a suicide.

He was running away from something he kept inside.

Not just that but a curse from North Africa? Shaman? CJ had baggage, I mean real baggage.

Could I call it bad juju?

I wondered why CJ would even have written his story. Maybe he was trying to cleanse his pain, his internal hurt. Did it work? I don't know. He never talked about it. I was definitely getting into his writings.

And his parents—he never talked about them. He made me his Executor and never said anything about his parents. It all had to do with the deadly tragedies in New Mexico. I dug deep into his diary entries. It appears that his mother gave CJ leeway and made herself available should he want to talk. He did not want to talk with her. She apparently had a strong bond with Sachy and the kids. He just wanted to get away from anything that related to Sachy and their kids.

CJ's father told him not to give up his business—build it larger—fill his life with it. But CJ had to get away from his New Mexico memories. He ignored his father.

He cut himself off from his parents as part of his technique to keep Sachy and the kids out of his thoughts. For CJ, I don't know what to say—big time hurt on every level.

Was he under a spell from Africa? Did the New Mexico shaman cure him? Who knows? He did his job well in SoCal; but... he did have a strange edge.

And, after thinking more about our times together in my Santa Monica office, I recalled CJ had a wood plaque on his desk with a verse with the 23rd Psalm of David: "Yea, though I walk through the valley of the shadow of death, I will fear no evil."

I asked him then. All he said was, "I'm just a Christian believer." Often he did not have much to say and as I recall this was one of those times. He gave no further religious belief details.

***

Nursery

...CJ continues...

The first couple years in Los Angeles were great. I was busy; and I liked my work in SoCal. All our projects had high budgets with the best architects and developers in LA. That meant we could use large trees and the best materials for paving, walls, lights, benches... including art works and water features on nearly every urban project.

I worked closely with Kurt and we won lots of built project awards. No office environment is ever perfect, but we worked through our disagreements and I was thoroughly engaged. Thoroughly engaged? My thoughts were on the design and construction of our works. That was what I needed. No thoughts of the past.

One day, sourcing large trees for the interior of a new shopping mall, I had to go to a huge regional nursery. I needed 6 matched nos. *Ficus retusa*, about 24' tall, 9' clear single trunks with nicely formed foliage crowns. The nursery grew its trees in natural ground and dug them as required. My job today was to select six—six that had all around 360-degree balance. They would be planted as individuals, not in a group.

I had learned a lesson from another SoCal landscape architect, Ruth Shellhorn—an excellent lesson. Each tree was individual and most often had a distinctive good side—a preferred face. That's what made walks through the nursery so much fun—looking for the best face of trees. But today was different. I needed the best face all the way around on six. I had to carefully inspect all faces on each tree.

Each of the size trees I needed would be dug and put into 72" boxes—each a 6-foot-square wooden box, 42" deep, sufficient to hold all the roots for the 24' tall *Ficus retusa*. So I was at the nursery to tag them for pruning, digging, low-light prepping for six months, then shipping to the Dallas, Texas project site.

The salesman's name was Julie. He took me in a golf cart out to see the trees. Julie talked all the way. He was old, thin, wiry, permanently suntanned and with facial wrinkles that wouldn't quit. Julie was one of those classic old time SoCal movie industry construction-business guys.

For things landscape, Julie was a Hollywood fast and smooth talker, full of stories going back to the original 1950s construction of Disneyland in Anaheim—how they moved huge specimen trees, bare rooted, including the 24-7 misting of everything so it wouldn't dry out. I listened to Julie's stories as we slowly rode up and down row after row of 20' to 25' tall field-grown *Ficus retusa*.

He assured me they had all been annually root pruned in the field. Then he affirmed that, on digging, there would be little or no impact on the recent growth. Anyhow, he said that they would prune them all to thin out the branches and leaves while maintaining well-balanced crowns. Julie ticked all the boxes while mentioning that before shipping, the trees would be then put under shade for six months to simulate their indoor lighting conditions. Shipping, he said, would be in climate-controlled trucks. Lastly, he suggested I come to see their pruning so I could be happy with their shape in the final two months before shipping.

As I was tagging the last one, his phone rang. After jabbering for a couple minutes on his phone, he cupped it and asked me, "CJ, that's the last tree—you've got all six, right? Mind if I leave to meet another client? In another field. You can get back to your car by just walking 1/4 mile down this row."

"No problem, Julie, I'd like the walk and look at some other trees in your nursery."

No sooner had Julie and his golf cart disappeared when I heard another golf cart. It was close, on the next aisle of trees;

but I couldn't see it. As it slowed down, I heard a woman's voice call out.

"Hey CJ! Is that you?"

I didn't recognize the voice.

***

Eileen

...CJ continues...

Who was talking? I walked around the huge *Ficus retusa* I had just tagged. Before I could see her, before I could say anything, she asked, "Looking for work?" I answered, "No, just tagging trees."

Then she said, "You don't recognize me? Casablanca? Those West African cowboys?"

I looked carefully. She was tall and thin. Long sleeve, embroidered, blue cowboy shirt, down to mid thigh over black toreador pants. It was Eileen.

"Eileen?" I was remembering. We studied Arabic (Darija) together in a full immersion Peace Corps course in Casablanca. What was it... 10 years ago? Maybe more.

"Yup, that's me. Have you forgotten me and that other girl, the one built like a brick shit house, Bree?"

I walked up to her, and she asked, "You finished with your work? C'mon, climb on board and let's take a ride."

"Yeah," I said and climbed into her golf cart. "Yeah, I remember you, and Bree, and the Casa Caper we pulled off. Bree? Yeah, she had some knockers, but she had a horrible time. She got caught up in trafficking."

"I heard."

"And was kidnapped."

"I heard."

"She came to Tangier and was looking for a guy you told her to find if she ever got in trouble."

"Yeah, she was naïve. Trouble followed her."

"You talk about her like she wasn't important," I said.

"People like her should stay away from international do-gooding."

"I understand that; but Bree had some good stuff going on."

"What do you mean?"

"As I remember... later the same night after we had done away with those rowdy guys, she told me about her landscape research around the Med."

"So you are still into all that?"

"Into it? It's my life; and Bree had these strange landscape experiences, things she heard in the landscape, that convinced her about fairies."

"That's my point about her naivety."

I had more to say. "No, really the events that night in Casa confirmed what she had 'felt' in the North Africa landscape—she said there was something dark and dangerous."

"Hang on! No, dark and dangerous—isn't that what crime is? Isn't that what keeps poor people poor? You're not going down that do-gooder hole, are you?"

"No, no, no! Bree was onto something—something that I later learned had gotten ahold of me—something dark, dangerous, debilitating..."

"What are you talking about?" Eileen's intense eyes showed her interest.

"After my six months in North Africa, I had become wounded emotionally, intellectually. Simple tasks had become impossibly complex and..." I had to stop. Memories... New Mexico... too much.

Then I said, "Let's talk about something else."

"CJ, I know the entire story. We know you've had your share of tough times. Nuff said. We've been watching and wondering when we could talk about your future. That stuff you were talking about—Bree and the Med landscape—and your ability to process those things. CJ, that interests me and the people I work with."

"What brings you to this nursery? You in the nursery business? What people are you talking about?"

"No. Government work. And it keeps me running."

"What a coincidence to bump into you..."

"No coincidence. It's you I am interested in. We need people like you, with your language and can-do experience."

"What do you mean?"

"Have you ever thought about changing your profession for something more active, more rewarding?"

"I'm still not clear about what you're saying."

"Intelligence. Working with intelligence groups against organised crime. We call it Information Operations."

"You're kidding! I'm into the landscape architecture world, period."

"We know; that's perfect, we can work with that. But if you ever want to get into something with a larger reward... do you have a business card?"

"Yeah."

"Can you give me one?"

I gave her mine and she wrote on the back before returning it to me. We continued riding through the tree nursery without talking. I looked at large, field-grown, properly pruned trees. All with balance and character. We rode through strawberry trees, *Arbutus unedo*, floss silk trees, *Choirisia speciosa*. Tens, no, hundreds of them. Inspirational specimens.

Then Eileen said, "We have big criminal, cultural, political and religious problems that need people with experience like you."

I thought for a moment, then blurted, "Eileen, listen, I had to go through all that bad stuff in Morocco, but there was a lot of other stuff, too."

"Like what?"

"People in Morocco—normal families, normal workers. Normal. I mean people living within their own homes, their own communities—protecting their families, preparing for the future—all the basics that work across cultures."

My eyes met her eyes. She was listening. I continued, "It's what made me conclude I had to live and work in my own home, my own neighbourhood, my own religion, my own culture, my own landscape."

"I hear you."

"We solved a cultural and criminal problem that night in Casa; and I don't want any part of life in those kinds of places. I want to build my own place in my own country." I didn't want to say anything about New Mexico and why I moved here—she had already said she knew everything.

"Listen CJ, I am not here to change your mind. But those types of problems we saw in Casa, in North Africa are problems affecting many cultures, hurting uncomplicated people. Those problems are finding their way to our shores and if you ever want to address them face to face, send me an email or call me. I've written contact details on the back of your business card."

I looked at the numbers, then put the card in my wallet and said... nothing.

She asked, "Can I take you back to your car at the nursery office?"

Riding back with Eileen, I found myself recalling the time on my term abroad design study in Morocco—how we had pulled a fast one on the West Africans who were harassing Bree in Casablanca. I surprised myself when I realized that I got some pleasure from those memories.

***

Kurt Says

I couldn't believe what I was reading. CJ and Tangier, CJ and Morocco—his experiences went way, way deep.

I knew CJ had been to Morocco as a student but this "CIA secret agent" stuff... a brand-new headline.

And his "paranormal" link between African djinn and New Mexico? Well, that was some real weird shit.

I read all I could about his time in Morocco and its effects on him. He thought he was possessed. Maybe he was. Maybe... no, it couldn't be... maybe there was some connection to Cairo. Both Egypt and Morocco are in North Africa. And the Sahara connects them... so does the Mediterranean Sea.

I chewed on that for a while. The different pieces of CJ's intense life experiences were confusing me. They were putting me on different paths that all had to end up in Cairo.

I had nothing about CJ's twelve months in Cairo. Then, I remembered I had an old friend, Cal, who was a high school teacher at an international school in Cairo. Needing more information to understand CJ's "end" in Cairo, I sent an email to Cal's school. I was desperate to find out more. It was a "hail Mary" request. It was a stretch, a hope.

Everything I had gathered so far was a downer. But the CJ I knew was energetic—the very opposite of a downer. Needed to get more info.

CJ was on some wild ride.

***

LA? Too Much

A couple years passed. My SoCal landscape architecture work, while successful, had become tedious. Regulations at municipal, county, state and federal levels were growing like weeds. They affected design. Like straight-jackets, they bound arms, tied our hands.

The people writing these regulations didn't have the creative fires or practical experience. Instead, these "activists" used spreadsheets and statistics as weapons. Some seemed to have a political agenda. Others were more favourable to mountain lions and coyotes than humans.

Yeah, we could challenge their regulations... if we wanted six months to three years upfront legal costs. And no client wanted that loss of time and money for a garden. A lot of clients look at the landscape costs of 10% of the total project cost and call it nail polish—thus months of delays arguing for a regulation exemption is not popular. Tedious? I was getting burnt out.

There were days... I would get wave after wave memories of Sachy from my LA intern time. She had come to visit me more than a couple of times; and we had shared wonderful sunsets over the Pacific Ocean from Santa Monica beach. The waves of memories became painful. So many emotions, so many project obstacles... I wasn't sure what to do. My design fire was weakening.

One evening at home, I was going through old business

cards when I saw Eileen's email address. I reviewed again our night with the West Africans in the Casablanca hotel—made me smile—the trick we played to save Bree. I thought, what harm in talking with Eileen? Maybe that kind of challenge might be what I needed. So, I sent her an email.

In response, Eileen invited me to Sunday Brunch with some of her friends and colleagues in the Golfers Lounge at the Trump National Golf Club in Rancho Palos Verdes. The golf course and the view west across the 26 miles of Pacific Ocean to Santa Catalina Island revealed the fullness of the SoCal lifestyle—a sweet combination of cultural and landscape realities. The SoCal landscape—relaxed, beautiful, both natural and well developed—inspired me and my work. When I looked out to Santa Catalina, my eyes and heart drew a deep breath of fresh air. I already had the windows open. The temp was 75°. But I had memories—long gone LA memories.

Driving to the brunch that morning, I reviewed my work situation in LA. Yeah, I had fun putting the soccer league together but... The LA scene. I put on the Black Sunday CD by Cypress Hill—that was the new thing, the new LA trend. Try to hide from that. Impossible.

Every contractor hired day labourers off the street corner. As I remembered my intern days in LA, the best contractors found the best day labourers, legalized them, and worked hard to meet the deadline-driven Hollywood TV and movie industry. And they became skilled craftsmen. They earned our respect; and they regularly built our high budget projects. Those were the guys of our soccer league.

But the street scene now? Not like then, when it was all about—laid back... suntan... yearlong summers. Now? Too much identity politics and regulation friction in your face in the public realm—environmental fascism bringing the threat of death back into our communities and family neighbourhoods... poisonous snakes, coyotes, mountain lions, bears. And on the job site where workers used to work hard to perfect their skills... now they claim to be victims asking for government reparations. Sad. Needed a change.

Needed something fresh.

***

Rancho Palos Verdes

...CJ continues...

When I arrived for brunch, Eileen introduced me to the surrounding people. First was Connie Smith, the Executive Secretary for the President of one of the nation's largest AEC (architecture, engineering and construction management) firms, headquartered in downtown LA.

Eileen gave me some inside background. "Connie, a real power broker, has been with the firm for forty years. At the office, everyone respectfully calls her Big Momma. She gets things done. But you should call her Mrs. Smith until she tells you otherwise."

Next was Eileen's female colleague in... I didn't know, some kind of intelligence agency. And the last was a grizzled but professionally well-dressed man, definitely in his late 50s, hair already white, and the square jaw of a boxer. His name? Will Clendenon. He was the Program Manager for the company's two-billion-dollar management contract on the West Coast of the Kingdom of Saudi Arabia—a new port, industrial oil complex and community on the Red Sea, 300 km north of Jeddah. That was how Eileen described it. I shook hands with all, exchanged business cards with Mrs. Smith and Mr. Clendenon, then sat down.

After we all ordered a round of drinks—the usual Sunday brunch relaxers, sparkling wine, Mimosas—then Mrs. Smith started.

"Ever thought about going overseas again—working as a landscape architect in a foreign country?"

I didn't know what to expect but I was looking for a change. I said, "Well, I suppose it would depend on my responsibilities. I am looking for larger projects with larger responsibilities. Can you tell me more?"

"We have huge new town/regional centre projects that need landscape architect managers. Mr. Clendenon manages the one in Saudi Arabia where we have a multi-billion-dollar project to build an industrial port and small peaceful new town on the Red Sea. You can find larger responsibilities there..." She looked directly into my eyes.

I couldn't believe what I heard. No more individual site projects. A new city! I said, "How would I fit in?"

She said, "For an entire new city of 200,000, we are in the early stages and we need landscape architects with broad experience and capabilities. If you're interested, call me at the office and we can arrange an interview."

Well, I had never imagined such a large scope of work. This sounded like a big-time challenge.

Mr. Clendenon began, "This new town is very important to the strategic growth plan outline by the King of Saudi Arabia. He has appointed a Royal Commission (RC) to oversee the project. A Saudi Arabian Royal Family Prince chairs the RC. And key members are junior members of the Royal Family. That is an important background to remember."

He continued, "Your record in Morocco and the US leads us to believe you have the skill set. Please understand the difference. Both countries are Muslim, but the Kingdom of Saudi Arabia is not Morocco. The Saudis are strict. They do not tolerate Western liberal behaviour or public Christianity. You'd have to live with that."

I listened. Everyone was watching my reaction. No public Christianity? I thought no problem—I only went to church on Christmas and Easter anyhow. Then I asked, "Just what would my landscape architectural duties be?"

Mr. Clendenon said, "Once you settle in, we'd expect you to take charge of the entire landscape program for this new industrial town from planning to design to engineering, construction and maintenance. Do you like the sound of that?"

"That's an enormous challenge and I need a challenge like that."

Mr. Clendenon continued, "You'd be a Field Project Manager in our Community Projects group. We have an entire engineering department on site to support that aspect of your work; but on all issues landscape, you'd be the man."

Mrs. Smith said, "The Kingdom of Saudi Arabia (KSA) is a long way from home. Could you manage that?"

"I've done that before in Morocco. I should be able to do it again. But..." I hesitated. I don't know why.

Mrs. Smith said, "As a bachelor, you will have generous leave options every six months and a 30-day home leave every 18 months. All airfare paid."

Stuff was coming at me hard and fast. I felt excited by the challenges; but I gave no thought to details. Then Eileen's colleague spoke.

She said, "Let's put the landscape architecture and personal stuff aside. We will need your help. Mr. Clendenon understands that you as the point man for all project landscape issues will give you cause to attend regular meetings in Riyadh. The Royal Commission members are all male, young, mostly well educated in Western universities, either in the US or the UK. We expect you to be social with them. Talk about sports as a common ground. No politics, no religion, no dating, no borderline cultural issues. We want to hear how they talk about competition and fair play. These guys will be the next generation of leaders in the Kingdom. Do you follow?"

"I hear but..."

"This is not complicated. We know you set up a soccer league for your contractors here in LA. You should be full of tales to generate conversation, right?"

"Yeah, sure, soccer... I can talk all day about that." I was starting to like this extra dimension to my work. This truly was the kind of new dimension and scope that could "fully occupy" me. That is what I wanted. That is what I needed.

Mr. Clendenon added, "We have a contact in Riyadh. A guy

who works out of an international consultant management firm, the Analysis Corporation in Philadelphia. He will meet with you as regularly as required to brief you on expectations from each Riyadh presentation."

"Presentation?"

Mr. Clendenon said, "Quarterly, the basis of these meetings in Riyadh is a financial and project status presentation. That is my part. The topics that fall to you will be developed on a meeting-by-meeting basis. You will have to think on your feet."

Mrs. Smith looked hard into my eyes and said, "Your record demonstrates your abilities in this respect. And you will receive an additional 15% uplift to your base salary. Do you have any doubts?"

It was all happening so fast; I didn't have time for doubts. I was jumping into a puzzle with moving pieces—conceptually, that was what I was hearing. My only brush with something like this—in Casablanca—was a thrill and fun. It sounded attractive.

After finishing a second round of drinks, Mr. Clendenon suggested we hit the brunch buffet. As we were walking up there, he said to me, "Get plenty of the bacon and ham..." He chuckled strangely, before adding, "You won't see any pork at all in Saudi. Enjoy it while you can. Same with booze and movies. Not a bar or movie house in the entire country."

That was a challenge. If I took the job, I would face innumerable cultural and professional challenges. Not my first rodeo; Tangier and northwest Africa had thrown all kinds of challenges at me—and I survived—barely, but I survived.

Indeed, this was just what I needed. To make a long story short, over the next six weeks, I met with the responsibles in the AEC head office four or five times before they made me an offer. My base salary would be 3.15x what I was making in Santa Monica.

They reviewed all the cross-cultural differences and then explained that I would live with my own sort, Western Expats, in a specially designed community—with schools, shops, excellent medical and recreational facilities. Not exactly like home, but the flavour of home. The Saudis were family people and among the Western expatriates the majority were also families. Sounded okay to me.

I did some of my own research online. There were very few accounts of life in the Arabian Peninsula—Burton, Burckhardt, Thesiger, Thomas, Lawrence. But I found a quite intriguing 15-minute multimedia depiction of the Arabian Peninsula landscape by a landscape architect who obviously knew the region. He called it a Botanical Sampler. I found it to be a sweeping overview of Araby and its ethnobotany. He made it sound seductive—the whispering sand dunes, the mangroves and the eerie... pirates... histo-geography... endless distances. Challenges! I liked it.

Here's what happened. I had an excellent job offer—scope of responsibility and salary package. In return they wanted me, when, from time to time, making presentations to the Saudi Royal Commission in Riyadh, to interact socially with certain "junior" members of the Royal Commission and share information I'd gather with a contact to be named after I arrived on site in Yenbo, KSA.

Seemed simple enough to me. I was not to speak to anyone about this part of my work, including all who had been present at the brunch. I thought, can do.

I was about to embark on a strange trip. Just what I needed. I'd never come to grips internally with the accident that killed Sachy and our three children; and LA had the ghost of those memories always just over my shoulder. In KSA I would have an enormous challenge in a strange landscape—new place with immense responsibilities. I was up for it. Next thing I knew, I was in the KSA.

3-Hello KSA

This is a Desert

...CJ continues...

I thought my time, more than a decade ago, in Muslim Morocco might have helped me to find my way in the heart of Islam—the Kingdom of Saudi Arabia (KSA). I couldn't have been more wrong.

Arriving by jet over the Kingdom of Saudi Arabia, I examined the landscape from 40,000 feet. Like the Med landscape of Northern Morocco? Not a chance! Seen nothing like it. As far as I could see, all the way to the hazy mid-day horizon—no greens, no rich earthen browns, no blues. No trees, no scrub. No lakes, no rivers, no creeks. It was all barren. Eerie? Stronger than eerie, it was, dare I say, otherworldly.

We were aiming for Jeddah International on the Red Sea, on a flight path that took us over the entire Arabian Peninsula. I saw desert like I'd never seen. None of the diverse vegetative greys, pale blues and silver greens, so much a part of the New Mexican Southwest US desert.

Couldn't believe my eyes. Soil? None. Water? None. Plants? None.

Overstatement? Hyperbole? No way! From 40,000 feet, it was all sand and rocks. From horizon to horizon—all tans, blonds and oxide reds, mixing—with a strange, hazy fearfulness. Why did I feel fearfulness? It was the endlessness of the entire scene—like I was entering an eternity of nothingness. Yeah, I felt a fearfulness—maybe an existential fearfulness.

Endless sky without clouds over endless landscape

without life—bound with an all-encompassing cotton wool, a threatening haze, a suffocation in the process. A landscape devoid of life symptoms... barren. A landscape empty... of life. Fearfulness? Huge uncertainties. Huge unknowns. There had to be something, a powerful something I couldn't see.

I recalled how I felt about LA, "...I had to get out of the LA tedium..." But here?

What had I gotten myself into?!

This appeared to be a landscape cursed. How else to describe the absoluteness of no life? This was the landscape of my new job?! I hadn't touched down yet and already felt an awkward disconnect.

Disconnect from what? The landscape? The landscape had always been my muse except northwest Africa. And, over the central Arabian Peninsula, my first feelings now? Pushed away... this new landscape pushed me away.

That was from 40,000 feet.

***

On the Ground

...CJ continues...

On the ground, life was no less shocking. I tried to settle in. It wasn't Morocco. It was a different world. No churches. Prayer calls five times a day on loudspeakers and all shops closed, shuttered for the duration of every prayer. I'd heard plenty of prayer calls back when I lived in Tangier, but here?! Very different world. In Tangier, life went on. Businesses kept operating. Shoppers kept shopping.

But here in Saudi, everything and everybody stopped for the prayer call. People in cars stopped at the nearest mosque, leaving their cars higgledy-piggledy in the middle of the road. Around the mosques, the streets, chock-a-block with parked cars, became impassable during prayers.

Because of no shopping during prayers, customers were ushered out of the shops. While all Muslims were in the mosque, the non-Muslim shoppers milled around on the streets. After the prayer, the shops rolled up their shutters for business again. It was as though time stopped. Everybody stopped and waited until the prayer was over.

That prayer call ruled the public realm. Easy to understand why there was no hippy trail through this country.

Think I'm exaggerating?

Let me tell you about what happened when I first arrived in KSA at the Jeddah International airport. My flight from LAX to Jeddah went via Schiphol. Hearing that good chocolate was difficult to find in KSA, I scheduled an overnight in Amsterdam.

I picked up a box of Droste select pastilles. Then I hopped on a fast train to Brussels—hadn't been there for years, since the bike trip before my term-abroad design study in Tangier—but I still remembered the fine chocolates. In Brussels, I picked up a couple bars of Côte d'Or with hazelnuts and a box of Leonidas Heritage pralines collection.

Arriving in Jeddah, I experienced complete air conditioned (AC) passage directly from the airplane to the elevator-bus and then to passport control. Never set a foot outdoors. Never a breath of outdoor air.

I was in 100% AC space for every aspect of my Jeddah arrival. I went through passport control, then picked up my luggage and went through customs. Very long, single file lines for non-Saudis at customs. Finally, my turn.

First culture shock—the guy was a young Saudi in officer kit. Had to open every bag. Take everything out, item by item. He paged through every book, looking for pornographic or offensive religious images, I figured.

Then, in broken English, he asked what was in those chocolate boxes. I said chocolate. He said, open them. Open them? Open them. So I opened them. First the Droste. He asked, alcohol? I said no. He said show me. I cracked one pastille and showed him it was solid. I smelled trouble.

Then he asked me to open the large box of Leonidas pralines. Long story short, he used his finger to crush every praline in his search for alcohol filling. Language issues all over the place. I gave up the protestations and stood slack jawed as all 40 of my pralines were squashed, one by one. It was midnight before I exited customs.

Their country, their rules.

Welcome to the Kingdom of Saudi Arabia, KSA, Saudi. But at least I wasn't surrounded by uniformed guys with machine guns. None at the airport and none in the cities. My Moroccan experiences with soldiers and their machine guns had left a lasting uncomfortable impression. So it was a relief not to see any in the KSA.

***

Getting to the Job Site

...CJ continues...

Enough whining—here's the rest of my Kingdom of Saudi Arabia arrival story.

After clearing customs in Jeddah, a Public Relations (PR) rep from my company met me. He introduced himself as Vivaswan. Vivaswan? I wondered, what kind of name? Had to be Indian. He spoke good English and had a calm demeanour. His facial structure? Never seen before. His skin was the darkest chocolate brown colour—a colour I had never seen among people in the US or Morocco.

He asked to see my lavaliere, corporate ID badge. I had it around my neck. He confirmed I was on his list of new employee arrivals. Before I could ask him anything, he ran off to gather others. When Vivaswan returned with them, he helpfully guided our transit with confidence to a regional flight, destination Yenbo.

Transit had some interesting first times for me. As I exited the terminal, I walked outside without air-conditioning for the first time. Along the guided walkway to the Yenbo plane, must have been only 50 metres.

I was naked in the face of the KSA/Red Sea climate. It was 2AM. I inhaled the first time the air of the Red Sea Western Region of KSA.

Why was I thinking it would be a Mediterranean experience? Coastal? Warm?

Anyhow, what struck my lungs was unique, uncomfortable. I

had never experienced this uncomfortable, sour combination of extreme humidity, extreme salty, extreme desert and off-the-charts heat—the middle of the night and off the charts—sweating. I was outdoors sweating at 2AM. Standing and sweating—hard to breathe.

All beyond healthy in the extreme. I got two minutes of Jeddah's coastal air. My body told me not to inhale deeply. I didn't argue. But the air had a character, an almost smell. A blend of sand, salty silt, excessive heat all coalescing into a not quite acrid... first time... and when I arrived in Yenbo, it was this way every day and night. Especially in the 40° at sunset.

I sought a fresh cool breeze and never found it. It was as if the sands had been in a constant stage of salt fermentation. The smell? Red Sea salt and Empty Quarter sand fermenting over millennia, whipped by shamal and stirred by djinn. Djinn? Yeah, djinn, that was the only way I could explain the fearful feelings that absorbed me when I observed the landscape from 40,000 feet. This was my new home, my new landscape. All agitated by my distant memories of the northwest Africa landscape—was Morocco still haunting me?

After six of us disembarked from the 40-minute jet to Yenbo, Vivaswan walked us over to a waiting corporate Toyota minibus. We put our luggage on board in a special luggage bin.

On the minibus, Vivaswan told us we had to wait a few minutes for a family that was on their way.

One by one, Vivaswan came to us, collected our passports, which would be kept, by our company, safely in a vault until R&R, home leave or end of contract. At the same time, he handed out an introductory brochure—a nice A4 size landscape format booklet filled with flash graphics and photos of Yenbo New Town. Beautiful photos of the Red Sea coast with mangroves, coral reef gardens and King Fahd port, the crude oil refineries and the landscaped community. I started reading.

The Kingdom has made substantial industrial investments for Yenbo New Town, envisioned as a major Western region Red Sea port for all exports from the Kingdom. With a primary centre for petrochemicals, it will become the world's third largest refining hub and the largest industrial city and largest crude oil export facility on the Red Sea with crude oil and natural gas supplied by cross-kingdom pipelines. Yenbo is on major shipping lanes to Suez Canal and developing markets in Africa and the Middle East.

New infrastructure projects include upgrades to the port, airport, electrical power, potable and industrial water, roads, sewerage treatment, schools, mosques, housing, hospitals and other cosmopolitan services and facilities.

Yenbo offers outstanding quality of life on the beautiful Red Sea. As a full-service city, Yenbo offers world class medical clinics and hospitals. The city offers beautifully landscaped residential areas and recreational facilities for families. Yenbo New Town is modern Saudi Arabia. In short, the new city is characterized by the best of modern conveniences with the interior and exterior features congenial to Saudi Arabian lifestyle. It is truly a quality environment, a modern city reflecting the distinctive tradition of Saudi Arabian Culture.

It was the same I had seen in LA when they had recruited me. It was boring bunf about this massive project; and that massive project was what I came here for. I came here to work, to make a city in the desert, green.

An hour passed, the sun had risen. Finally, the missing family climbed aboard and we were on our way. The minibus windows were already too hot to touch. The AC was blasting.

I was more interested in the landscape. It had a burnt-out look—too much sun—too much brightness. No trees. No shrubs. Forty-five minutes driving through the same. My senses? Felt an oppressive nothingness. But hey I came here to fix that—use my landscape architecture skills for relief.

***

67

Yenbo (Al Nawa Village)

...CJ continues...

The sunrise hadn't helped. The outdoors didn't even look fresh. Even with the minibus AC blasting out on high, I was suffocating. Now, with my feet on the ground in real life, despite all the detailed briefings my new company had given me in Los Angeles, I wasn't sure where I was going or what to expect. But I cradled a little hope—that my skills would be used.

I looked again at Vivaswan's Yenbo welcome pack. Despite the boring bumf, it was an attractive graphics package. The best part of the pack was a map of my destination—Al Nawa Village.

Al Nawa housed everyone from our company, everyone from the Royal Commission and the top managers of all consultants and contractors.

Al Nawa was the "constructor's village" while the rest of the new town was under construction. It was the only part of the new town that had housing—built and serviced.

It was just past 7AM as we arrived in Yenbo. The minibus—I called it the welcome wagon—took us past the headquarters tent of the RC for Yenbo. Then we were dropped at our company's headquarters, the space frame, the HR department. We were divided into two groups—bachelors and marrieds.

Al Nawa Village had seven camps, neighbourhoods or Haiis, as they were called. Haii 7 had the Royal Commission Tent, an imposing tent (looked to me like it could have been drawing on

Saudi Arabian historical reference) and our company's main headquarters. Vivaswan called the headquarters the "Space Frame". When I asked why, he told me that the headquarters were all under one very high roof that architecturally and structurally was called a space frame.

Three neighbourhoods, Haiis 2, 4 and 5, were for marrieds only. Haii 3 housed the bachelors and Haii 1 temporarily housed recently arrived bachelors. Haii 6 had the mosque and retail frontages—it was the village centre.

Vivaswan gave me an upgraded Royal Commission Yenbo al Sinaiyah ID package then drove me and a couple others to Haii 1.

He took me to my room and told me to take it easy for the day. I was thankful for that. Seemed like I had been travelling 72 hours straight. I was tired, hot, hungry and needed a shower. Vivaswan would collect us the next morning for an 8 o'clock appointment.

My accommodation was fully furnished, felt like a sport youth hostel—nothing fancy—just the basics and a short walk to an employee cafeteria to which my ID provided entry.

A typical Haii 1 accommodation was in a building—like a double wide construction cabin. Inside there were six single rooms, a common hallway, a toilet room, a shower room and a maintenance room.

Each room had a bed, a desk, a chair, a wardrobe and a bookshelf. AC was central for the entire building—in fact everything everywhere indoors was air-conditioned. Every vehicle had air conditioning. Hell, I used to think AC was a luxury. Even in West LA, we didn't AC every building. But here, I was learning, AC wasn't a luxury. It was a necessity. It meant survival for people like me, the Western expatriates.

At the centre of Haii 1 was the employee cafeteria and a small commissary. The cafeteria served three meals a day. I used my photo ID to access it. Reminded me of a large college cafeteria. Walk through line, serve yourself drinks, nothing fancy. Rectangular tables for six—thirty to fifty tables total. It was huge, busy and noisy during service hours.

Haii 1 was an interim solution. It held new bachelors until

studios in the bachelor Haii 3 became available. The Haii 1 population was fluid. I never knew who would be my recent-hire neighbour.

On the day, it was a weird guy who had sat by himself in the back of the minibus. Tall, 6'3", thin as a beanpole, broad-brimmed cowboy hat, Levis, wide leather belt, cowboy shirt and cowboy boots. Did I say cowboy all the way?

I had taken a sweaty walk around Haii 1 after dinner and just returned to my building. As I entered my building I saw the cowboy in the common hallway area. Previously, he had taken an interest in the young, small Bangladeshi boy who was assigned to keep the common areas clean. I had thought little about it. But this evening, when I entered our building, the cowboy was leading the Bangladeshi into his room and then turned his music player up loud.

I went directly to my room, grabbed my soap and towel and headed to the shower room to wash off the salty sweat from my walk. In other words, I minded my own business.

I couldn't wait to get my own Haii 3 studio.

In less than a week, HR moved me into my own Haii 3 studio—kitchenette, entertainment nook, study corner, private bath—it was wonderful, austere, small like a hermit's shelter, only comfortable. I liked it. My new home. Everything was a challenge. I was engaged. Just what I was looking for.

***

Org Chart

...CJ continues...

My second day in Yenbo, Vivaswan met me at 7:30 and we walked to the "Space Frame", a large, airy, modern Bucky Fuller-like high ceiling, column-free building. It was the sprawling hub of my company's Yenbo activities. Vivaswan guided me, through the expansive "Space Frame", to the Community Projects Directorate. Along the way, we talked.

I asked, "Where is your home?"

"India."

"India? Where exactly?"

"Kerala, do you know it?"

"No, tell me."

"Beautiful, peaceful, most south India, sandy beaches, coconut trees everywhere... here we are. Everyone is waiting for you."

The meeting table was full with five men. Vivaswan introduced me to the man in charge, the Community Projects Manager, CPM. I shook hands, and he welcomed me, offered me a seat at the foot of the table. I sat, looked at the men around the table. They all had grey and white hair. I thought they all looked retirement age, except for one dark-haired guy. He was the landscape architect from the Engineering Department. I learned later that many senior personnel from my company on this job were here to get a nice pay packet before retirement. They were not wasters; they were all qualified managers.

The CPM began, "Welcome to Yenbo New Town, we all call

it Yenbo. Our company has been an integral part of the city's development since 1976. That includes the master plan and the management of all infrastructure design, construction and administration for the new city. This is a mega project with complex engineering ventures having billion-dollar budgets and decades-long schedules.

"For your daily context, Yenbo has two parts—industrial and community. The community is where you will work. And the Royal Commission, the RC, let me side track a moment—there are many Royal Commissions out of the capital, Riyadh. The King authorizes Royal Commissions for the most important projects throughout the Kingdom of Saudi Arabia. The King appoints members of the Royal Family to sit on the boards of each Royal Commission. At the topmost level, they control budget, schedule and payments.

"They fund and manage this Yenbo project; and they expect to see a green community—one of them said, like Santa Barbara, California—white buildings and lots of landscaping—do you follow?"

I nodded.

"That is your job—landscaping—the community; the place where everyone lives. We expect your broad experience in Southern California landscaping will allow us to meet their expectations."

That sounded straightforward enough, I thought—a green city in the desert? A challenge—definitely.

The CPM paused for a moment and stared into my eyes, before continuing, "Around this table are the people you report to. My Deputy Director (DD), your Principal Project Manager (PPM), your Senior Project Manager (SPM) and the landscape architect from our Engineering Department with whom you will regularly liaise."

They all handed their business cards down the table to me.

"Henderson is your SPM. He will set you up and help you interface with all involved in landscaping. Questions?"

I understood. I had no questions. The CPM had given me a broad yet concise overview.

"Then we are all done here. Henderson will show you to

your workstation and the rest is up to you. Welcome aboard."

On my way out with Henderson, the Engineering Department landscape architect joined us.

He said, "My name is Amelio, and I graduated in landscape architecture from Michigan State—you?"

"Me, also from MSU—when did you graduate?"

"15 years ago—we'll have to get together and talk about old times—how about I pick you up in front of the Space Frame at noon and we'll have lunch together."

"How can I find you?"

"I've got a red Jeep with a green racing stripe that says 'Keep Saudi Green'—can't miss it. No one else has anything like it. See you at noon."

"Sure thing—see you then."

Then he split.

Henderson walked me to my workstation.

I commented about the high ceiling in the expansive "Space Frame" structure.

"Damn near the size of a football field," he said.

I checked through the office supplies and stuff.

He said, "Take the next two days to get up to speed with the landscape context of our work."

"Who is the best source for gathering that information?"

"You'll want to sit with Bertram and Hans, two planners who assembled all the regional landscape data on which we have built our landscaping program."

"Where can I find them?"

"Talk to Matthew. He does all your secretarial work. He can provide phone numbers for you to set up your meetings. Bertram and Hans have been here for years. They both know people and processes. There is one more important item. Two weeks from now, you are required to attend our in-house program on International Project Management. I'll send you the schedule later today."

It was noon before I knew it. Headed over to the main entry. Yeah, there was the red jeep with the green racing stripe shouting "Keep Saudi Green". I climbed in and Amelio drove us over to the Camp 3 canteen.

I said, "Mega project? And I am so far down the ladder with landscaping responsibilities?"

"The CPM didn't give you all details," Amelio said. "Our company has more than 2,000 managers on site with many divisions—each deep with management layers and support personnel. Your division, Community Projects, then there's Construction, Infrastructure, Regulation and Control, Business Development, Municipality with Planning, Administrative, Technical, Public Services and my division, Engineering. We have every discipline imaginable plus document control—get the feeling that you are one bee in a huge beehive? That is the reality."

I wanted complex and more responsibility—well, complex I had.

Over lunch Amelio explained the difference between a landscape architect in the Engineering Dept. and a landscape architect in Community Projects. In summary, I organized the scope of projects and the hiring of consultants and Amelio reviewed their design submissions.

But that wasn't what caught my attention about Amelio. He was some kind of born-again Christian. He told me he spent all his free time driving north in Saudi Arabia near the Gulf of Aqaba where he hiked the landscape he called the Wilderness of Midian.

He said it was the landscape of the "Burning Bush" and the exodus—he couldn't stop talking about it. Interesting, but it ruined my lunch. I tried to change the subject—to learn about soils, water and plants; but it would not move Amelio from his old-testament biblical history. Amelio was loquacious. Before we finished lunch, he told me in too much detail about his three-year Turkish cross-country trip Istanbul-Konya-Mt. Ararat. I was thinking this was Amelio's hippy trail story until he got into Noah's Ark at Mt. Ararat then across Iran to Teheran—Isfahan where he followed the path of Vita Sackville-West until Afghanistan Kandahar, Kabul, Peshawar, the Khyber Pass and Pakistan where he built up his interest in carpets.

I interrupted, "Excuse me Amelio, but I have to ask... the decal on your Jeep—Keep Saudi Green—I don't see any green to keep—just arid tan sands—what's up?"

"We're both landscape architects, right? With appreciation for nature, the natural environment, right? Well, when I say green, I am not talking about the colour green, I am talking about the existent Bedouin culture that has lived this desert landscape for thousands of years—do you follow?"

I nodded but I thought how could someone be hired to plant this new to-be-stable community when he had dominant sympathies for the native landscape and its go-where-there's-rain nomadic communities?

Enough, I thought. "Shouldn't we get back to work?" I shut Amelio down when he returned to carpet details—not my kind of guy—self-centred, preaching (to the choir in my case) and preferring the nomadic landscape. Real shared conversation was impossible.

I couldn't wait to get back to my office.

I had an appointment with my SPM. I liked Henderson. He was grey-haired, prematurely grey, and he had an energy that I came to understand epitomized the efforts that many put into their work here in Yenbo. Before we finished, Henderson took me over to the secretary pool and introduced me to Matthew.

All the landscaping projects were going to be under my control. The depth and breadth of this massive on-site management team... seemed excessive—too many layers everywhere—but we were building a new town and running it. I'll see as I settle into the real work.

***

The Next Day

...CJ continues...

I always thought of planners as professionals who built nothing. In my experience, they most often impeded design and construction—costing the developer losses of time and money. They had design ideas, but no design experience. Few had construction or maintenance knowhow.

And the landscape? They, like so many others, most often thought landscape architecture was just gardening. But I came to know the planners I was to meet in Yenbo New Town were different—they had, what many call, vision. I would call it, experience, broad experience.

Matthew, providing secretarial services for me, arranged a meeting in our offices with two key planners, a Brit and a Swiss. Both countries had a good 1,000 years of civilization, landscape, villages and towns. Had to respect that history.

Brits? I had my opinions. They always thought a Yank's education would never prosper in Britain—some overheated leftover from 1776 and 1812—old story that never has died.

And the Swiss? Frugal, very proud of their independence and their very careful way of doing things. For the Swiss, everyone else was an outsider—not to be let in—not to be trusted. Yeah, I had doubts about my first meeting with my corporate colleagues—true internationals.

So, in the afternoon, I met the two professional planners, Bertram, tall and a tad on the heavy side, from the UK and Hans, shorter and looking fit, from Switzerland. I was pushing

40, and these guys looked to be well into their 50s. The UK and Switzerland both have highly active local planning boards protecting green space and traditional architectural heritage, but what about the desert?

I knew both countries were small but both had extremely varied sub-cultural variety. Their countries were geographically and climatically blessed with the moisture and soil that permits plentiful self-sufficient agriculture. And both were accustomed to taking meticulous care of local details.

That was what I knew... but what about this vast desert, the salty Red Sea, the lack of topsoil, the lack of rain and people of nomadic tradition as residents?

I met Hans and Bertram in a small meeting room in the "Space Frame". After collegial greetings and handshakes, and after they gave me their business cards, Bertram asked, "What do you need?"

"I'd like to have access to background environmental studies (surveys plus analysis) on climate, soils, geology and water supply."

Hans said, "All those are in the Document Control Building in Haii 3. They have a library there."

I pulled out my plan of Al Nawa Village and asked Hans to mark its location with an "x".

Then I asked, "Is there an executive summary on how to move forward with landscaping based upon those background studies?"

Bertram reached into his briefcase and pulled out the Royal Commission Directorate General of Yenbo New Town Developmental Guidelines. Less than an inch thick, it was an A4 size document with plastic cover and wire binding.

He put it on the table, opened it to the Table of Contents, and pointed out the relevant sections.

He said, "You should read: Water Provision, Community Landscaping and Environmental Protections. That will get you started. This copy is for your personal use."

They had been helpful, so I asked, "What do you do for recreation—your free time in Yenbo?"

Hans said, "You must have been told about the mangroves

and the coral reef. Many people spend their weekends on the Red Sea coast among the mangroves or snorkelling the coral reef. Others hang out at the Haii swimming pools."

Bertram said, "We have a Red Sea Philatelic Society. We explore the landscape history, especially the old Istanbul-Medina railway built by the Turks. We schedule outings on the weekends. Sometimes we organize trips to see Nabatean ruins up near the Jordanian border. There's plenty to explore and see. We meet the first Wednesday in every month, if you'd like." Bertram was friendly in his cool, British way.

I asked, "Any big picture items you'd bring to my attention?"

"Glad you asked," said Hans. "We have something for you—a welcome gift." He reached into his backpack and pulled out a book with a ribbon on it.

"You might find this interesting reading."

It was *Life between Buildings: Using Public Space.*

Hans said, "We are sure you have read *Pattern Language, Design with Nature, The Image of the City* and..." I think I heard a snigger, "Jane Jacobs' *The Death and Life of Great American Cities*; well, Jan Gehl's work welcomes you to this side of the ocean." That got another discussion going—Yenbo greenbelt, greenways, parks, local, neighbourhood, district and city centres.

I asked, "What about this hot, arid, sub-tropical climate—who wants to walk or bike ride in this climate?"

Bertram said, "Green means shade—make sure your consultants understand that."

"And there is a road and public transportation network," said Hans, "... no shortage of fuel in this country. It is about options—autos, busses, bikes, walking—they are all available."

"But this is a city for Muslims—how do all these Western ideas fit?"

"Simple," Bertram said, "the fundamental metric is a 10-minute walk to the local mosque—we planned everything around that, including only a 10-minute walk from every residence via greenways to local parks. But the cultural centre around which all shopping residential and recreation is built is the mosque and its easy accessibility—you know prayer five times a day."

I had to let that sink in.

My time with the planners was useful. But I was still vague on, how can I say it—the horticultural details of plant life in this city.

***

New Towns

...CJ continues...

At the end of the day I went back to my bachelor flat, paged through Jan Gehl's book before carefully reading the Yenbo New Town Developmental Guidelines, especially focussing on Water Provision, Community Landscaping and Environmental Protections. I was starting to get a feel for what these two planners had been doing—what they were about.

I examined their business cards—more initials after their names than I could immediately recognize. I went over to the Computer Centre to go online. Long story short, the ones that I could understand: Bertram RIBA (Royal Institute of British Architects) and TCPA (Town and Country Planning Association); and Hans BSA (Bund Schweizer Architekten) and SIA (Swiss Society of Engineers and Architects). So much for initials but they helped in real life.

All kinds of developments were happening in the world of planning processes. In the old days survey, analysis, design—these were the foundation of planning. Then Ian McHarg put the ecologically based layers together to drive design. Then one of his students, Jack Dangermond, took advantage of computer developments and set up data gathering, analysis and mapping software. But despite those advances—the intent of planners has always been melding the social science with natural science.

And in the end, whether old school, eco-design or geo-design (still in its infancy), the cloudy mysteries of human connections with nature are still to be resolved. Every planner struggles to combine culture with science. There will always be unknowns in the process whether by humans or human developed software.

It was 10PM when I finished online. As I stepped outside it felt like the temperature was still over 30°C with Red Sea coastal humidity at least 60%. I walked over to the Camp 4 Commissary, open till 1AM. Commissary? New thing for me. It was smaller than Ralph's in West LA. Smaller even than Trader Joes. It was strange—narrow aisles, lots of products that seemed unorganized to me. The employees were different here in Haii 4 than Haii 1—either sub-continentals or Filipinos—always helpful, always smiling, but I couldn't find what I was looking for. I was hunting for some ice cream when I bumped into Hans. He asked how I was, showed me where the ice cream cones were and suggested we go outside if I wanted to talk.

Outside the commissary was a small, protected, open courtyard, enclosed by other community shops with its edge surrounded by a continuous heavy duty wood trellis on pre-cast concrete columns. The trellis was covered with all kinds of sub-tropical vines, all new to me (I came to know them as *Antigonon leptotus*, *Clytostoma callistegioides*, *Doxantha unguis-cati* and *Quisqualis indica*). In the centre of the courtyard was a recirculating fountain with a bench height wall containing the water. We sat on the edge of the fountain and ate our ice cream cones.

I asked Hans about his planning experience and how it relates to Yenbo New Town. Hans said, "It really starts with the landscape and social contexts of the project in question. For example, in Switzerland overall we have good water, good soil, amenable climate but vast amounts of very steep terrain. The country has supported itself with agriculture over centuries, therefore we preserve agricultural landscape. Our problem is over densification of cities and how to accommodate population growth without losing agricultural landscape. We have invested in transportation and communication to facilitate everyone's quick and easy access to the countryside." He paused, looked me in the eye... I was listening carefully.

81

"Here," he said, "our landscape and social contexts are greatly different. The government asked us to build a new town that would be not only the envy of the world but also respecting the local/regional customs/culture."

"How?" I asked.

"Nothing is certain in the planning world, where we try to unite architecture and landscape architecture with the inherent social variety of people."

"I hear you, but where do you start?"

"There are ancient and modern approaches to new town planning—much of this has been in the UK. I'm sure Bertram can give you details—the UK has much more available space for new towns than we have in Switzerland. They were trying to make London a better place in 1829 with John Claudius Loudon 'zones of country', 'breathing zones' or 'breathing places'. That may have been the inspiration for Ebenezer Howard's garden cities, greenways and greenbelts. And after WW2, the UK had some great planners who have worked to find successful balance between the landscape, the artefacts and the people. Patrick Abercrombie, Frederick Gibberd, Geoffrey Jellicoe and Peter Shepherd. Here at Yenbo, we have started with their principles:

- low density housing with private gardens;
- the use of green belts to control urban sprawl; and,
- the use of open space networks to separate neighbourhoods, while also providing land for parks and networks of greenways (multi-use footpaths and cycleways)."

It all sounded good to me; but I still wondered about nomads in the city. And I recalled the failures in the US of our urban renewal projects in St Louis, New York, Chicago—I brought that up to Hans.

"This social structure in Saudi Arabia is considerably more regulated than your country, the UK or my Switzerland. There will be social pressures for adapting to this new town. But like every other plan—over time adaptations will be made according to social behavioural patterns. There is no sure thing in town planning—except perhaps that there needs to be plenty of people spaces at people scale everywhere. We are providing that 'outline' structure with local, neighbourhood and district centres as well as a city centre. People on this Arabian Peninsula are accustomed to people scale as you can see in their old medinas. For our people scale in the outdoors we are expecting you to make them green, sustainable and shady."

We had long finished our ice cream cones. It was near 11PM and I had a long walk from Camp 4 (Haii IV) back to my bachelor flat. I said to Hans that I looked forward to working with him and thanked him for the background. We shook hands and I took off.

As I walked home, I recalled something of John Brinckerhof Jackson's thoughts on landscape. "Nature, ecology, and landscape are important reference concepts for landscape architecture. Traditionally, all three have been considered polar opposites from culture or humanity, in a dualistic relationship." I struggled with his duality. And Hans said this duality was guesswork in town planning. And I wondered, could landscape actually be the pliable dynamic interface between humans and nature? If so, what would that mean to me as a landscape architect designer?

But something kept inserting itself in my thoughts. Nomadic way of life on the Arabian Peninsula. Nomads. I thought—these people are first generation country boys, what some in the US call "Red Necks". These are people who know how to survive in the harshest of landscapes—the sands of Arabia—and they have for centuries... millennia? The government wants them in single family residences in a new city? I guess in return for dependable water, health, work and education—not a bad deal?! But were the nomads ready for it? That was Amelio's schtick—Keep Saudi Green. Weird.

***

Bobby Busch

...CJ continues...

I still had an important unresolved task—horticulture. I headed over to the Construction Department office. I had to do some digging. Found out that landscape construction and maintenance were being managed in their own site office by a guy named Robert (Bobby) Busch. The secretary looked at his org chart, then looked at me saying, "Busch? Don't you know, this guy is a dedicated member of your team!?"

I was shocked. "Let me have a copy of that org chart, and where is his office?"

The secretary marked my map with an "x"; and I was on my way. My next stop was Henderson's office where I asked, "Is this right? Does Busch work for me?"

"Not exactly. He works for the Construction Division. They dedicated him to our landscape group because all our design work, when it's approved, becomes construction documents and Busch manages all the landscape construction projects—as well as the follow-on maintenance. Do you see?"

I understood. The size and complexity of the design, engineering, building and operating of this new town was definitely going to keep me busy. As I headed to Busch's site office, I started thinking it through.

What I had learned before I got here—no design with a set of construction documents (plans and specifications) is ever complete. There are always the unexpected, the unknowns, the surprises that emerge during construction. Therefore, the decisions made during construction can make or break design.

What does that mean to me in KSA? Here's how it works. Design and construction are administratively separate. Design management is in the Community Projects Division. Construction management is in the Construction Division. The Construction people manage all construction contracts— civil, structural, infrastructure, architecture and landscaping.

That group was the largest. They handled the largest, most complex projects and obviously the largest budgetary percentage. The completion of those projects on time related directly to our company's payments. That meant there was enormous pressure to complete construction projects according to the schedule. Cash flow. Can't slow that down and keep your job.

I had to become best friends with Bobby Busch the Landscape Construction Manager and his team who handled installation of the landscaping projects. They had the responsibility to notify me of any field adjustments having a design impact. That is a broad mandate. It is a mandate, however, secondary to cash flow. How often might I hear about field condition design changes? I wanted to always be kept in the loop. So I became friends with that construction management team. We had to have "immediate-response open-communication" lines.

How did things change in the field? Utility alignments, utility access, emergency vehicle access, additional entry access to buildings, expanded building footprints—stuff like that—always occurring.

Then there was the procurement of site furnishings and anything else not produced within the KSA. Things that depended on international shipping. Then there were alternatives that saved money. Anything that looked similar yet cost less would be savings for the RC. We had to consider it without impacting the construction schedule.

Hell, back in SoCal, site furnishings were as easily accessible as buying a pack of cigarettes at the corner 7-11. Here everything could become a festering boil on the project process. Furnishings from Germany? From the UK? From Japan? From India, South Korea, Australia, China, the Union of South Africa? Companies from every one of those countries were in KSA seeking a KSA partner.

Our company established a legal buffer against delays from that rapidly changing field of play, which, despite our plans otherwise, regularly occurred on every project.

That was the big picture. I didn't know what to expect as I entered Bobby Busch's site office. He was the only Westerner. Indians, Pakistanis, and Sri Lankans populated the office. A construction office populated by sub-continentals, Eastern Country Nationals? Smelled like an Indian restaurant. The secretary motioned me to a door in back. Busch had his own office.

I introduced myself. He was American, my age, a graduate in landscape construction from Mississippi State—a Southerner—good ole' boy. Chewing and spitting. One office wall was covered with horizontal bar chart schedules of work under construction—looked like Microsoft Project—date delimited, expenditures, etc.—all the basics. A second wall was covered with a large whiteboard—looked like procurement items and status.

I showed Busch the document the planners had given me. He chuckled and said, "Do you really want to know how it works out here?"

I was game. "Fill me in."

Busch said, "I'm not interested in your design stuff—only plants that grow and do not become a maintenance headache."

"That makes sense—but growing the plants—tell me about soil, water and hort basics."

"First thing, our installation contractors have a 12-month establishment maintenance period."

My jaw dropped.

I asked, "12 months, hell, in California we only had 1 month maintenance for the installation contractors. Why the difference? It must have to do with climate."

"It's more complicated than that—I'll get into it later... but regarding maintenance, there's more—we are really hard on them. They must replace any failures within 24 hours of notification. We also monitor their on-site nurseries to assure health and size are proper. Everything in the nursery is under shade cloth. You got time? Let's climb into my jeep and I'll show you around."

Busch drove us right to the edge of town. I couldn't tell. It was all a flat plain, blindingly bright and sandy/silty—with the dark reddish-brown Hijaz mountains still quite a way off in the distance.

"This is it," said Busch, "the edge of town—how do I know—it's the drainage channel. We dug this. When it rains, a lot of surface water fills the wadis, seasonally dry riverbeds, and turns this plain into a lake. This drainage channel intercepts it, keeps Yenbo from flooding—drains it all to the Red Sea."

He continued, "The flat lands between here and the Hijaz—those are our sweet sand resources. We've tested the crap out of them—they are perfect nursery sand—excellent pH and drainage but no organic matter, have to add organic matter and fertilizer. But after that, plants grow like champs. Wintertime temps never drop below 50°—stuff never stops growing.

"And the water? We irrigate every square metre with tertiary treated sewage effluent, and you know what that means—nursery sand, warm winter temps and sewage effluent, plants grow like wildfire—they never stop growing."

"So," I said, "no trouble getting that Santa Barbara year-round green look the RC wants, eh?"

"To say the least!"

I liked Busch's straightforward answers, so I asked him, "What do you do for fun here—you single, like me?"

"Nah, that's another story. I'm married, no kids, wife's with me—she's originally Palestinian but carries a Jordanian passport—that's the long story bit—maybe another time. I've got to get back to prepare for a progress meeting tomorrow AM."

I liked his hort-based landscaping summary—for the first time I felt some confidence that the basics of the green city were doable.

***

The Work

I took the in-house International Project Management course and after two years I became comfortable with how all the processes worked and who were the daily movers and shakers—the people who got things done quickly.

Despite the tedious SoCal work out of Los Angeles, the real reason I came to the Kingdom of Saudi Arabia was to get away from my memories—the New Mexico unspeakable. It worked most of the time.

What enabled it to work was my new job—and it was a bear. Some things were like my commercial projects in Los Angeles but much, much larger—two factors of ten larger in both scope and cost. In fact, everything about my work was two factors of ten more complicated. That's the simplest summary.

But whether the work subject was water, soil, plants or labour—planning, design, construction or maintenance, it was all complicated. It was all without established precedent. From here on, my work descriptions and comparisons become very complicated. They are curiosities for landscape architecture groupies.

I'll start with the office. Let me compare my office and staff in LA with my office and staff in Yenbo. In Los Angeles, our firm was small. Some might call it a boutique firm. We had only five people and everybody did everything. A team of all-rounders— designing, drafting, scheduling, bidding, inspecting, billing.

In Yenbo, we had a dedicated department for each of those

activities, and a support Engineering Division of nearly 100. In Yenbo, I had my own team with representatives from each department, plus our own secretary. We had a dedicated scheduler, a contract administrator, a dedicated construction manager, a dedicated legal rep, a support engineer and a support landscape architect. I oversaw them plus the long-range scheduling of all new landscape design work.

About the work process, that is how a design moves through construction into maintenance. In Yenbo, everything began at zero. In LA, we had established contractors, established material suppliers, established nurseries, and an established process of bidding, awarding construction and maintenance. Worked quickly, smoothly and silently like a well-oiled machine. Rarely a glitch.

In Yenbo, we had no established consultants, no established contractors, no established materials suppliers, and no established nurseries. But we had an established set of processes. Those processes took time and manpower. The minimum time to process any contract through to award was 9 months. Nine months!

Consultants, contractors and materials suppliers had to submit their qualifications (usually packaged in a number of thick A4 size portfolios) to our Purchasing and Contracting Department (P&C) who carefully reviewed all details to determine—qualified or not.

My project management staff had its work subdivided into three separate domains—pre-award, award, and post-award. We worked through the 9-month sequence of pre-award activities wherein we established the technical and physical scopes (carefully detailed definitions) of the work, then reviewed the portfolios of the approved consultants and contractors to determine those best suited to receive bid documents.

The second domain was bidding, negotiations, and award. Finally, our last domain of activity was the post-award activities. We assured that the work executed met the contract scope of work, a window that normally extended 18-24 months.

We contracted out design to consultants who, after their approved design, prepared construction contract documents.

Including design, construction and maintenance, we had at any one time at least five major projects in post-award. The range of typical projects included urban street landscaping, urban park landscaping, greenbelt landscaping and recreation island park landscaping. We were busy.

The work was enormous and complex. This job was everything I hoped it would be personally and more professionally. It took me right to the basics: soil, water and plants. No pop-culture fads like SoCal, just the basics.

Let me try to make the materials of the landscape understandable. The understanding is exquisitely complex because it blends the large geographical scale with the small site scale. Soil. No soil because there was virtually no vegetation. And no vegetation meant no organic seasonal degradation to blend with the sand that was everywhere. No organic matter. No compost material. All sand.

And there were, for this discussion, but two kinds of sand. Salty silty sand along the coastal plain edge of the Red Sea, and sweet sand inland about ten kilometres. Where there was sweet sand and an oasis—a ground water source of minimal salinity—there were date palms and shrubby growth. Rare indeed. Highly sought after by everyone, but I have digressed.

The new town was on the west coast. The main purpose of the town was to build a deep-water primary and secondary oil industry port. This was to export Eastern Region oil, via overland pipelines, without the troubles of the Strait of Hormuz. The port was located away from any mangrove and coral reef communities. In order for a deep depth port to be achieved, a reasonable amount of dredging and filling had to be accomplished along the coastal salt flats.

On the landward side, filling and compacting of up to three metres was required for later road and building construction. The salt plus compaction was unfriendly for ornamental plant growth. The Royal Commission demanded green ornamental plants for the community of 200,000 people. So, for each tree and shrub planting, the compacted salty fill had to be excavated for the planting pits and replaced with sweet sand and amendments.

Hey, wait a minute. No natural plants—yet make it green. There were no nurseries. Yeah, you can bet I was busy. Nobody had ever selected the all-too-often not-found native plants for nursery propagation. And the Royal Commission wanted a green city year round. That determined conceptually the types and numbers of plants and the amount of water required.

Let's hold on for a moment and talk about water. You can do your own research about rainfall frequency in the Hijaz eco-zone of the Western Region of Saudi Arabia. I saw no rain at all in my first four years.

I must insert that for this landscape the presence and absence of water, of rain, led to the Bedouin lifestyle. They had to move to where the rain had fallen in any one year in order to find the evanescent forbs on which their goats, sheep and camels could exist. So, if rainfall was not sufficient annually for a Bedouin family, how was water to be supplied for a city of 200,000 people? Not to speak of irrigation for green city landscaping?

But there were more "rainfall" dangers. When rains came, they were usually so intense as to flood our entire coastal plain. To protect against that, a civil engineering drainage canal bordered the entire inland boundary of the new town. Busch had shown me that.

In the end, for something as essential as water? In LA, we relied on pipes bringing water from rivers 400 miles away. Here, that was not possible. There were no natural lakes, no natural rivers, and an unpredictable saline water table.

For our Yenbo potable water supply, we built a massive combination power and desalination plant. The Red Sea was the source. We also built a massive sewage treatment effluent plant which cleansed, purified and recycled all the new town used potable water. We then pumped tertiary treated sewage via its own dedicated pressurized pipe infrastructure solely for landscaping irrigation throughout the city.

I don't want to get too much deeper into the weeds with these descriptions, but these are the basics here and everywhere an Arabian desert landscape architect works. Water has to be dependable and respected. We used the desalinated water twice—once potable in the house and second as treated sewage effluent (TSE) for landscaping. The effluent for landscaping irrigation became a unique policy-driven design aim called "TSE-only, with zero discharge into the Red Sea". So how much TSE was needed for each landscape project? How much should be allocated for each tree and shrub at installation and during mature growth? And what should be the basis of the calculations for those figures of cubic metres per day? My challenges were welcome and many—so much deeper than anything I had faced in Los Angeles. I relished my work.

Now, the plants. Where did we get them? Oh, life had been so easy in SoCal where over decades we depended on six to eight well-established contractors and scads of dependable large and small nurseries. But here, who was dependable for hundreds of workers, and millions of plants worth tens of millions of dollars? There was not an existing landscape industry of even a small scale—not to speak of the enormous needs for a new city scaled for nearly a quarter million inhabitants.

That was where our Purchasing and Contracting Department came in. They were in charge of all procurement. They made sure it was legal and according to project processes and needs. To keep the playing field level, all contractors were required to house their workers on the site in a specially provided neighbourhood for contract labourers. All to reduce any abuse of workers, which was a good thing because finding hundreds of landscape labourers with experience often meant sourcing farmers from Sri Lanka, Bangladesh, India and Pakistan—people who had never even seen automobiles before arriving on our job site. I kid you not.

And each landscape contractor established his own nursery on site and bought the plants accordingly. Because each planting pit was sweet sand with amendments, and the irrigation water was TSE (rich with fertile nutrients) and the winter temperature never dropping below 50°, the young plants grew unbelievably fast and established quickly.

I thought the growth rate of plants in SoCal was fast, at least compared to the Midwest where freezing cold solidified the earth every winter. But in SoCal, there was no topsoil—so

I was already accustomed to soil enrichment and replacement for trees, shrubs, groundcovers and grass. But here there was salty soil around every planting area and, due to non-stop insolation, a very high transpiration rate. New challenges everywhere.

This was a new world for me and every day unexpected complications arose.

***

The Local Culture

...CJ continues...

White or black. Couldn't be much simpler. Men or women, none of the Saudis in our Yenbo project or urban Saudis in general performed labour, work as I grew up knowing it.

Then who in urban areas, workers? Labourers? Always Eastern or Western Country Nationals. The Saudis? In public, they were always clean and dressed either in black, the women, or white, the men. Men always in white *thobes* (full length robe-like gowns) with white or red checked headdresses (*ghutras*). The *thobes* were lightweight versions of Moroccan *djellabas*. Women always fully covered in black *abayas* top to ground—head, hair, face, arms and legs.

Different world, my friend. Minimum, absolute minimum social interaction. That was the Kingdom of Saudi Arabia's urban life. I, a Western Country National bachelor, a true outsider without a hint of social interaction with Saudis in public, never got comfortable. I trained young Saudi men, as interns, on the job; but never a smidgen of jolly social exchange. In fact, I rarely saw full *abaya* Saudi women in our New Yenbo public.

Maybe that was alright. One less thing to distract me from my work. In KSA, the non-Muslim foreigners were clearly outsiders. Just the opposite of my time in Morocco and Tangier especially where everyone on the street wanted to get into my life.

The first time I went to the gold souk in the old part of Jeddah I found a node of two or three medina byways. These were the narrow pedestrian-only medina byways. Tightly clustered, 30-40 shops made the node.

The byways were without lights. The shops provided lighting through their front windows. At this node, all the shops were gold shops. I'd never seen anything like it.

Each of the gold shops had bright halogen lights in their picture windows. Each window chock-a-block filled with vast varieties, treasures of women's 22-karat gold jewellery—so much brightly lighted gold—ceiling to floor in the window and everywhere inside the shop. The glittering aura told the magic of gold.

Whenever I was in Jeddah, I would revisit... night-time only... the glow, the glitter, the beaming aura. I made the mistake once of trying to visit these shops in mid-afternoon 40+° heat. I learned they were always closed, nothing to see, shut up tightly no less than 4 hours from mid-day prayer until after sunset prayer.

At 10 o'clock at night, the warm glow of 22-karat gold was soothing even in the horrid Jeddah night-time Red Sea humidity. That was the first time I saw as much medina souk activity as I had experienced every day in any Moroccan medina.

In the Jeddah gold souk at 10PM every night—inside every brightly lighted gold shop was at least one cluster of eight to ten black *abayas* around one white *thobe*, all examining 22-karat gold ornaments for the women.

The only time I saw a Saudi woman's face was once in a second-hand white metal and silver jewellery souk in the southwestern inland border town of Najran where, on the side of a street, were a bunch of women vendors dressed like 19th Century Bohemians, no face coverings, no black—never could figure that one. Najran? On the border with Yemen—maybe that was Yemeni influence.

There must be some kind of cross-cultural middle-ground between the pushy Moroccans and the hidden Saudi Arabians. Or maybe not. Neither of these places was my home. Why should I think it could be? Like I've said before—their place, their rules. Finished.

Or is it? Something is attractive about both these strange places. Maybe it is nothing more than a "variety is the spice of life" experience. I learn new things. I like that. But there is much more that I don't understand.

My job and its daily pressures worked like a cocoon to shelter me from the cross-culture unknowns—and I'm okay with that. And making a difference? I am turning a plant/water/soil free landscape into an enjoyable community resource that mitigates this intense desert climate. Simple as that. Complex as that. That is making a difference.

***

Kurt Says

What a picture!

CJ gave me insight to his work, landscape and cultural environments that the best travel documentaries never quite hit. He was absorbed.

As I read, I felt the CJ I knew—always seeking a challenge and finding an intelligent solution. He liked hard work. He was in the game; but it was clear that the horrendous family accident in New Mexico had left him wounded inside.

Overall, I was relieved to find that CJ was into his KSA work. His postcards never indicated otherwise. What happened to change all that?

CJ got his bigger responsibilities but he also got bigger admin issues and cultural issues—were these a positive or negative leading to Cairo—was he frustrated, depressed or just old-fashioned CJ problem solving—and what about design? Was this new location better?

4-My Routine

My Original CA

...CJ continues...

On the project, as I was building a strong team, the key person was my Contract Administrator (CA), a guy out of Purchasing and Contracting (P&C). In fact, my CA was key from the beginning.

A bunch of personnel changes happened my first month on the job in Yenbo. There was a RIF, a reduction in force that removed Amelio from Engineering, decimated the ten-person senior landscape group and axed a whole slew of middle management types. The thinning was a benefit to me because a lot of the middle management types were only interested in managing their own turf—not at all team players in interdisciplinary cooperation. Those guys made a habit of kicking dirt in the face of landscape people (last ones in on the job with the smallest construction budget, that was us).

RIFs roll through our company in Yenbo like earthquakes. Everybody feels the rumble. They are caused by downward fluctuations in the world oil price. Watching trends in the price of oil on the world markets, we can guess a RIF might be coming but there is never forewarning.

After that initial RIF that put me in charge, the only remaining guys were two juniors plus the CA. That CA, and he was an older guy, gave me someone who had the connections—gave our group some seniority, some gravitas.

But... he was a bit of an odd duck. He was a Brit, though brought up in the US. He actually held an American undergraduate degree in landscape architecture from U Penn.

Then he moved back to the UK and did a second undergrad degree in quantity surveying. He taught in the landscape architecture program at a university here in KSA before joining our company here in Yenbo.

He told me the entire story himself when I first arrived in Yenbo. Crazy. He, about his time as a KSA university instructor, told me parents would come to threaten him whenever he gave grades lower than a "C". He saw little future for home-grown Saudi landscape architects. And that was where my Yenbo story really got interesting.

Over the next 18 months, as our workload increased, I built a supporting team of seven more. During this same period, my "odd duck" original CA left the kingdom, moved to Cyprus. Just as well. He had tried to squeeze me out. He wanted complete control over contract negotiations for all consultants and contractors. Didn't even want me in the room during negotiations. His approach reeked of impropriety. I forbade it. We were always in conflict. Glad to see the back of him, truly a prickly guy.

Talk about prickly? That was the weather most of the year. 35+° till midnight. 80% salty Red Sea humidity every sunset. AC? Running 24/7/365. The outdoors hummed with hard working AC units. Everyone always seeking shelter from the climate. Air-conditioned cocoons, anyone? Challenges! There were a few and I was into them. Now, I needed a new CA.

***

Work and Recreation

...CJ continues...

Without a CA, I was without contractual protection. And why did I need protection? I, we, were all under massive schedule and deliverable pressures. We had weekly progress meetings with the SPM to highlight emerging problems and monthly progress meetings with the CPM. We had to present each project timeline for deliverable progress and projected completion. If we weren't on schedule with deliverables, we would be publicly chewed out, ground up into raw meat. We had to perform. And the CA was the sharpest tool we had.

Most important of his jobs—on all contracts under my purview, he had to make sure that all landscape contractors and consultants met all RC process and financial requirements.

This is where I learned the difference between RC labour camps and off-site labour camps. Long story short—the RC labour camps set standards in safety, health and quality for labourers and supplies. Thus, they were an expensive part of any contract. Some contractors got away with off-site facilities; and that is where trouble began.

Trouble? These were unfortunately, pirate contractors— low overhead costs for their housing, materials and staff—the management taking higher percentages for profit while quality of their work was sub-standard. That's the general picture for our large-scale city construction where networks for labour, support goods and services had no established presence.

Consultants and their designers brought their own problems. They didn't stay in labour camps—but I often wished they did so they could truly learn the local landscape.

We had a lot of consultants from the UK doing landscape design. In order for them to be qualified to tender services here in Yenbo, they had to prove they were at least 51% owned by a Saudi Arabian entity.

Once they managed that, the next issue we uncovered was the British landscape architecture language. They used different vocabulary to describe landscape, design, and the processes. Different to our Yank ears. They used that vocabulary as a launch for subtle and gross sledging meant to undermine our authority. In the end we approved or disapproved their invoices. We used that power like a choke hold on their weak performance.

They often did the work in the UK with a skeleton team—rarely meeting schedule. We found that result too frequently. So we tweaked the payment conditions and built in surprise visits to their UK offices to assure both progress and quality.

After persistent schedule and quality difficulties, we further adjusted the contract conditions such that the UK team members had to be situated in their KSA partner office here in KSA.

The battle was ongoing because most consultant team members did not want to live even for short times in KSA. Those consultants ultimately lost their approval for Yenbo projects.

We were always under big pressure to meet our company's schedule because that was key for receiving timely and full payments to us from the RC. So we pushed the consultants hard. Ultimately we were successful; but, after design, construction brought another set of challenges.

In the Western Region of Saudi Arabia, on my Yenbo project, street trees were part of the infrastructure work. That was the first time I had seen on a competitively bid, huge project scale, plants being grown in the used empty tin cans normally thrown out from labour camp kitchens. Always rusting, the cans were lucky to have drainage holes.

Pirate contractors always stacked these sub-standard plant containers cheek-by-jowl to save on land rental costs. Plants were hand watered seemingly by chance. And pruning equipment? Just never around. I could see that my SoCal nursery standards would not apply here. I'd have to adjust.

The captain of these pirate landscape operations was invariably a French, Belgian or Afrikaner character. These guys had meanness carved all over their faces—a kepi blanc, French Foreign Legion escapee. They were at least suitable for a starring role in a Werner Herzog movie, men of neither scruples nor fear. Everyone who worked for these captains was a day labourer at the cheapest rate. If the day labourers would have come from farm backgrounds in Bangladesh, or Sri Lanka—eh, never such luck.

I had struggles everywhere. But struggles? That's my work. I enjoyed having to solve them.

Speaking of struggles, I had them with people supposedly on my own team—civil engineers and structural engineers. These guys hated to have me, the landscape architect field project manager, the gardener in their eyes, question their schedule or over-engineered work. Reminded me of years ago when I set up a loosely linked team of engineers, friends, back in New Mexico—the teamwork was good but... the... family disaster deaths—don't want to say more about that.

Here in Yenbo even though we were all on the same team, some of these engineers acted like I was taking food out of their mouths. We all had schedules to keep—"to keep" meant our company being paid on time by the RC. But some of these engineers always had excuses why their design review of my landscape architecture consultant work could not be done on time, meaning I would have to take the blame for delays in RC payments to our company. That would be the end of my job—on the way back to the US. Weasels, these engineers were.

I needed a willow cricket bat from the UK or a "Louisville Slugger" baseball bat from the US to convince them—that worked sometimes, or I arranged for extra front-end lead time—so when they delayed I would still meet my scheduled deliverables.

My work often seemed like stealthily moving pieces around on a chess board. I liked the challenge—people and professions—cheating attempts on so many levels, my own team, the consultant teams and the contractor teams, all to make a green city.

Yeah, I was busy and yeah, it was intense. Ten-hour days, 5.5 days per week. Options for relaxation? Every six months I had a travel-paid nine-day vacation. In between, I made my studio flat my cocoon. Music, writing on design. I had no recreational interaction with the locals. Hardly saw them.

We also had holidays according to the Muslim calendar—Hajj and Ramadan—local three-day breaks. I rented a car one Ramadan and drove around old Yenbo and Al Wejj—everyone in those towns slaughtered their own lambs and the day after, every dumpster and trash can was overflowing with bloody entrails—every street, every alley—couldn't hide from it. The towns looked and smelled in the heat of the day like outdoor slaughterhouses. Everyone living there was inside celebrating. On the streets and alleys, I saw only scraggly, short-hair cats. These cats, with tails, ears and eyes damaged by inter-feline street warfare, were wild scavengers, feral, definitely not house cats.

So much for local holidays. Needed Western recreation—went to the UK or Amsterdam on my every six-month scheduled holiday—absolutely essential.

***

Cocoons

...CJ continues...

Hermit shelter or cocoon? Any difference?

My job was a cocoon. Maybe other people felt the same; but the truth is everybody took, as often as possible, a break outside the KSA. The closest, most popular short haul was to Cyprus, a partitioned island in the Eastern Med. Others went to Jordan, but Cyprus felt, so they say, like you were out of the Muslim world. That was Greek Cyprus, not Turkish Cyprus.

What about the rumours? Rumours about an Arabian Peninsula country that overcame the desert. The land that grew agriculture to support its own population? That was Israel. But if our passport had an Israeli stamp in it, we could not re-enter the Kingdom of Saudi Arabia.

When I say my job was a cocoon, that is to say it kept me so occupied that thoughts of the past never entered. But 24 hours in a day and I can't be thinking about my job full time. What to do?

My company supported a book library, and a CD/DVD library. The book library became my hangout because reading books were my magic garden—my trips into Never-Neverland. But I also found books on regional craft, jewellery and dhows. It was easy to get into books. DVD movies? Not so much. And I got involved in local clubs.

I became a regular attendee at the monthly Red Sea Philatelic Society meetings. Most important to understand was who attended these meetings. Nearly every meeting, 40-50 attendees, was 100% expatriates, Western and Eastern. From time to time, a high-ranking Saudi from the RC would attend, but not regularly. All the regular members were into buying sheets of every new stamp the Saudis released.

Often there was a short AV presentation by a member regarding a recent field trip. Then people would break up into smaller groups to share snacks and talk about their own interests.

Discussions about historical events in the Hijaz were wide ranging and linked to stamp collecting. Lawrence of Arabia, the Turks, and Western Region politics were popular topics.

I sat one evening with the Brit planner, Bertram. We talked over tea. We got on pretty well.

Like most senior and committed planners, Bertram was big time into history. In casual conversation, he easily covered Sumerians, Babylonians, Persians, Greeks, Egyptians, Romans, Turks, all well-established cultures with arts and architecture influences along the fringes of the Arabian Peninsula.

I felt like I was hearing a masters lecture when he spoke.

"Beside the *mu'allaqaat* (oral tradition), Petra and Medain Saleh are the only extant physical record of a past the desert sands have erased," he said.

Then he summarized, "Around the edges of the huge deserts of Arabia are clues to mysterious past civilizations living here. The explorations of those edges are active."

This hunt for clues inspired me.

Bertram said, "Aristotle wrote that democracy is possible only within homogeneous ethnic groups and that despots have always reigned over highly fragmented societies. Along the edges of these massive deserts, we are looking at both."

On this evening, Bertram couldn't stop. Next, he got into Islamic historical influences, especially pre-Islamic Arabia— something about which I knew little. But it was a landscape subject, and the portly Bertram had quite a few years of Saudi Arabian landscape under his belt. I was thinking... pre-Islamic, was that including pre-Christian? I asked him and he answered as a British professor would speak to a neophyte Yank student.

108

"Christopher, the sands are deeper than Islam, deeper than Christianity, deeper than Judaic history, deeper than we can imagine. Mysteries underneath mysteries."

He noted my interest and continued, "From the Arabian Peninsula's southern coast, Arabia Felix up through the Levant, there were routes."

"Who has found them?" I asked.

"No one has actually found them; but they are the subject of pre-Islamic oral histories."

Bertram continued, "It is logical. Goods from India and the Far East and from Central Africa made their way along the coast to places that are nowadays known as Yemen and Oman. Camels, caravans, moved these exotic goods overland to the Levant and then by sea again, around the Mediterranean."

"Anyone can make up stories—how does anyone grant authenticity to them?" I asked.

"There are records, poems, many oral but some written 2,000 and longer years ago. Some are well known, others less so and are under study. They are called the *mu'allaqat...* and there are others... others that make the longer history of the Arabian Peninsula a shape-shifting mystery."

"Mystery?" I asked then continued, "Like how long were humans living in this god-forsaken death-wish climate and was the climate always like this and where did the people come from that populated these deserts?"

"Now you are getting the picture, Christopher. Before the Nabateans. Not very far from here, around Medain Saleh, there are remnants that some say are older than the pyramids, older than Stonehenge."

"What?!"

"There is ancient rock art up there. Ancient..."

I didn't know where this was going. All I heard was something that I would call landscape mysteries. I wondered, what does this landscape hide?

"Tell me more."

"First of all, Christopher, the local people, the Bedouin and their descendants have lived through it all—the sands and all it carries. These people are strong, tough, independent and resilient." Bertram paused, measuring my reaction. I was his student. Then he continued.

"Second, on a geographic and much larger paleontological scale, it is more about faith in your sources, but there are remnants of pastoral civilization before the 'Fertile Crescent' just north of here."

I was interested, but I didn't have the faith.

Bertram continued, "You have seen the photos of Nabatean architecture—Petra in Jordan, and Medain Saleh here in the KSA—carved from stone, haven't you?"

"Yeah, last month I saw the presentation. It looked like some kind of Greek or Roman architecture."

"Those carved façades are on the northern edge of the Arabian Peninsula—on the edge of the Levant—the eastern Mediterranean coast.

"And then we have more mysteries."

Bertram paused, using the momentary silence to good effect before he continued. "The question is why none of them conquered the peninsula."

A quick answer sprung to my head. "No water, all sand."

"That is obvious. But nomads, the Bedouin, have lived for centuries, millennia, on this peninsula, in the landscape—can you sense some mysteries here?"

"How do you see it, Bertram?"

Then Bertram hit it big when he said, "Beneath every ancient mystery of the origins of human civilization, the place wherein their hidden roots lie is... the landscape."

That I could get a handle on—that interested me. And then older memories surfaced. I recalled Bree's experiences on the edge of the Sahara—the ones she told me about when I met her in Morocco. Very inhospitable landscapes that had a negative vibe—but where did the vibe come from? And here was a pre-Islamic presence that had remarkable skills—where did it come from?

Well, these discussions were a cocoon of their own. I enjoyed them. They gave me new perspectives—insights into people, their culture and their relations with the landscape. That's an exploration of the unknown that has infinite dimensions.

It intrigues me. But it is not my work. Work is one cocoon. Explorations into the roots of human/landscape interactions are another cocoon.

Being on this project in the Western Region of Saudi Arabia had its attractions—but I was a Westerner. And there was nothing Western about the Western Region of Saudi Arabia.

***

Qaaba

...CJ continues...

In Yenbo, on the television there are two channels. Saudi Channel 1 always in Arabic. Saudi Channel 2 in English. Both, on the five prayer calls every day, cut to the mosque at Mecca for the prayers. And on the Saudi second channel, in English they refer to the King as the Custodian of the Two Holy Mosques. Two holy mosques? Yes, one in Medina-the Prophet's Mosque and one in Mecca-the Sacred Mosque.

How many Muslims in the world? By some sources, approaching 2 billion. So 2 billion people bowing five times a day in the direction of the holy mosque in Mecca and its Qaaba. That's got to be some powerful magnet. What is it? And what is the source of the power? Could it have landscape roots?

A frequent explanation is that the Black Stone was placed in the Qaaba by Prophet Abraham, after it was presented to him by the angel Gabriel. Angel? The stone is recognized as to have come from heaven. Online research on such an important feature is difficult to filter. Stories are varied and the reality seems to stretch back to "before written records".

I tried to deep-dive my online research hoping to get into the pre-Islamic landscape roots. I always ended up learning more details about the centre of Islam—the Qaaba, a stone building at the centre of Islam's most important mosque and holiest site, the Masjid al-Haram in Mecca. Understanding its place in Islam was my starting point.

The Qaaba, or cube, is known as the House of God, the

most sacred spot on the planet earth. When a Muslim prays, he bows in the direction of the Qaaba in Mecca.

The Qaaba, a cubic building, elegantly draped in a silk and cotton veil, is the holiest shrine in Islam. Prayer five times a day and the hajj (pilgrimage to the Qaaba) are two of the five pillars of Islam, the most fundamental principles of the faith.

Upon arriving in Mecca, pilgrims gather in the courtyard of the Masjid al-Haram around the Qaaba. They then circumambulate (*tawaf* in Arabic) or walk around the Qaaba, during which they hope to kiss and touch the Black Stone (al-Hajar al-Aswad), embedded in the eastern corner of the Qaaba. This has been my summary of the fundamental religious Qaaba basics.

Black stone? In the Qaaba? What was it? Where did it come from? And why was it important? This had the makings of some kind of landscape mystery.

I had run across the writings of the Swiss Titus Burckhardt years ago in Morocco. He, having accepted Islam, also travelled the Arabian Peninsula, making a detailed description of the Black Stone in his 1829 book *Travels in Arabia*:

"It is an irregular oval, about seven inches (18 cm) in diameter, with an undulated surface, composed of about a dozen smaller stones of different sizes and shapes, well joined together with a small quantity of cement, and perfectly well smoothed; it looks as if the whole had been broken into as many pieces by a violent blow, and then united again. It is very difficult to determine accurately the quality of this stone which has been worn to its present surface by the millions of touches and kisses it has received. It appeared to me like a lava, containing several small extraneous particles of a whitish and of a yellow substance. Its colour is now a deep reddish brown approaching to black. It is surrounded on all sides by a border composed of a substance which I took to be a close cement of pitch and gravel of a similar, but not quite the same, brownish colour. This border serves to support its detached pieces; it is two or three inches in breadth, and rises a little above the surface of the stone. Both the border and the stone itself are encircled by a silver band, broader below than above, and on the two sides, with a considerable swelling below, as if a part of the stone were hidden under it. The lower part of the border is studded with silver nails."

Then, visiting the Qaaba in 1853, Richard Francis Burton, a noted linguist and observer of cultures, wrote this description of the Black Stone:

"The colour appeared to me black and metallic, and the centre of the stone was sunk about two inches below the metallic circle. Round the sides was a reddish-brown cement, almost level with the metal, and sloping down to the middle of the stone. The band is now a massive arch of gold or silver gilt. I found the aperture in which the stone is, one span and three fingers broad."

Others take a more mystical approach:

"The Black Stone was held in reverence well before Islam. It had long been associated with the Qaaba, which was built in the pre-Islamic period and was a site of pilgrimage of Nabataeans who visited the shrine once a year to perform their pilgrimage.

"The Qaaba marked the location where the sacred world intersected with the profane, and the embedded Black Stone was a further symbol of this as an object as a link between heaven and earth."

While:

"Islamic tradition holds that the Black Stone fell from Jannah to show Adam and Eve where to build an altar, which became the first temple on Earth. Muslims believe that the stone was originally pure and dazzling white, but has since turned black because of the sins of the people who touch it. Its black colour is deemed to symbolize the essential spiritual virtue of detachment and poverty for God (faqr) and the extinction of ego required to progress towards God (qalb)."

and:

"The nature of the Black Stone has been much debated. It has been described variously as basalt stone, an agate, a piece of natural glass or—most popularly—a stony meteorite. Paul Partsch, the curator of the Austro-Hungarian imperial collection of minerals, published the first comprehensive analysis of the Black Stone in 1857, in which he favoured a meteoritic origin for the stone.

"Robert Dietz and John McHone proposed in 1974 that the Black

Stone was actually an agate, judging from its physical attributes and a report by an Arab geologist that the stone contained clearly discernible diffusion banding characteristic of agates.

"A significant clue to its nature is provided by an account of the stone's recovery in 951AD, after it had been stolen 21 years earlier. According to a chronicler, the stone was identified by its ability to float in water. If this account is accurate, it would rule out the Black Stone being an agate, a basalt lava, or a stony meteorite, though it would be compatible with it being glass or pumice.

"Elsebeth Thomsen of the University of Copenhagen proposed a different hypothesis in 1980. She suggested that the Black Stone may be a glass fragment, or impactite, from the impact of a fragmented meteorite that fell 6,000 years ago at Wabar, a site in the Rub' al Khali desert 1,100 km east of Mecca. A 2004 scientific analysis of the Wabar site suggests that the impact event happened much more recently than first thought and might have occurred within the last 200–300 years."

But those religious and pseudo-scientific descriptions are just part of the story. And the rest of the story is where the mystery and my interest deepen:

"The Wabar craters are impact craters located in Saudi Arabia first brought to the attention of Western scholars by British Arabist, explorer, writer and Colonial Office intelligence officer St John Philby, who discovered them while searching for the legendary city of Ubar in Arabia's Rub' al Khali (Empty Quarter) in 1932.

"Philby had heard of Bedouin legends of an area called Al Hadida ('place of iron' in Arabic) with ruins of ancient habitations, and also an area where a piece of iron the size of a camel had been found, and so organized an expedition to visit the site.

"After a month's journey through wastes so harsh that even some of the camels died, on 2 February 1932 Philby arrived at a patch of ground about a half a square kilometre in size, littered with chunks of white sandstone, black glass, and chunks of iron meteorite. Philby identified two large circular depressions partially filled with sand, and three other features that he identified as possible 'submerged craters'. He also mapped the area where the large iron block was reputed to have been found. Philby thought that the area was a volcano, and it was only after bringing back samples to the UK that the site was identified as that of a meteorite impact by Leonard James Spencer of the British Museum."

This area of the Rub al Khali, the Empty Quarter, has always been rife with legends of buried in the sand civilizations—Wabar, Ubar, Iram, Omanum Emporium and others—thought to have been destroyed by a natural disaster, or a punishment by God. TE Lawrence focussed the legends, calling it a hunt for Atlantis of the Sands.

The more I dug into this "Atlantis of the Sands", the more oblique it became. The truth, as I figure, is first and foremost, the sands rule this peninsula because the sands erase human activity no matter how sophisticated modern technology is. Back to the Black Stone and its home, the Qaaba.

"The meteoritic hypothesis is viewed by geologists as doubtful. The British Natural History Museum suggests that it may be a pseudometeorite; in other words, a terrestrial rock mistakenly attributed to a meteoritic origin.

"The Black Stone has never been analysed with modern scientific techniques and its origins remain the subject of speculation."

All of this leaves me somewhat confused. I am not one of the faithful. For the faithful and to most of the world this Black Stone inside the Qaaba is the religious center of the Arabian Peninsula. To me it is a mystery and I am inclined to say, rather it is the desert landscape that is the most powerful.

And the question regarding the power of the Black Stone in the Qaaba? No answer. A definite cultural and landscape mystery. This is the spiritual context of my landscape work in the Kingdom of Saudi Arabia.

***

Design

...CJ continues...

Speaking of cocoons, I live for design. And design? I have always tried to fit my landscape and garden experiences into my approach to landscape architecture design. Those experiences are essentially and always linear, moving from one destination to the next—like reading a book, like listening to music.

In summary, landscape is the root. Thinking about landscape and design together weaves a delectable cocoon for me. When I am into landscape and design, I am in a special cocoon—a place where discrete parts of linear experiences reorganize into transforming inspirations. In those moments, nothing else matters.

In my shelter, my studio, I reviewed my notes from back in Morocco, through New Mexico and SoCal to structure a suitable design path for the work I was doing in Yenbo.

I disagreed with popular tropes in contemporary landscape architecture such as
  - The Digital Trope: faster is better;
  - The Social Trope: consensus solves all; and,
  - The Environmental Trope: sustainability as the "secular supreme".

I was not a standard LA guy, riding the crest of the pop-art wave. These tropes were the very things, developing over the past twenty-five years, that I saw were undermining the original, solid foundational core of landscape architecture. And what was that landscape architecture core? Understand the regional and local landscape in all natural and social dimensions, then problem solve for a solution to inspire users.

I was searching for an angle or a series of links between humans and plants, humans and gardens, humans and landscapes... and I sensed there must be some repetitive thread or theme connecting humans to the landscape—something more than gravity. I imagined, weird as it may seem, that music might be connective tissue between humans and plants.

After much thinking and too much re-thinking over months in my Haii 3 studio, I came up with some basics. They were my attempt at "Design Protocols"—a six-axiom definition of landscape architecture:

- In the beginning there was one: landscape. Landscape harboured danger for humans.
- Humans constructed shelters. Then there were two: landscape, and the shelters in the landscape.
- And today still, humans essentially move through the landscape from shelter to shelter.
- Architecture is shelter.
- Landscape is everything else in which the shelters sit.
- Landscape Architecture is the dramatic craft concerning the quality of experience, during the movement of humans from shelter to shelter through the landscape.

So how did I apply those axioms? In my own New Mexico business I tried to apply what I learned in Tangier but the realities of each project—who pays the bills, who builds the project, who maintains the project—forced me to rethink what was design.

In Yenbo, I had to make sure everything grew and was healthy—that was my first priority. And I wasn't the designer, I was the design manager. Each landscape consultant had to prepare the landscape architecture design. I had to give them guidelines, their scope of work.

And that was quite a challenge. Fortunately, I could draw upon my experience teaching landscape architectural design when I taught courses in SoCal. I had already broken down the practical bases and built a simple, trackable path for new landscape architecture designers.

In Yenbo, I had to translate that for professional use. We had landscape architecture design consultants from the US, Canada, the UK, Australia, Germany. I had to make it understandable to each of them. That was a challenge in and of itself.

US to US had its own challenges; but the US giving design instructions to Brits—they didn't like it one bit. But they wanted the big design contracts so they agreed—only to take issue with every small thing once we awarded them the contract. I needed the "Louisville Slugger" again and again.

It was easy to solve getting from A to B in the landscape. I should have said you have three choices—geometry, natural or a blend. The climate amelioration was a shade and wind direction problem. But the irrigation was a science and craft all its own—evapotranspiration rates, time of day, season, frequency, amount. Those all had to be solved on each project and fit within citywide structures of water provision and allowances.

In the end the fundamentals of humans moving through an awful and intense climate was the central point—needed shade and ventilation. And extreme weather occurrences—we stopped flooding. Extreme heat and wind came when it came. This was the Arabian Peninsula, home of the Empty Quarter—hot, dry, windy, scarcity of life—we weren't going to change that. Amelioration.

And design? Hardscape, art, plants? We tried to be open to art in the context of local/regional traditions but the climate was undeniably the most powerful influence.

I could live with that very traditional approach to landscape design. It had to solve that local/regional climate problem for the new Yenbo urban dwellers. What was a struggle were the consultant designers who played word games, made word salads to get their way. Design has always been an amorphous word, an amorphous concept, an amorphous process. It's arcane really—it arises as someone's idea and nobody knows where an idea comes from—all of a sudden it arrives in our heads. It definitely has alchemical roots.

In reality, design is just another way to say "I like it" or

"I don't like it". Good or bad—it is what I say it is. Design is surrogate for survival of the fittest. That is what every discussion on design becomes—survival of the fittest.

My job as design manager was to direct and control those discussions and results. I loved the responsibility. This was why I sought an enlarged professional challenge.

**

Kurt Says

Okay, CJ's work day was ten hours. And his work week was five and a half days, every week. That's a long, hard haul. And his Haii 3 accommodation? Hardly looked better than a prison camp. At least he had a room to himself. No Trader Vics, no cinemas, no bars, no night clubs. Hardship, but he had his reasons. And he must have had some goals. Though I wonder. Money? Vacations? Power? Design?

He had natural recreation around him on the Red Sea coast—mangroves, coral reefs, beaches; but he never talked about anything but the sands—the silica. I don't know, if I can add a little humour—maybe he was inhaling too much "spice". Humour aside, design was CJ's spice.

He always ranted on design. I really had to use a hard filter on his rants. But he did win design and built-project awards for us. And I was curious about what inspired him, where he was headed with design.

I remember one little design battle we had when I brought up the infamous "Bagel Garden" from the late 1970s. If I remember correctly, it caused so much debate, so much consternation that the editor of our professional Landscape Architecture Magazine (LAM), lost his job because he published it.

On the day with CJ, as I remember it, I started, "that bagel garden, that was good stuff, gave everyone an alternative to naturalism in the landscape..."

CJ exploded, "Alternative? On the issues of maintenance and plants, the designer who has become famous from that bagel garden just ignored them because of their cost—totally irresponsible. Then to say that makes a good garden solution for poorer people?"

I said, "She also said she was trying to make sense out of nonsense."

CJ jumped right back at me, "Gardens are someone's art joke? Her excuses were her art. Ha! She thinks she is making a difference for less fortunate people? And she doesn't discuss the simple front yard or back yard growing fruits, vegetables and flowers? She gives up food and portals for an individual's art ideas? How can anyone support that? No wonder the LAM editor was fired."

On the day, CJ went on and on about making a difference and plant portals. I turned on my hard filter.

Truthfully, he was hunting for the holy grail. He wanted to make a difference, like all of us. He wanted to make something beautiful that "works"—and that alone was good enough for me.

I told him, "Save the holy grail for the alchemist."

To see CJ getting into design again in Yenbo? That was a sign of strength and health. I wondered about how his death in Cairo was verified. I wondered if it was just paperwork cleared out of someone's full inbox.

The more I read from his KSA design writings, the more I sensed a business opportunity. Maybe I could learn something from his design musings to keep my firm on the cutting edge. Selfish? Am I selfish? I'm a businessman. The business pays for my food and shelter.

***

Alan

In my first six months on the Yenbo project, just after the original Reduction In Force (RIF), they put me in charge of the severely pruned landscape group. I had a visit, a strange visitor.

I had forgotten that I was to expect this guy. His name, Ali Hussain; he said, "Call me Alan." His business card said Senior Manager, Information Operations, The Analysis Corporation, with offices in the US, Europe, Africa, the Middle East and the Far East. He had a phone number and a PO Box in Riyadh.

He looked like a cross between Pakistani and Iranian, Middle East brown skin, dark brown eyes, thick black hair and beard—medium build, maybe 5'10" tall. He said he had an office in Riyadh for a consultant company out of Philadelphia, working as a program oversight consultant for the Royal Commission.

His English was good, university level and only a slight Middle East accent.

He introduced the subject. "My responsibility is administrative. I provide high-level implementation schedule oversight."

Then he said, "I am here today, expecting to be briefed by you on the RIF impacts to the landscape program schedule."

I was wondering what this guy was all about, when suddenly the light went on for me—this was the guy Eileen's team told me to expect. He was my local information-gathering contact.

He was distant and subtly pushy. But, worst of all, he wanted my bolshy CA in our meeting. I stood firm. Told him I handled all things landscape. If he had a problem, he should talk with Will Clendenon, our Program Manager. Alan agreed; and there was no further discussion on landscape responsibility in the Yenbo New Town.

After that rough introduction, here's how it worked. Alan visited 10 days before each time I had to go to the KSA capital city, Riyadh, for an RC presentation. He came for what we called a dry run—where, the week before, we practiced the RC presentation.

In a general way, he would identify with whom I should talk at the associated social events. At the events, I spoke about football, usually with junior members of the Royal family. Then in the week after the presentation, he would visit me to hear me describe what I heard. Never knew what was going on and never was under any pressure. At least that was the way I understood it.

It was easy talking with young Royals about football. The Falcons were their national team. They had won the Asian Cup numerous times. They aspired to be in the World Cup. And about Yenbo, they all wanted Yenbo New Town to be healthy and beautiful for the Saudi families who would work and live there.

At first I tried to use my Darija dialect of Arabic from Morocco; but I soon learned that local Arabic dialect and jargon was so different... so we used English because most of them had university educations from English speaking countries. All in all, I got on well with them—we talked football non-stop. These sports discussions gave me cultural insights which were useful in my Yenbo parks and recreation contracts.

But then it changed—not the Saudis but my contact. Alan wanted me to be more aggressive. He asked me to make sure I spoke with specific older RC members. Then he asked me to introduce specific topics—personal meets that would focus on social behaviour. I was no longer comfortable. Talking about family members, wives, sisters, young girls, young boys—didn't seem right. I didn't cross those lines.

Then sometime later, it got worse, he asked me to wear

a wire. I said no way. He backed off. After work one evening at that same time, I bumped into Will Clendenon at the Commissary. Asked him to talk about Alan. He suggested we walk over to the soccer pitch where a game was in progress. I related the details of Alan's upgraded requests as we walked.

Will listened. Said nothing until I finished the entire story. Then he said, "Sometimes silence is the strongest position."

I took his words seriously; and it was a good thing I did. The next two RC briefing quarters Alan kept pushing the wire and the personal meets on me. He even threatened me with a salary deduction. That was foolish because I knew, backwards and forwards, all the details of my signed/countersigned conditions of employment, my MOA, memorandum of agreement. I was on firm ground. He had no play in it at all. Alan pushed, I said nothing. He had no response, no power. I just kept talking football with the young Saudi royals at the Riyadh RC briefings.

Despite those rough spots, I never had to wear a wire. But the story wasn't over.

***

JeanClaude Arrives

...CJ continues...

Not much later, when we were having our dry run practice for the quarterly RC Riyadh presentation, another guy came with Alan. Alan introduced him as his colleague. They definitely were not chums.

And the new guy, at first glance he looked like the character "Murdock" from the old TV show, *The A-Team*—a loosey-goosey character who wasn't into the jargon of building and running a new town. Alan said he was an American, but his name, JeanClaude Thibaut—anything but American. I came to find JeanClaude sharp as a tack and a deep thinker. But he was bizarre—like a geek.

It seemed as time went on that this JeanClaude guy took over from Alan. That was a relief because JeanClaude, while weirdly detached, put no pressure on me to be socially invasive with the Saudi RC members. And he took an oversight interest in all landscape plant subjects—actually, he, in his own weird way, was a breath of fresh air. It was a relief for me not to be pressured on the info gathering. I continued talking sports with the young RC guys. JeanClaude took notes at my briefings and just stayed out of the way.

He said little at our first dry run; but 3 months later, after his second dry run, I had, in the evening, a knock on my studio door. As I opened the door, it surprised me to see JeanClaude. Not accustomed to visitors, I stood there for a moment in a daze. He spoke first.

"*Mon ami*, you are not inviting a colleague into your home?"

I didn't know what to say. Alan never had been a guy who would "drop in" like JeanClaude had just done. I welcomed him into my little studio. I asked him if he'd like something to drink—all I had in the fridge was orange juice and milk.

He reached into a paper bag and brought out two litres of Rauch red grape juice.

"Perhaps you'd like what I prefer," he said as he handed me the two bottles. "Put them in your refrigerator, they are best chilled."

"Are they pure or homemade? I've heard many people use Rauch to make their own wine at home."

"Wouldn't do that myself, out of respect for Saudi culture. You might wonder why would they maintain their sobriety? Because of the landscape, what it does and what lives in it. Chill the grape juice and we will have a chat."

And we sat down. JeanClaude told me that he was sub-contracted to The Analysis Corporation, Middle East, out of their Vienna Office. He told me he only takes their job opportunities when they coincide with his ethnobotanical interests.

I asked, "What are your ethnobotanical interests here in KSA?"

"We'll talk about that later. The grape juice should be just cool enough now."

I went to the refrigerator and poured two glasses.

"You may wonder why I stopped to see you."

He was right, but the question was on the rhetorical side.

"Wait a minute," I said, "I appreciate the freedom you have given me during the quarterly Riyadh RC briefings."

"You don't want to dance with the devil," he replied. I had no idea what that meant.

I started, "What..."

He interrupted. "I read your writings from Morocco. You got into the edge of ethnobotany and ethnobotany keeps me. It is my raison d'être."

How did he get my writings from Morocco? He had a mesmerizing way of speaking—thin French accent, deep voice and gravitas covering each word. I calmed and just listened.

"In Morocco, you were on the edge of the Sahara and the edge of dark West Africa. Now you are on the edge of the Arabian Peninsula, whose arid deathly heart is the Empty Quarter. And here, like there, djinns are djinns. Let me introduce you to the ethnobotanical threads of meaning in this region.

"First some background. I saw that in Morocco, you were bemused, even flummoxed, by the landscape forces that enveloped you. I understood from your writings that you found in the plants of your Tangier gardens a metaphysical path that took you to peace. Is this not so?"

"Yes, that is an accurate summary."

"Even though you had horrendous side effects from what you and others around you called the 'evileye', right?"

I nodded my agreement.

"Let's look how that relates to our current situation, *mon ami*, okay?"

Again I nodded.

"First, some current accepted wisdom. Together, the *djinn*, humans and angels make up the three sentient creations of God. The Quran mentions that the *djinn* are made of a smokeless and 'scorching fire', and they have the physical property of weight. Like human beings, the *djinn* can also be good, evil, or neutral."

I listened. I was surprised that an administrative analyst from Philadelphia talked about ethnobotany in the most arcane and esoteric terms when referring to the landscape.

"Have you gone inland, crossed the Hijaz mountains to the Nejd, yet?"

I shook my head.

"The sands whisper." He paused and looked at me. While refilling our glasses, he said, "The Saudis hear them; but they will never talk to you about them."

Now, I had questions.

JeanClaude read my mind and said, "Not yet."

***

The Second Bottle

...CJ continues...

"When I read your Moroccan writings (*Tangier Gardens*), I was intrigued by your explanation of human suffering with a unique turn of phrase, '...threw the baby out with the alchemical bath water'. In part, that is why I am here, *mon ami*.

"You are a landscape architect, into ethnobotany and alchemy. You are a rare animal. West Africa. North Africa, Arabian Peninsula. Those all have ancient roots in the landscape.

"Let us stick with your writings for the present. The road to Santiago de Compostela that your good friend was about to follow has an established alchemical history, revealing secrets to Nicolas Flamel. We should not get into too many details."

I listened. I had never found a professor at university or a professional colleague interested in discussing these topics.

JeanClaude continued, "Why do you think there is so much confusing and contradictory information about alchemists and alchemical research?"

He paused. I sensed that was a rhetorical question. I was right.

"I will tell you, *mon ami*. Portals. Your portals—you had difficulty describing what actually happened to your consciousness when traversing your plant portals—why? Because they are what alchemists were working with—what they were trying to explain and learn about. Isn't that in your colloquialism 'some heavy shit'?"

I said nothing as all he said began sinking in.

"The alchemists' allegory? Plants changing human perceptions, plants causing human transmutation. And so, here we are. The Arabian Peninsula, rich in everything but soils and water. Rich? You may wonder? I am not talking about sand, oil or minerals."

He paused, then said, "Before we go further, CJ, let's open that second bottle of grape juice."

"I used to drink grape juice as a kid but it was so different, Welch's, it was called."

"Concord grapes, *Vitis labrusca*, CJ—native to North America. That's what you were drinking. These are European, *Vitis vinifera*."

"Let's get back to the Arabian Peninsula and its landscape."

"Patience, my friend, we were speaking of millennia of human existential explorations, not one of your project presentations to the RC.

"Roots. The roots of this peninsula have traceable linguistic identification including Arabic, Latin, Greek, Persian and Egyptian. They all have been blended and explored by the people of this peninsula. Deep and rich."

And I thought my time in Morocco got into deep roots. I said, "Do you not blend landscape roots with cultural roots when you define ethnobotany?"

"Exactly, *mon ami*. Let me tell you about the Emerald Tablet—the link between this peninsula, the Greeks and the Egyptians."

"Emerald Tablet?" I asked.

"Yes, it is simple, mon ami, and it is non-different from what you learned in Tangier. It is simple—the answers are in the green."

"Answers?"

"Maybe I should say, the path is in the green. Deep history is riddled with unexplained events, don't you agree?"

I nodded.

"There is no need to hide from anything—answers and strength are in the green. Just do it. Just follow the path and you will find your strength and answers. Even the Saudi flag is green—why? Where did that come from?"

I asked, "But what about this project, this peninsula..."

He knew this question was coming. "We are getting there, *mon ami*, we are getting there. This peninsula is old and rich very unusually. It is multi-layered puzzles within the beauty of Bedouin-spoken Arabic. Its written and unwritten contain a deep feeling of intimacy with nature in the Arabian deserts—vivid imagery, exact observation, and shape-shifting unknown sources generating a bottomless... endless... timeless reality.

"You would do well to hold that as the base as you develop a green city amid this desert."

This was a funny conversation. It was vague, but encouraging.

"So let me say that I have read Alan's notes about your complaints."

JeanClaude paused and looked me straight in the eyes before continuing, "...no plants, no nurseries, no horticultural skills—that is your work. What are you thinking is your job? Get a suntan?"

I thought I saw a smug grin forming from the corners of his eyes. He moved ahead saying, "Those are problems for you to solve. Listen, my friend, build a city botanical garden, build a city nursery, start a joint program with a university and a trade school, hunt for and propagate native plants—do not try to tell me nothing grows here—the rare native plants are all drought or salt tolerant—find them, work with them, and start a local irrigation test facility. Set up those programs and I can assure the funds for your company's operating budget." Then he paused.

He had quickly opened a bunch of doors I hadn't even seen. I felt a growing enthusiasm for my work. Then just as quickly, he became socially collegial again.

"We have not finished the grape juice or this conversation yet. You wanted more that related to your projects? Let us look at oases. Tell me what you know."

"Oases? They are undependable sources of water that can support date palms and minor agriculture when they are fresh.

They are geologic/geotechnical phenomena related to slow fluctuations in the water table."

"Close enough. Now let me enrich that with historical stories from before the *mu'allaqaat* (stories that attach themselves to the heart).

"The *mu'allaqaat* are written. What I am about to explain are oral only. You know the bible story of Lazarus?"

"I know what I learned in Sunday school... years ago. Tell me."

"Jesus brought back the dead Lazarus to life. I will say a little more because oases, here in this land so very rich in existential history, are still a magnetic energy. They reach back to a time before our current world—knowledgeable people from the Indian subcontinent speak of those times as the age of truth. But in recent millennia many people speak of oases as scattered places where grievous injuries and diseases can be cured.

"Some say these oases were part of civilisation prior to the whispering sands. Due to bad behaviour, abuse toward others and abuse of the landscape, humans were cursed to become *djinns*. And the *djinns* who did malfeasant, if I can translate with flexibility to English, are known as the league of shadows."

"But most important for your work, *mon ami*. Listen carefully. The majestic date palms, still found in many oases, are the centres of Bedouin family life. They are the remnants from that prior civilisation. Never take oases or date palms lightly. They are environmental touchstones (*baraka*) for the Arabian Peninsula people."

If I wasn't slack jawed, I sure felt like it. The grape juice was finished and so were our talks.

From that personal face-to-face meeting, I learned clearly JeanClaude was big into an existential ethnobotany. I looked forward to talking with him, but we hardly saw each other. He kept his distance.

And in reality, that was the least of my responsibilities. The other things? I was fully engaged with design, design management, man management, project management, technical oversight of horticulture, irrigation and maintenance—and I added the botanical garden and nursery as projects critical to the New Yenbo landscape. I did not have any free time. And I liked it.

***

Kurt Says

Was CJ really into the CIA stuff? Not much to it—Alan and JeanClaude. CJ wrote little about it; but from his notes it was clear that he liked his info gathering responsibilities, his football talks with junior Royal Family Saudis.

But, this guy, JeanClaude, he planted some Egyptian seeds in CJ's mind. No doubt. Maybe some fertilizer too. Because the first seeds were planted in Morocco, according to CJ's references about the medina streets always filled with the melodic songs of the Egyptian singer Umm Kulthum.

CJ's next couple of years were an expansion of his first days and years—intense climate, weird co-workers and no cross-cultural interaction with "locals". CJ had his hands full with his work. He took shelter in his studio and his vacations to Western Europe every six months.

Struggles he had; but I don't see a person on a path to suicide or a person depressed by his professional choices. He was on the run, on the run from the memories of the personal family disaster years ago he had experienced in New Mexico.

And CJ was hunting for the holy grail of design. He was always trying to make something beautiful that "works". Nothing new there. To me it's clear, he still had not found "the path". Nevertheless, his continuous searching for it reminded me how he always found a unique design angle on the projects we did at my office. But that was secondary. What happened to him?

So, if I rule out suicide, where does that leave me?

He had an accident, was lost, was murdered, or he took

himself off the grid. Accident? No reports from hospitals or doctors? If he was lost... CJ never got lost... he had a great geographic sense no matter where. But off the grid... his choice... but then what? He left his rental car. So he was likely on foot. Can I guess that authorities contacted hotels for their guest lists? Not likely. All I can conclude from reviewing his writings to this point is that he must be alive.

But I have no real proof. On this mystery I wasn't getting anywhere. I decided to go surfing. The ocean, its waves, the fresh air and sun always cleared my head.

5-Gordie

My New CA

...CJ continues...

Yenbo had become my home. But not exactly. Why? Difficult for me to explain... Morocco... here... not the same, but both with threatening undercurrents. In Morocco, everyone on the street always touching me, always trying to get me into their lives—why? Whom do you trust? In Yenbo, Old Yenbo on the street was Saudi land. It was never-never land. Never see. Never touch. Never understand.

Old Yenbo—a small, centuries-old dhow port on the Red Sea for African Hajis on their way to and from the holy Muslim cities, Mecca and Medina. Over centuries, it was forever a smallish cluster of dilapidated coral stone buildings—and in the 20th century, hardly changed, the port of TE Lawrence.

That port was not satisfactory for international oil tankers, thus I was there to build a modern port and modern city—Yenbo New Town, 25 kilometres south of Old Yenbo, on the road to Jeddah. Our project was changing the region—everything new—buildings, roads, systems and populated with non-Muslims.

At work though, everything went smoothly most of the time, once settled in, learning office protocols, etc. Everyone there knew me as CJ. But my work in Yenbo New Town was missing a key element. I badly needed a Contract Administrator (CA).

Once I got through the problems of my original CA, the over-the-edge-of-propriety, self-centred guy, I hired Gordon Howe as my CA. He became the last piece, the key piece of my team of ten. My team really got together then.

That made my project work real and solid. CAs controlled who was an approved consultant or contractor. And they controlled the flow of money—payment for services rendered by consultants and contractors. I was glad to have Gordon, my own guy, in that important position.

He was a team player. Together, we built a legal regulatory and contractual framework to control every Saudi riyal spent on every landscaping contract. That was all new for me because in SoCal we knew everybody who worked for us and they knew us. Control was simple then.

Here, nobody knew anybody; and we had to control rigidly the contracts, the purse strings and the work schedules. For Gordon and me, it meant crafting detailed measurement and payment clauses along with line-item accountability. Significant challenges. Great fun. Great successes.

As Field Project Manager, I handled the team of ten. I ran my own group; but that small team was within our huge, 2,000-person expatriate corporate presence.

All my 2,000 co-employees worked under the same corporate administrative umbrella structure, part of the cocoon—that of the world's largest American engineering and construction management firm. Together, these were the managers of the planning, design, construction, and operations of Yenbo New Town. These professionals managed construction labourers and a community of 50,000 persons.

My life there had its own special reality—virtually no contact with local culture and distant contact with my home culture. We rarely saw Saudi men, always dressed in all white, and even more rare was the sight of a Saudi woman, always dressed in all black. Black and white culture? I kind of liked it. See black—do not engage in any way. See white—all is well.

The shops? They were all staffed by other Middle East Levant Arabs or, more frequently by Eastern country nationals. Saudis owned the shops but never worked out front. Eastern country nationals? Indians, Pakistanis or Filipinos often ran the shops. Inside that setting, life could be as normal as you and I find our own daily lives. I was "comfortable", though it was not like home, not at all... comfortable as long as I could get my every sixth-month vacation to the UK or Netherlands. Yeah, I had my share of cultural cocoons to get by; but my job was challenging and fully engaging—my job dominated my life.

Work weeks in Yenbo were based on the Muslim holy day—Friday, the religious day of rest, *lyum al j'ma*—mosque day. For all expatriates, the work week was Saturday through Thursday—not really life as Americans know it. So Yenbo was my home but not my home; and when my new CA Gordie arrived, he brought welcome links to Michigan, where I was born and attended college.

***

Sports Bonding

...CJ continues...

I always tried to get close to the guys on my office team. I tried to create mutual bonds of trust. It was the same for Gordon. Soon after he arrived on site, I went to him at the end of the workday (mid-day) on a Thursday (same as Saturday back home). I said, "Say, Gordon, want to go watch some kids' soccer?" Kids' soccer was the biggest public community sport among Yenbo expats.

"... let's do it!"

Regarding professional sports, Gordon and I both had Detroit roots—I went to Michigan State (MSU); Gordon went to the University of Michigan (U of M)—I had always been a sports fan—Gordon had played sports.

As we walked over to the soccer field, Gordon and I compared sports notes. I said, "Gordon Howe, your name— c'mon—so famous, your dad must have been a huge Gordie Howe fan, you know who I'm talking about..."

Gordon laughed. "Of course, you mean—the Canadian in the National Hockey League—holding just about every Detroit Red Wing scoring record in the 50s, the 60s..."

"... yeah, yeah, that's right..."

"Yeah, Dad was a huge Red Wings fan—and he named me Gordie."

"As I remember from your CV, you played hockey, that figures, and football, right? At the U of M?"

"Yeah, offence in hockey—defensive back in football."

142

"How'd you get through it all... engineering and playing big-time sports—especially two sports?"

"CJ, c'mon, it's simple... it was just discipline—get up every day and do the routine."

After a pause, a big smile spread across Gordon's face as he said, "Hell, CJ, now I understand... you went to that party school, MSU, and you did what everyone up there does, party! Right, partying is a full-time sport at MSU, right?"

Both of us laughed.

I looked at him. We were about the same age. Gordon was a solid 6' tall and 220 lbs, a sturdy and dependable presence. I thought about the directness of Gordon's words, "get up every day and do the routine", then I said, "Me? After making my weekly time for partying, I had my hands full getting through landscape architecture—I worked a job part time, 3-4 hours a day for a couple years, but, when push came to shove in my last year, I had to quit the job and the parties, just to get all my school projects done."

As we watched the soccer coach set the kids up for skills drills on the artificial turf, I, enjoying the earlier ice hockey back and forth with Gordon, continued, "You remind me of the old NHL (National Hockey League), lots of hard skating, it seems like you getting through U of M was all hard skating."

Gordon said nothing. He had an innate humility—at least, that was how it seemed in the beginning.

"The old NHL," I continued, "was all Canucks. Even though most of the teams were in US cities, the players were all Canucks, right? They embodied the hard-work, never-say-die spirit of the sport, you know?"

"Yeah, I know what you mean," Gordon agreed. "In sports, you get an immediate result for hard work and skill improvement. Funny, I got results on the ice, or on the field, week after week. At the end of the game, the whistle blows. Bam, I got the result. Win or lose. In the classroom, though, the actual result from the hard work didn't come until years after—took long-term dedication."

I thought about my new hire—dedication to get through school, dedication on the field and dedication on the job.

Committed and dedicated... this guy's okay.

As we watched the kids playing five-a-side on half a field, I concluded—if anyone embraced the old-fashioned hard work Canuck ice hockey ethos, it was Gordon—I'd call him Gordie, the American Canuck. The Canuck? He'll be an excellent addition. I needed a guy like him—someone stable, someone trustworthy, a dependable clear thinker who had similar cultural roots.

***

Indo-Pak Restaurant

...CJ continues...

Generally, in Yenbo al Bahr, Old Yenbo—retail stores staffed by Pakistanis and Indians played Bollywood music; while stores staffed by Middle East "Arabs" (Egyptians, Syrians, Lebanese, Jordanians) played Umm Kulthum or Lebanese singers in the style of Umm Kulthum. But old Yenbo has always been known as a fishing and pilgrimage port. East African Islamic pilgrims have for centuries arrived from across the Red Sea (less than 150 miles) by dhow in old Yenbo. I wondered why there were no stores staffed by East Africans.

On the edge of Yenbo al Bahr, the Indo-Pak Restaurant was not part of any chain. It was a one-off. It was like all the clothing shops, tech toy shops, grocery stores and a lot of other small restaurants—required by law to be at a minimum 51% Saudi owned. Only Eastern country nationals did the work. That was life just outside the edge of my work cocoon.

A few months later, work between the Canuck and me had settled in pretty well. We took the Yenbo New Town community minibus the twenty-five kilometres into old Yenbo for dinner after work, to a place called the Indo-Pak Restaurant.

Indo-Pak Restaurant? Yes, that's its name—but you have to know who was cooking to know what you might find. All cooks had this in common—always guaranteed hot—Sub-continent hot and Middle East hot, both off the American scale, big-time heat, big-time burn.

The Saudi families love the hot food, as much as the Indians and Pakistanis. And in time, the restaurant learned how to offer a "mild" version for Westerners—though it was still hotter than anything from back in the Midwest USA. Even though I liked this restaurant, it was always a "fast-food" type experience, a change of pace. It never impressed me with enough culinary gravitas to encourage me to take a trip East to the Sub-continent.

Like all public restaurants in Saudi Arabia, it segregated the seating, family from bachelor—bachelors could not see into the family section, and vice versa. They always filled the place with customers, and served big plates of food—decoration was cheap, price was reasonable. We had finished a refreshing cooling-down dessert of room-temp rasagulas, scrumptious, small balls of curd soaked in sugar syrup, and were waiting for our Nescafé. We talked about our family backgrounds.

I explained, "Me? An 'only child'—dad got prostate cancer— no longer able to have kids the old-fashioned way. Caused a lot of friction in our house... separation... divorce..." I paused... didn't want to say more... drifted... until the Nescafé arrived, then asked, "Canuck, tell me about your family."

Gordie said, "I had a twin brother. He left home at 18, joined the Army, became a Ranger... 1990, went to the First Gulf War. Then funny thing, he gradually became more distant—heard from him less and less—just kinda dropped off the grid... I figured he went deep under, or joined a private sector security firm, haven't heard from him... must be ten years, maybe more, don't know if he's alive or dead." Gordie laughed with a tinge of sadness when he added, "I couldn't even find him when I got married."

"Married? I didn't know you were married?" I was going to keep this part of the conversation one sided.

"Used to be," Gordie said reluctantly, then slowly looked away, up at the TV on the wall. The Indo-Pak Restaurant always had movies on the bachelor side with the sound up loud— either modern Bollywood or old India black and whites from the 50s. Tonight, as Gordie looked up it was an old movie, sub- titled in English, with a soft, melancholy, lost-love passage of tabla and sitar.

I followed Gordie's eyes and ears, then broke the movie's spell. "Tell me, Canuck, your marriage, what happened?"

"Well," the Canuck started slowly, "... had a real bad run of it about five years ago—just really getting through it now. I found a nice girl, sweet girl. We were right. Then, as my parents were coming to the dress rehearsal for the wedding, they got hit head on—automobile accident—both killed instantly. That hurt... that really hurt... a real effing bone-cruncher... we put off the wedding for a month—found out how much we really meant to each other. Got married—did not try for kids for three years. We worked—established our home—ahhh, those were great years."

My own memories and hurt quickly welled up inside... I swallowed it all as I listened to his story.

He continued, "Then we were ready to go for kids. She had a smooth pregnancy, everything normal—but when her water broke, some kind of bleeding started—she needed a transfusion, the transfusion blood or something wasn't right; anyhow an aggressive bacteriological infection had entered their main organs—both her and the kid. Our baby son died in twelve hours, and she died two days later—effing devastated.

"Eh... that was five years ago; but I'm up on my feet now and skating again. I'm glad to be out here working—a new world for me. I needed it."

His story brought back too many memories. Wife and kids. All lost. The thoughts hurt. Hurt too deep. Couldn't talk about it, yet.

We had more in common than I had imagined. I remembered long after, clearly what the Canuck had said, "On his feet, and skating again." I guess we both were. It helped that night, and every time I remembered those words. I kept my thoughts to myself. He was convinced to move forward with his life and I too... in my own way... or so I hoped.

***

147

Millionaires

...CJ continues...

Old hands, Western expatriates, used to say that for six years in Saudi Arabia, back in the 1970s, careful saving could make you a millionaire. Not because of kickbacks or any other illegal activities, but just because the contract conditions and bonuses were so generous.

Savers, the people who could save a million in six years, took all their vacations in Cyprus—no Africa, no Europe, no US, no Far East. All local living costs in Saudi Arabia were covered—local transport, furnished accommodation, utilities, kids' schooling and health. And the bonuses for contract completion were as much as the salary itself.

Though nobody was becoming a millionaire these days, a bachelor contract every eighteen months still required Western expatriate bachelors, like the Canuck and me, to take a vacation every six months, which included round-trip business class airfare to London. At the end of each contract was thirty-day home leave, which, for me, included round-trip business class airfare back to Los Angeles. These air trips were paid in miscellaneous airline vouchers that I could use to go when and wherever I wanted. Then, at the end of each contract, on my total base salary for the entire eighteen months I received a 35% cash bonus uplift. Not bad.

In my first couple years, I used my allowances wisely and had saved. Even though I was an LA "got-it-together" guy, I still had a taste for cross-cultural experience—the kind that foreign travel offered. Rare positive remnants from my old design study term abroad in Morocco, I figured. But maybe an obscure ancestral branch—I had a great-uncle who had spent the last decades of his life in Egypt. But that was far removed—truth was I had never really thought about it. Different cultures were like jigsaw puzzles—always a challenge. And I liked that—but in a limited sense, nothing too strange.

My dad had pushed me, as a youth, to be out of debt and be financially well organized. That made my time in KSA financially comfortable. So, when I travelled, I always chose well-established, five-star hotels. I could have a filtered cross-cultural comfort level in the hotel, and then venture into the local culture at the depth and time of my own choice.

Aside from revisiting North Africa and Southern Europe, places having climate with long periods of heat and aridity—plants that, with irrigation, might make Yenbo their home—I always went West. The idea of going East had never really attracted me. In the end, six months at a time in the Middle East left me thirsty, thirsty enough for generic Western culture—the Netherlands, the UK.

***

East vs West

...CJ continues...

Gordie had been working with me for a couple of years when one evening, I was over at his studio apartment. The Canuck had tabled his first batch of homemade wine, and we were uncorking for the obligatory taste test. Wine taste testing can go on all night.

Homemade wine—to get around the Saudi no-alcohol rules—almost everyone brought in the ingredients, when coming back to Saudi from vacation and home leave. Back home in Yenbo, they laid up batches of wine, fermenting from locally available grape juice, Austrian white or Austrian red. Some used to say that the Religious Police, the *Mutawa*, came by in the pre-dawn hours, sniffing the used grape juice bottles in the trash cans, just to catch Western expatriates with alcohol!

According to the law, and the individual employment contracts, guilt would mean within 24 hours the Western expatriate would be immediately ended from his job, on a flight home and expelled from the Kingdom, forever. But no one had ever been caught in New Yenbo. And few worried.

This night, hey, the batch was beginner's luck—at least, that's what I told the Canuck. We drank freely and talked about vacations, rest and recreation, R&Rs—backwards and forwards—theories, costs, etc. We both agreed that first for each was a hose down—getting together with a girl, making sure the plumbing still worked.

And you may wonder about this subject? Let me remind

about the social context of the expatriate workers like Gordie and me. The whole men-women thing was weird. There was the black and white public face of Saudis—all Saudi men always dressed in all white *thobes* and all Saudi women always dressed in all black *abayas*. In the Saudi public realm? Black and white.

Then in our offices there were no women, not a single one. All men all the time. You may ask, what about the married expatriates? The married men? Their wives were home wives. They did not work. At work, in the office there were no hairdos, no lingering glances, no coquettish conversations, no perfumes, no short skirts, no tempting cleavages. Some called it prison. For others like me and Gordie, it was called work—serious work.

We had a workplace for work—not a workplace for male/female flirting. May seem weird but we were men and men are men. We talked about how to relieve sexual tension—especially since it involved leaving Saudi and going to another country.

I said, "I go to Amsterdam—need the West—the museums—the art and architecture bookstores. I know my way around the Amsterdam red-light district, the brown cafes—it's an easy hose down—no commitments. Just do the job—know what I mean, Canuck?"

"Yeah, I hear you; but there's something soft about the ladies and their culture of the East. I took a chance going to Bangkok for the first time. Now, I know the place—and I like that extra service attitude. I leave refreshed—they are somewhere between business and the real thing. It's definitely better than a business-only hose down. They relax me physically, emotionally. Very nice."

The Canuck continued, "There's one lady I see regularly. She's about twenty-five. Beautiful girl—Malaysian—Chinese descent, she's trying to make her future... this girl, Kaytee... let me tell you... for me, she just might be my light at the end of the tunnel..."

I listened, felt discomfort from those words. This was a path that I, personally, never wanted to go down. Then I said, "I dunno, Canuck—you know there's lots of stories—guys been misled, tricked by girls from the East. Hey, who can blame them—they just want the money to help their families. Look out, Canuck... beware..."

My voice tailed off as my own hurt—accidental death of wife and kids—my own uncertainties—bubbled up. I had sympathy for Gordie, didn't want to talk about it. So I quickly bottled it.

I absorbed the landscape. Gordie absorbed people. We were different; but in our Western work cocoon in KSA, we became friends. And even in that cocoon, I could withdraw.

Gordie looked at me, shook his head slowly, said nothing. Cultural roots run deep—they are strong—both discrete and most often discreet. They hold on tightly. He clearly thought I did not understand.

And I thought maybe deep down, Gordie was still in emotional deficit, a lingering long-term shock from the loss of his parents, wife and child. I could understand that.

***

Landscape, West or East?

...CJ continues...

We refilled our glasses.

Then, changing the subject, Gordie surprised me, though maybe I shouldn't have been surprised, when he said, "CJ, about these cross-cultural differences that send us out of KSA for basic bodily functions... do you think as we arrived by air the first time, that we had any inkling just how strange the cultural differences, the cultural restrictions would be?"

"From the air? Is that your question?"

"Exactly. From the air."

"That is interesting because I had some unusual first-time perceptions that day I flew in."

Gordie said, "C'mon, tell me."

"The first obvious things were absolutely no water and no plants... as far as the eye could see."

"Me too."

"But there was also something strange in the atmosphere... a kind of haziness where the sky and the barren landscape met..."

"How do you mean?"

"I didn't really know what to think on the day; but after a couple months on the ground, I came to think there was something strange about the light—the sunlight that enables healthy plant growth—and there was no plant growth. I defined this place as a place where light hurts—where intense sunlight frightens. I asked myself, how does that impact the people who call this place home?"

We opened a third bottle. Poured each other full glasses.

Gordie said, "Sounds interesting... but without conclusion... right?"

"Yeah, you could say that."

"Maybe that's the difference between you, a designer, and me, a bean-counter."

"Huh?"

"Listen, When I flew in I saw something totally strange to me as we were approaching to land. On the barren landscape... there was a road here and a road there, but little traffic. But what caught my eye was spiderweb traceries of paths crossing over one another and getting closer and closer together as the edge of town approached. As we got lower, I could see here and there on that tracery the dust clouds behind white Toyota pickup trucks, travelling at speed."

I was spellbound listening, then I rephrased what Gordie had said, "Spiderweb traceries of omnidirectional straight-line tracks from endless desert leading to and converging on the edges of paved urban centres..."

He continued, "I thought these people wanted to get out of that desert landscape so fast that they took the shortest straight-line distance to their destination and each trip was different. Was it fear? Was it practicality? No gas stations. No rest stops. Just a beeline to the destination."

"And you thought...?"

"I thought this culture is so foreign that even the basic use of the automobile—which you and I grew up with—is beyond my understanding. How can we know what to do to help them live in a new town—Western style?"

I said, "Hang on, Gordie. It is not such a disaster. It is not so one sided. The original urban planning included workshops with local leaders. The result? The core of all city planning was the local mosque."

"What do you mean?"

"If you break down every residential area you will find them based upon local mosque size and located to a 10-minute walking radius. The local mosque becomes the centre of the neighbourhood. Adjacent to the mosque are shops, health services and schools. You've got to admit that has some local resonance—never see that kind of centralized planning in our country."

We tried to keep the conversation straight; but finishing the third bottle of home brew, we had had more than our fill for the night.

***

Moussy

...CJ continues...

Sometime later, we had been working together for maybe four years. Gordie and I, after work on a Thursday, the end of our work week, walked over to the Haii 4 commissary. We were shopping for something different and Haii 4, the neighbourhood of senior management families, was known to have the widest variety of groceries.

Anyone could use any commissary; and each commissary had enough freedom to have unique stock items. Gordie and I each had our own private studios in Haii 3. We were planning to spend the night relaxing and watching the tube. So, after work, as Gordie and I strolled through the Haii 4 commissary, we found, in the drinks cooler, six-packs of Moussy.

"Moussy? That's beer, isn't it?" I asked. "What's it doing here?"

Gordie looked at the packaging and said, "It says non-alcoholic beer. What do you think?"

We both had our roots in the sports and beer culture of Detroit and were immediately attracted to beer.

I said, "Let's give it a go."

Gordie picked up two six-packs and said, "If we're going to try it, we might as well give it a fair trial."

I said, "Let's hope they haven't boiled the piss out of it like Stroh's did with their beer in Detroit."

As we walked over to Gordie's place, sweat poured off our brows. The temp just at sunset was still above 30° and the breeze gently coming in off the Red Sea pushed the humidity to intolerable. Gordie called it a "humid stank". After that five-minute walk, we were ready for a good cold beer—even though the salty humid smell of this hot, acrid air was not the cold iron and steel of our Detroit memories.

Back at Gordie's studio, we put the Moussy six-packs in the freezer while we dumped a couple of potato chip bags into a large bowl. Once the Moussy was properly cold, we moved it to the fridge and cracked open the first two. Cool, refreshing. We slipped into the past—the memories of cold beer with friends in the US.

We sat on the sofa, put our feet up and turned on the TV to watch a soccer match in the Saudi Football League—always on the Arabic-only SaudiOne. Didn't hold our attention long. I liked soccer but Gordie—it was his studio, thought football was American football.

The prayer call interrupted the match—the match went on in real life—but on TV, the five prayer calls per day always interrupted the programming. Typically, while the prayer call was chanted, the live camera showed the large numbers of Islamic pilgrims (*umrah*) circumambulating, counter-clockwise, the Qaaba (house of God) in Mecca. He muted the TV and started talking about a trip he had taken recently for P&C. He had to make a site visit to a couple of suppliers wanting inclusion on the Yenbo New Town bidding lists.

He got up and went to a drawer of his desk and said, "Boy, did I see some strange stuff on that trip. We drove south of Jeddah but via the Asir mountains—they run parallel to the coast continuously south a couple hundred klicks, 9,000 feet above the Red Sea coastal plain.

"It was a different world. We were above the heat, above the horrendous coastal humidity. Let me show you some of my photos.

"This was in the Asir National Park, tallest peak 3,000 metres, elevation-wise like the Swiss Alps, but no snow. The Royal family has its summer residence up there."

I asked, "You been to Switzerland?"

"Yeah, I took that 'one week to see all the sights of

Switzerland' on my way over here. Lots of ice, snow and water there—forests and tourists everywhere—but look at this next shot."

"Baboons?"

"You bet, hamadryas baboons, you know, the ones that always look like they have a chip on their shoulder? I saw a clan of them. I saw them trooping along the top of an adjacent rocky hill—they look like mean SOBs—wouldn't want to mess with them.

"But that wasn't our destination. We had to go down onto the sun-baked littoral Red Sea plain almost to the Yemeni border—Jizan, a smallish port town, was the supplier's home."

"Jizan?"

"We saw two things that blew me away—you need another beer?"

"Sure do. This goes down nicely. If I didn't know any better, I'd think I'm getting a buzz off it..."

Gordie looked at the fine print on the label which he read out loud. "... alcohol free might mean up to 0.5% alcohol. Do you think the Saudis read that?"

He brought over a couple more beers and his photos.

He said, "Look, this is a grass hut, saw maybe a dozen of them on the approach to Jizan—looks like savannah Africa, doesn't it?

"And this weird-looking tree, what do you make of it—one guy told me it was a baobob, what do you think?"

"Yeah, that's right, looks like a young one, *Adansonia digitata* most likely..."

"Don't you wonder, CJ, how does Africa—its plants, its culture—how does it get to Saudi Arabia, how does it take root? Across the Red Sea? Hell, even Moses needed the help of God to cross it!"

***

Do-gooder?

...CJ continues...

"Hang on, Gordie, I'm not really following. Nothing mystical here—Red Sea dhows have been running the edges of Africa and Arabia between Sinai and the Bab al Mandeb for centuries—plants and climates similar on both sides of the Red Sea, no? And, for just as long, Old Yenbo has been receiving African Muslim pilgrims."

Gordie said, "I don't dispute that. But in the bigger picture the culture of the people who are Bedouin (nomadics), who live in a huge and impenetrable arid desert, next to places where aggressive baboons roam, next to places where grass huts make sense, and what are we doing—even though we are building local mosques everywhere around them we have a high-density suburban world based on Western cultural standards—there is something inherently unsound about this."

"Huh?"

"Since when does the blend of Africa and Arabia yield San Fernando Valley, Pasadena or even Dearborn, Michigan? Unsound at the most basic."

I was perplexed. Gordie made sense; but if we acted on those conclusions, we wouldn't be working here. I thought maybe the beer was affecting him, maybe not; but I was enjoying it and I was still thirsty. I got up and went to the fridge.

"Want another, Gordie?"

"Why not? These aren't bad. Are you feeling a little buzz?"

"It sure has something more than water in it. I like it."

I took a long drink, then sat down and dug into the potato chips. I was still flummoxed by what Gordie had said. I didn't know what to say. So, I took another long pull on the Moussy.

Gordie said, "I see the good things you've done at work—like forcing consultants to acknowledge the fast growth of plants here—saving installation and maintenance time and money..."

"You mean like those oleanders, pampas grass and henna, planted as whips one metre apart that grow in one growing season to 3m height and spread?"

"Yeah, like that. But I wonder about some of the other design instructions. I understand when you instruct the consultants to approach their planting design not as an extension of the adjacent eco-system—the adjacent Empty Quarter nothingness—but as though we are building a huge oasis, luxuriant with plants and water to support a huge population of 200,000. I understand that instruction but I don't understand when you instruct not to do planting design like salt and pepper or like plane geometry... what, CJ, are you asking them to do?"

That question hit me like a one-two punch. Gordie worked for me and he was second-guessing my design instructions to consultants—that was the first punch and the second punch had me back on my heels. What was I asking them to do?

I fluffed off the first one as chit chat between friends—no big deal, but the second? What was I trying to do?

The Moussy must have been getting to me. No, it was definitely getting to me—tasted pretty good. Gordie got two more out of the fridge.

I was still bumbling over his last comments. Answers did not come. In my mind, I was all sloshy... I was... words started forming...

I answered, "I was trying to make a place where the Saudis could become enlivened by the beauty of plants."

Gordie said, "Beauty of plants? These are people of the impossible desert life for generations. When they see a plant, they know there is water. Survival. And if a plant can grow, it better be useful—dates—date fronds, henna. Absolutely the basics, the fundamentals. What are you trying to do? Sounds

160

like an idealistic do-gooder..."

"Do-gooder?!"

Gordie said, "Didn't you hear our instruction from the Royal Commission? Green and white city—like Santa Barbara—they had a simple image for us to execute. They were not trying to inspire their people into some artistic ideal. They just wanted their people to be happy and proud of the wealth of water and green in their daily lives."

I was still caught on his words "do-gooder". I had never thought of myself like that. But he was right. In this strange place of oil riches and barren, lifeless landscapes, I had become what I had always chaffed over—a do-gooder, an idealist run amok—chicken with its head cut off.

I had no words. I was speechless. I tried to turn it over in my head.

Words finally came. I said, "Gordie, you and I are here because we are the best at designing, building and operating huge, complex landscape projects. This is no backyard garden. This is huge and our task is to succeed in doing it. The Saudis want something green, efficient, sustainable and successful. Who else can do that?"

Gordie nodded. I took that as agreement with what I had just said. I think that alcohol-free beer was getting to him, too. I felt internal strength and clarity returning.

I said, "You may not understand all the weird comings and goings of the design world and its jargon, but you should rest assured that I have boiled down this jargon for the strange international, multi-cultural, English-as-a-second-language domain in which we operate. That's my work, Gordie."

We both finished our beers and Gordie went to the fridge for a couple more. For the rest of the evening, we watched Saudi Division One football on the tube.

But as I lay down to sleep that night, our exchange on design took over my thoughts. Design was one of my cherished cocoons. Design was my life. The do-gooder label stuck in my head. Why? Because that was indeed what I was. Hubris writ large? Maybe I never left LA?

I thought about Kurt and the design debates we had. He

was not too different from Gordie—practicality ruled. Back in LA with Hollywood, TV, movies, fashion, style—design ruled. Everyone in that land of plenty was looking for the cutting edge of design. But here, even with the wealth from oil, this was not a land of plenty. Rules different. Landscape different. Priorities different.

I laid awake thinking about design, my interests, my travel/foreign culture experiences... I have always seen design built on a concept from observation of local natural and social landscape realities. And from those observations, I physically, emotionally and intellectually linked my selection of the plants, the paving, the water and all other physical design components. But then my Moroccan experiences took me a step beyond—into an arcane territory—that could carry the user to blissful enjoyment. But the practical world of clients and regulations tempered my hopes for transcendent design. Real life had hit me once, and through Gordie, hit me again.

Real life lesson, though depressing, had hit me upside the head. I'd have to live with it. Then I thought, even back in the US I had to bend to the whims of every client, everyone who hired me whether in New Mexico or SoCal. And here, as Gordie rightly saw, it was the big natural and cultural landscape that should drive my work. He was right. I had gone off the rails.

But work is work. I can do that. And design? It is like a wild horse. Needs training. Needs discipline to be useful. And style? Style of the training or style of the result? Design style? I need to re-think a few things.

***

Skin of the Earth

I drove out of town via construction haul roads—not in use because it was mosque day—*lyum jma*, Friday. Six days a week, 18 hours a day these haul roads are heavily used. Construction haul roads are not paved. They are a calcium-based dust, regularly watered and compacted hard from very heavy truck use. The trucks move dredged and cut material out of town. And other trucks haul in sweet desert sand, 7.0pH, in for landscaping.

I drove away from the Red Sea coast and its burdensome coastal humidity. I parked just beyond the inland edge of the Yenbo New Town development. The inland humidity was so low I couldn't feel it. But because of that I could feel the direct heat of the sun and its enhanced reflection from the blinding, reddish beige desert sands. My trousers, my hat, all the outer layers of my clothes were so hot, I didn't want to touch them. What do you think? Summer sun on the Arabian Peninsula, just a hair north of the Tropic of Cancer—30°C, 40°C, 50°C? I figured at least 60°C. Too hot to touch. I had one bottle of water with me and five more in the car, where I kept the AC running. There was no shade, no trees, only the odd piece of scrub... and lots of sand, stones and rocks. That's the context.

I walked. I needed to clear my head. The Arabian Peninsula desert landscape. The lack of variety, the lack of diversity. It was simple. It was clean, that's just how TE Lawrence described it—he was right on. No wind, no artefacts, no trash, just

163

nature's facts of life. There was raw topography—flat plain, barren mountains and a simple skin—sand. That simplicity, that cleanliness was like a meditative state that I entered into.

And my thoughts: nature, landscape, culture, town planning, design. They roamed freely in my head. That was good. I let them roam because if the arid tropical heat and light did not interrupt, I thought they would settle according to their reality in life.

Gordie was right about designing for myself or for the people who would be living here. But what happened to me in Tangier, in the gardens, amongst the plants? Did I not experience a transcendent reality? Did I not get taken, did my consciousness not get taken to an experience beyond words? What is wrong with me trying to design so that all humans can access that same conduit I did?

Who are the people I am designing for? What is their context? Nomadic history. People of these very sands. Struggling for water, for food. And we, we are giving dependable water, dependable food. What else for them?

We, ourselves, were once nomadic, struggling in the landscape for survival, shelter and food. Was it only the urbanizations of the 14-19th Centuries that gave us the freedom to sit down? To sit down and realize that nature and beautiful landscape inspired us. Regenerated us.

And new towns of the 20th Century, did they not all have in common the interlacing of landscape (green) bands into humans' daily lives? And did this not also drive the planning for Yenbo New Town? Small scale design is something the residents may grow into in their own time. But now, their new home is a large oasis—large enough with all provisions for safety, shelter and good health. Discussions of beauty? That is for the residents. We are not omniscient to the point of dictating their daily lives or foisting our unique ideas of beauty upon them.

Beauty? What about beauty? Beauty in the modern West vs beauty in the Arabian Peninsula.

What is beauty? What is nature? What is landscape? How are those linked to human culture, to human behaviour? The

164

answers throughout human history have always been vague word-smithing to cover what appears to be indefinable. And many people who try to define that indefinable are subject to mocking: like James Lovelock and his Gaia; like Bree, her Sahara experiences and Faery land back in Morocco; and my evileye from northwest Africa and the Shaman cures in New Mexico.

Beauty and meaning, are they eternally separate? Meaning, could it be simply a mental construct that many humans seek instead of God? Words often found as identifiers in the landscape—sacred... contemplation. Sacred and contemplation in the landscape? I think there must be something very basic in the landscape that does not require academic research to feel, experience and even understand.

My purest idea of beauty is that it must include the portal that carries the viewer into the realm of transcendent glories. But... that's me and my culture. Again Gordie was right, I shouldn't impose that on people at home in their own culture.

Shouldn't I ask, with the massive digital and commercial media inflow of Western culture, when do local people change? Or do they? How do cultures change? And in which time scale? Days, weeks, months, years, decades, centuries or... ? Guesswork. Word-smithing. I've got to keep it simple. Or hubris? Am I going to change the world? Am I going to change the people of Yenbo New Town? Of course not.

I'll just do my job. What does that mean? Not just sprinkling plants around like from salt and pepper shakers. The designers (UK, US, Australia, Germany and Canada) I manage will have to produce the quality I know. Make ground floor rich because that is all most people see. Inviting people in—architecture urban environments, parks and gardens. Open space is more than hardscape/softscape, more than putting in plants, gardens and ecological balance—it is about places for people in their daily lives—landscape floors in urban settings—entries to buildings—evolving materials to highlight changes at entries. The scale of my job, my city-wide responsibility excites me. But...

On my own I can't stop wondering about the gap between

culture and landscape, between nature and man. There is no gap between nature and man. Man is part of nature.

My transcendent plant experiences from Tangier gave me a clue... no, a hope. I think I can find something in plants in the landscape that is a discoverable conduit linking that heretofore indefinable connection between culture and landscape. Could landscape actually be the malleable dynamic interface between humans and nature—what? Can't see the forest from the trees? Even in the Arabian sands?

My own experiences were that the landscape is, in simplest terms, a conduit, a Jacob's ladder to realms beyond human descriptive powers, beyond this world of the five senses and emotions.

And on beauty—every culture on every continent has, in detail, shown its respect for beauty—and all are different. So what is beauty—an emotion? An aura? And what is an aura? How is it communicated? Via emotions or something more subtle still? Chakra energies? I struggle to understand beauty. It is a deep well without light, without definitive end, without conclusive finality.

I figured that in general, until the human need for food and shelter in the landscape is no longer primary (24/7/365), the appreciation of the landscape for beauty may not be possible.

***

Kurt Says

Design cocoon, work cocoon, cultural cocoon? I don't really get CJ's cocoon thing other than he was running away from stuff.

What stuff? CJ's talks with Gordie made it clear that inside CJ still hurt deeply. He had never been released from the death of his wife and kids in New Mexico over a decade ago. And second, he was running away, or rather hiding from the awkwardly strange culture all about him. So his cocoon was his personal safe space into which he could relax and forget about the difficult things life had thrown at him. And now?

CJ needed the cultural comfort of someone like Gordie—similar roots, similar values. It was a positive for CJ's cultural cocoon in Yenbo.

But the more I think about it—maybe there is something about CJ's need for cocoons. Maybe they were his comfort for emotional boil-like growths festering inside him.

Maybe they were the roots of what? Something that would finally push him over the edge? Suicide? Nah, he had too much design and discovery fire burning inside him. He was stronger than suicide.

This whole do-gooder discussion. Hell, I'd been through it even before I first met CJ. For me, it was simple. It was people who out of hubris wanted to spend my tax money on their own kickback projects in foreign lands.

I get fired up on this subject. They are narcissists. They cover themselves saying they are making a difference. Making a difference? Hell, at the least they are modern thought-imperialists. And most often they are fattening their retirement accounts while pampering their own ego. These people are grifters. In our USA economy with too much idle wealth and idle time, they are cheaters.

I'm surprised CJ put so much into it. And Gordie, he had a point. Practicality of local context and local landscape should rule.

6-The Thin Strip

A Rogue Day

...CJ continues...

Gordie told me later he had nothing personal against me; rather, his comments had been about our business. But me, I was never the same. His words had opened my eyes.

Gordie and I carried on at work most professionally. Weeks turned into months, and the months rolled on. It was more than two years later when a strange day, like a rogue wave, broke over me.

No different from every other workday these last six years in Yenbo New Town, this day had begun at 6:30 in the morning in the Al Nawa Construction Village. I was at home in my Haii 3 bachelor studio. I grabbed a quick orange juice, toast, and coffee. Then I walked five minutes to my office to start work at 7AM.

I enjoyed my somewhat cool and always sunny early morning walk to work. In fact, I enjoyed the entire physical geography of the place. The landscape included the Hijaz coastal mountains—rugged, naked, dark russet red, jutting up 500 metres high, only ten kilometres inland from our new town site. Below the Hijaz mountain ridge, we were in the Tihama, a wide, gentle, flat coastal plain. Both the Hijaz and the Tihama were nearly vegetation free and always swept by drifting red sands which, hither and thither, grew into attractive sand dunes. And at the Red Sea coast, there were rich subtropic waters-edge ecosystems—teeming mangrove colonies and surreal coral reef gardens.

This geography could not be found in the descriptions from any tourist office or website. Yet, during eight months of the year, it was a landscape paradise—coolish mornings, coolish nights, but never below 10°C. In these so-called winter months, it was warm enough every midday for a summer-like swim and a fine tan—always plenty of sunshine.

However, during the four to five months of true summer, that was a different story. Despite the aridity of the inland desert, the prevailing winds from the west over the salty Red Sea meant heavy saline humidity. That stifling humidity coupled with the realities of the Tropic of Cancer daily 45°C temperatures strained everyone's resources, drained everyone's life energy. Physical movement was too much. Even thinking was hard in the heat and the humidity of this tropical climate.

But once I arrived at my Haii 7 office, I may as well have been in Southern California. Everything appeared to be USA-normal. The large, high-ceiling space frame was filled with Herman Miller high wall cubicles, all in desert earth tones, arranged department by department. And the office infrastructure? Great HVAC, spotlessly clean, modern communications, brightly lighted to the levels of the best American engineering standards.

My company of 2,000 employees in Yenbo New Town were all males. No female employees. The only female contract employees anywhere in Yenbo were Western country nationals—nurses for female health or teachers in girls' schools. And they were all family status.

On the day in question, I stopped by the secretarial pool for my department and said good morning to Matthew. From India, Matthew was a Kerala Christian. In fact, most of the male secretaries came from Kerala. They were well educated and skilled in office procedures, processes and equipment. They word-processed correspondence and maintained digital and hard copy files. Best of all, they had excellent English language skills.

I greeted, "Say Matthew, how did India do yesterday against Pakistan in the 'One-Day International', the ODI? Did you guys get your clocks cleaned?"

"Why no, sir, quite the contrary, as I am sure you must have already heard. In fact, the Program Director's Office may declare a local holiday on behalf of the stunning cricket India played."

I said, "Congrats, but at least, it must have been close..."

"Not a chance. We gave them a good lashing!"

I enjoyed these sports dialogues and laughed at the "lashing", then said, "Okay, okay, when you finish revelling in the newspaper accounts of the match, please pass the Arab News paper to me... oh... and by the way, please call me when the Canuck comes in, okay? I need to get with him before noon, agreed?"

"Yes sir, will do."

As my contract administrator, Gordie reviewed, for legal contractual compliance, every communication in and out from me. He was my "canary in the mine" on schedule and budget issues, not only contractual but also corporate. Together, the two of us made a strong professional team in a difficult international contractual environment. Gordie was without doubt unequalled as my right-hand man.

In my office in the Haii 7 space frame headquarters, I went through my normal morning motions, checking my schedule of activities on pre- and post-award projects, then reviewing documents on file at Purchasing and Contracting. After updating program reports for monthly senior management internal review, it was after 11:00. I called the Canuck's office. No answer.

I walked over to see Matthew. On the way, I checked the "Sign Out Log". The Canuck had not signed out for the morning.

"Say, Matthew, seen Gordie yet?"

"Nothing, sir. I checked his office, and he has not been in today."

"Listen, if he's not in after lunch, call him at home, please."

"Yes sir, will do."

I knew that the Canuck, with some of his contract administrator friends, had just cracked open a batch of homemade wine last night. Usually, when someone cracked open a batch, those involved might not be exactly punctual the next morning. This was how I figured the Canuck was late.

At the end of that same day, I stopped by the Canuck's studio. It was dark. I knocked on the door. No answer.

When the Canuck did not come in the second day, I called his place a couple times, without an answer. At lunch, I went over once again to the Canuck's apartment and knocked on the door. Again, no answer. After lunch, I went over to Human Resources (HR) and reported the unusual situation.

The next morning when I arrived at my desk I found a message from Matthew that HR was waiting to speak with me. At once I called HR. HR had initiated a wellness-check and from their after-action report they informed me that yesterday afternoon, Gordon Howe had been found dead in his bathroom, an apparent suicide.

Things moved swiftly from there. HR handled the government, corporate and family details. I was in shock. Shock is strange—a kind of uncertainty overload. The shock stunted my questions. I went with the flow.

HR tech people had confiscated Gordon's office computer. And HR then asked me to clean out Gordon's desk, the remains of his office. Funny, when you clean out someone else's desk, you never know what secrets you may find. I went through every drawer, every storage cubicle, every cabinet, every folder. The Canuck knew how to separate personal from business. There was nothing personal anywhere in his workspace, except in the top desk drawer.

I pulled out a thin... a folded something. I picked it up with my hands, unfolded it, stretched it out... a long strip. It was definitely not work related. It appeared to have been, originally, a tourist map of Thailand; but carefully trimmed, so that it was only about one inch wide, and maybe thirty inches long.

It was a slice of a map, a thin strip—north to the top, with a red felt-tip circle, drawn around Bangkok. On the unprinted back of the map, I found two names hand written, Creed and Kaytee Cheng. It was the Canuck's handwriting. I recognized Kaytee as the girl whom the Canuck had talked about when he took his R&R trips to Bangkok.

This thin strip gave me a small, strange slice of memory from my colleague and friend; but I did not know if it had value. Looking at the map, I thought it was a remnant to be discarded, ...or a clue to be resolved. This was all I had. There was no note with Gordon's body. The whole thing was mysterious. But I respected Gordie, despite our disagreements from time to time.

I wondered whether this girl, Kaytee, apparently from Bangkok, played any part in the Canuck's suicide. Shock does not allow questions. It warps logic. It impinges reason. Waves of shock, waves of uncertainty and sadness all simultaneously beat against me.

***

Haircut

...CJ continues...

The suicide, the authorities called it that, left me with no recourse. I did not feel right... maybe something was missing, maybe something was missed. But, the bottom line—indisputable—Gordie was gone. Dead. Just administrative paperwork at the corporate office now.

But I couldn't really let it go. I made an appointment to see Will Clendenon, the Program Director. The meeting was brief. He took me aside and suggested simply to let everything run its course—HR would handle it. For me, it was tough. Gordie the Canuck and I were different, but we were friends. I felt things that I should have said to him had been left unsaid. Unfairly cut off.

I grasped at loose threads... or at least one. The thin strip... the map and its names. I thought it over and over... back and forth... without clarity over the next days until I made my regular barber visit.

I went for my haircut in the Haii 3 local centre. I had a Lebanese barber, Mr. Safwan, a contracted service just like everything in Yenbo New Town. Mr. Safwan was an old-fashioned barber. For him the haircut was a special service to each client—a time for psychological recharge—a time for aroma and massage therapy.

For me, the colognes and talcs in Mr. Safwan's shop were a dreamy trip back to my almost forgotten Los Angeles barber. Mr. Safwan's selection... so sweet... so soothing. The Pinaud

Clubman talc, the Virgin Island Bay Rum, the Old Spice, the original Azzaro for men—together they created an aromatic aura for me. When I was in the chair, I could relax, I could think and afterwards I always felt refreshed. I recalled the Canuck used the same barber. I brought it up to Mr. Safwan.

"Say, Mr. Safwan, good morning. How are you?"

"Fine, Mr. CJ, and you?"

"Tell me, Mr. Safwan, you cut the hair for the Canuck, right?"

"Beg your pardon, sir?"

"Gordie, the Canuck, Gordon Howe, you cut his hair, right?"

"Oh, Mr. Gordon, yes sir, like you, he was a regular."

"You've heard, haven't you?"

"Yes, sir."

Mr. Safwan finished preparing my shirt collar for the cut, made sure the cloth cover and tissue band were properly in place, ruffled his fingers through my hair, then began with his scissors—rhythmic cutting—the very sound was dependable—trustworthy.

Sitting comfortably in the chair, I was thinking about the Canuck, then I said, "Strange, wasn't it? Suicide... nobody had any idea why, no note, nothing... worries me, thinking about it."

"Yes sir," Mr. Safwan said while he continued cutting.

"I found an unusual map in his desk. A bit mysterious, this map showed only Bangkok, and two names, Creed, and Kaytee Cheng."

Mr. Safwan stopped cutting. "Did you say Kaytee?"

"Yes, Kaytee. Have you heard that name before?"

"Yes, I have, sir. Mr. Gordon always talked about Miss Kaytee. He was thinking to marry Miss Kaytee."

I was stunned. The Canuck had said nothing serious about marriage. I thought to myself, was the Canuck truly going to get married? How close was he to this girl? But the Canuck knew how to keep quiet about things. Maybe I have a responsibility to contact his lady friend... to close this loop?

I chewed on that for a couple more days, thinking that maybe I should try to close that loop for my deceased colleague and friend. Fiancée—she should know. I called HR to see if I could get access to his computer. They would not release it; but when I told them my interest in Kaytee Cheng, they helpfully offered to do a search. Nothing.

I had not quite convinced myself yet when I was called in to see the Program Director. I thought this wasn't normal. Maybe it had something to do with the Canuck?

I walked over to Will Clendenon's office. It was a reduction in force, RIF time. The price of oil had been going down to where the Kingdom of Saudi Arabia had to reduce and slow down its development and implementation schedule. Sometimes these RIFs were rumoured in advance. This one was not.

I was given my thirty-day notice. Will told me I should prepare a final status report; and that JeanClaude from Riyadh would visit me one last time to be briefed.

The Program Director was as understanding as he could, under the circumstances. He thanked me for the info I had gathered regarding the young Saudis, the good sports vs the politically motivated. Then he told me that the company might reinstate my position—maybe—maybe. But my job was finished. The realities of international contract work hit me hard.

I was knocked flat. Battered again, another rogue wave. First, the Canuck dead, then RIF'd from my job!!! My future became now and it was uncertain.

I needed relief. I needed to numb that feeling of being kicked in the groin, hard... twice in ten days. To my home wine closet I went.

On my way, I grabbed a loaf of bread, English mustard and a wedge of English sharp cheddar cheese. When I looked into my wine closet, I saw two bottles of homemade red I had been saving for a special occasion. I grabbed them both. It took the first bottle to get numb. Finally, halfway through the second bottle, thoughts formed.

Before long, I was convincing myself, thinking... everything considered, and since I have the time, I'll close the loop left open by the Canuck's death. He and I both had lost our families and he seemed to have gotten over it when I hadn't.

Maybe Kaytee was the reason—but he committed suicide.

Conflicts in my thinking. I'll find his girlfriend, ask her some questions, make sure she knows he has passed away. Then I'll head to Europe for a leisurely late-spring-into-summer extended vacation.

As I drained my last bottle of that particularly excellent vintage home brew, I concluded, "Yeah, that should work."

Over the thirty days I had to prepare to leave Yenbo, I spent most of my time with HR and packing out my own possessions. I had storage lockers and my bank facilities in Amsterdam. Though I was emotionally upset with the strange turn of suicide and RIF events, the logistics of departure went smoothly. During my last week, I had an exit interview with HR, who reminded me to get my CV updated in their corporate system.

Then, the day before my departure, the Program Director contacted me and asked me to see him in his office. He told me JeanClaude had stopped in his office and reported that he was satisfied with the work and final report I had done for him. Then Will thanked me for my service and asked how he could get in touch should an opportunity arise.

That was a professional honour. Anyhow, when I went to sleep, my last night in Yenbo, I did not know what my immediate future held. Uncertainties filled my thoughts; but I was up for the journey, my personal pilgrimage. I needed to do something for my friend and colleague, the Canuck, Gordie Howe, even though it meant going to Bangkok, Thailand.

***

African Hajjis

...CJ continues...

In order to depart KSA, I had to get to King Abdulaziz International Airport in Jeddah.

On the outskirts of Old Yenbo, our firm was upgrading the local airport, and it was temporarily shut down. So, I arranged a long-distance taxi and raced on the 300km trip overland, from Yenbo New Town to Jeddah. It was nearly three hours of tedious flat roadside landscape with nothing but sand, rocks and more sand—and every so often, a wadi, a dry flat riverbed of more sand and rocks.

At 10AM we left Yenbo, heading due south. The sun was high and bright—blinding. At noon we crossed the Tropic of Cancer—no signs, just a mental exercise. The sun was at its apex—burning metal, plastic and window glass—blinding by refractions from the sand and salt fines in the air. Despite tinted windows and sunglasses, my eyes squinted, trying to escape the brightness itself, and inevitable fatigue from that brightness.

Two and a half hours in an air-conditioned metal box when the outside temperature was pushing 40°C and window glass at 60°C—don't touch! We did two and a half hours along an undivided highway where the history of speeding and sleeping at the wheel was told by burnt out roadside wrecks. So numerous.

There were so many abandoned wrecks. It was said you could walk on them from Yenbo to Jeddah without ever stepping on the sand. I could verify that. Yeah, there was tension. There was anxiety. There was no beauty. There was no water. There were no plants. There was blinding sunlight, haze, and heat. And we were in a hurry.

Finally, the airport. I rushed. My taxi had been late. And along the way, the taxi's AC stopped working. The Jeddah traffic had been horrendous. The airport terminal was jammed. I tried to hurry but African Hajjis were everywhere. It was that time of the Hejira year. Every Sub-Saharan African Muslim Hajji, with recently shaved black head under virgin white cotton skull cap, had within arm's reach at least eight large, re-used cardboard boxes and four large Ferrari sports nylon duffel bags taped, strapped together, all bursting, filled with goods—shopping booty to carry home after their Haj pilgrimage trip.

Some Hajjis were wrapped in the full ascetic white Haj garb; but most of these black African pilgrims were heading back home to normal life, decked out in their loud, colourful, native tribal dress. Waiting for their departure flights, they were sleeping, either draped across their boxes and bags, or just flat on the floor, everywhere. Along the terminal aisles, there was no room to even walk. I would never have planned a vacation during the Haj; but this time, I had no choice.

My thirty days to depart had expired on the day—I had to make the flight. My stomach twitched. Blood pressure throbbed through my carotid artery. Sweat rolled down my forehead. Anxiously twisting and pushing my way through this tangled jumble of African sights, sounds, and smells, I wove my way toward my departure lounge.

In the last month, my life had fallen apart. My cocoons had been ripped open. My tolerance had been shattered. I had nothing left, nothing in reserve. But a thought tried to surface on my way from Yenbo to Jeddah—maybe Gordie's eye opener, his death and the RIF were a lifeline for me. Maybe I needed to get out of all my cocoons. Maybe going to Bangkok to find Gordie's fiancée, Kaytee, would be my life saver. No time to think that through.

My Jeddah:Dubai:Bangkok flight had already been called. First class had already boarded. As usual, there was a scrum boarding in coach class. The airline staff ushered me to my first-class seat, free of the scrum and without delay.

**

Jeddah-Dubai-Bangkok

...CJ continues...

The airplane, no matter which class, always an oversized cigar tube. For me it was a cocoon. I relaxed and thought about the main memories, aside from Gordie, I had from Yenbo. Bertram and JeanClaude had spoken to me about existential roots in the landscape. Existential roots in the landscape? They spoke about something ancient and deep in the desert—something deeper than Islam. Well, those thoughts took me back to New Mexico. They took me to my university years, JB Jackson's writings and his uncertainties about connections between culture and landscape. Existential mysteries.

Something, an historical force, an existential mystery threaded through the Arabian Peninsular deserts. It had nothing to do with my design puzzles. It was where landscape went so much deeper than landscape architecture. Made me recall the description from Bree, the Peace Corps horticulture enthusiast from my Tangier gardens days in Morocco. She was very convinced by her own first-person experience that the Sahara exuded negative vibes—serious as she was, I never could grasp that.

And JeanClaude's words—an insight into my future career? I didn't know. He was right when he said, "You are a landscape architect, into ethnobotany and alchemy. You are a rare animal. West Africa. North Africa, Arabian Peninsula. Those all have ancient roots in the landscape." So many thoughts, so few answers and very little clarity.

As soon as we reached cruising altitude, I asked for wine. The stewardess reminded me that no alcohol could be served while we were in KSA airspace; but as soon as we would take off from Dubai, the service would be normal again. Thirty minutes later, after our short stop in Dubai, the stewardess returned and served wine.

I had just flown out of a personal Saudi Arabian disaster. With the suicide of my friend and right-hand man, disaster had once again blown me over. I felt obligated to notify Gordie's fiancée. I was on a quest taking me to Thailand with uncertain and perhaps unknown/unlikely results.

The whole suicide and KSA job RIF scene had gotten to me. Relief to be putting it behind me, so to speak. My Kaytee quest beckoned; but for the moment I needed any kind of deep cocoon—wine and sleep would do the trick. I chugged the wine; and I put my seat back, my feet up, determined to sleep on this six-hour haul to Bangkok.

After six years in the deserts of Araby, my mind was filled with its landscape images. The blazingly tropical Red Sea sunsets of the KSA Western Region coast. The dreary, sandy Tihama coastal plains, denuded of trees, stretching for kilometres from the shores of the Red Sea to the sharply formed and dramatic though barren rock of the Hijaz mountains.

As I started dozing, I was wondering about the reddish orange sand dunes, tucked around the dark russet red rock bases of those mountains... places which I had often explored on foot during weekends when... my memories and imagination intertwined as thoughts... which gradually became my dreams that damn sure could have been reality. And I descended into the cocoon of all cocoons—dreamland.

I felt the sand giving way under my feet. It must have been that dry quicksand of the desert I'd heard about. Strangely, I did not feel panic or fear. I was slowly sinking through the sand, like the sand had larger air spaces between the grains and could not support me... I felt, not out of control, but like I was moving down at the speed of a slow escalator.

As the sand reached my chest, my chin, my nose, my eyes...

my breathing and vision had not been affected. My downward speed had increased, but I was still upright.

If I had gone under the sand, how could there still have been daylight?

I could breathe, and what was it I was seeing?

The light level was low, but enough so that I could still see. It was cooler and there was humidity. It reminded me of the large, centuries-old, university buildings in London, just barely tolerable low light, huge spaces, high ceilings that always disappeared into some historically ambiguous, uncertain details, dissolving into distant mists...

In front of me there was a lecture hall with the doors open, and a lighted lectern. I could see inside... who was lecturing? And on what? I tried to look in, but my movement forward could not be impeded. I could not slow down. I could not turn around. I could not go backwards.

My movement felt more like an airport people mover, except I was moving down. But wait, my feet were moving like I was walking... I could not tell if I was moving vertically or horizontally and suddenly, I was dizzy... getting dizzier... losing all orientation of up and down...

Fight the flow... or... go with it...

There was someone next to me. I turned. I could just see the rear three-quarters of a hooded figure, in a dark brown coarse wool thobe? No, it was like a winter Moroccan djellaba, deep hood, well over his face.

I asked, "Can you help me? Where are we?"

The djellaba'd character agitatedly spit out over his shoulder, "Shaikh will fix, Shaikh will fix."

"Shaikh?" I asked, "Shaikh who?"

The djellaba'd man disappeared around a corner. I followed and was confronted by another large double-door entry to another lecture hall... this time with a large crowd, dimly and indirectly lighted all about. I saw a spotlighted lectern at the front... who was that lecturing and what was he saying?

Serious, the lecturer sounded like he was serious. Who? What?

Before I could process any thought, I became aware, in my

peripheral vision, of a growing uproar... I strained to turn my head to look... there was a huge crowd in the hall and way up high, in the fourth balcony, a major ruckus with banners, "Don't Cramp Me Style" banners... rowdiness... Rastafarians, Indians, Pakistanis, Sri Lankans, South Africans, Australians. It looked like a Cricket World Cup crowd... all trying to shout down the speaker...

I heard, I heard... it was in English... but there was too much rowdy noise. What was that he was saying... he was saying, "... and the importance of green to landscape architecture is..."

What, what? The crowd noise interrupted and the speaker... I couldn't believe my eyes, who was the speaker... it looked like... it was... it looked like Will Ferrell... all hell was breaking loose... cricket gloves, stumps, bails, pads, caps, all were being thrown from the balconies...

Ferrell shouted, "What do you think this is, some kind of fucking holiday? We are serious here."

The crowd went wild... someone came up behind Ferrell and started trying to wrestle the microphone from him... it... it was... no it couldn't be... the guy was threatening, shouting, "Don't walk through MY words!!!"

It was, no, not Al Sharpton... no, it looked like Eddie Murphy playing an Al Sharpton part... was that Eddie Murphy on stage trying to elbow Will Ferrell from the microphone... and this time he got the microphone and yelled, "Got to show some respect!!!"

Eddie Murphy and Will Ferrell were wrestling and shouting over each other. "Don't walk through my words, got to show some respect!!!" The crowd was screaming... it was wild... chaos reigned!

From the back of the stage dozens of short, Star Wars-type sand people in black, fine wool burnooses, with large, oversized hoods, emerged, each with an old English Bobby truncheon... all at the same time converging on the melee at the lectern... both Ferrell and Murphy were still yelling at each other, "... you ain't heard me out yet, you ain't heard me out..."

Before I could even assess satire and reality, I moved along and almost bumped into the djellaba'd man still mumbling...

"Shaikh will fix, Shaikh will fix."

I tried to grab him to talk; he slipped away into a lecture hall saying, "See the Shaikh. Shaikh will fix."

I didn't know any Shaikh... and now the lighting was from a very high clerestory. I looked up to see the sky and the light source was so high up it was like a visual pins and needles experience in my peripheral vision. I was blacking out... vertigo had descended on me. My knees weakened. I looked up again at the clerestory and saw twice as many pins and needles. This time they were moving, they were beckoning me; they were calling me... increasing and decreasing in brightness, throbbing in my head and causing me a shortage of breath. Then I blacked out.

As I remember, the dream continued, and I was sitting in a seat, a lecture hall seat, in the front row with two lighted lecterns directly in front of me. The lecterns each had a speaker, and each speaker had his name plate in front of the lectern.

The man speaking was Professor Dr Franz Hartmann, gaunt, balding with white hair and wire-rim glasses, talking about the history of landscape architecture and its purpose being to preserve and protect those landscape experiences that captivate and inspire humans to higher goals in life.

Professor Hartmann then said to us all, "I am sure you would all like to hear what the Shaikh has to say on this subject." I held my breath. The crowd rustled with anticipation.

Professor Hartmann continued, "As soon as the Shaikh finishes his ablutions, I am sure he will comment." The other lectern occupied my attention.

There was a heavyweight man, dressed in white robes, bald and bent over a bowl, taking water to his face, in ablution style, slowly and deliberately massaging it over his shaven head, then over his forehead, as if purging himself of all that could be unwanted.

The Shaikh's name plate read, not Shaikh, but Colonel, Colonel Walter E. Kurtz. Taking a clean white towel to his face, he spoke while daubing off the water.

Even still, his voice was clear, "Envy, pride, avarice, lust, anger, gluttony, sloth..." The crowd was alert. He put his towel down and looked out for the first time over the amassed crowd, and continued, "My students, these are immortal; and above all, we must clean our own doorstep..."

I could not begin to address these words because the face and the emotions of the Shaikh were the face and the emotions of Marlon Brando as Colonel Walter E. Kurtz in "Apocalypse Now".

I turned to the "student" next to me. It was the dark brown djellaba'd man, his hood still well over his face, who said to me, "Shaikh is good, Shaikh is good."

I looked over my shoulder at the rest of the large numbers of "students" in the lecture hall and saw more dark brown djellabas dotted here and there, always with faces hidden within the shadows of the hood. Even more disconcerting was the diverse group of "students" taking up the rest of the seats. They looked like garden gnomes, live garden gnomes... like iterations from "Snow White and the Seven Dwarves". I felt trapped as never, couldn't think, couldn't breathe, couldn't move.

Then the stewardess shook me, handed me a warm towel, and said, "We are beginning our descent to Bangkok."

I was shaken. I was leaving the sands, the winds and the desert mysteries behind. Except for my dreams.

***

Kurt Says

This dream—it went on and on. I laughed at all CJ's television and movie references. But honestly, I think it was him reliving all his issues in landscape architecture layered with, intertwined with his unique Saudi Arabian experiences.

After all, he just had two big-time losses—his best friend and colleague, then his job. That's enough to shock and stir up dreams in anyone.

I asked myself why. CJ was examining his purpose in landscape architecture, his disappointments and his uncertainties. All his instabilities resurfaced—Morocco, New Mexico. He was bummed.

Now, CJ was on a hunt for Kaytee, but, why? Honestly, I didn't know what he was looking for. Hope? Release? What I was sure of... he was uptight.

7-One Night In Bangkok

Two Nights

...CJ continues...

And now... Bangkok. On this trip, I was a first-time pilgrim. My pilgrimage had a quest, a goal; but I moved around like a tourist. Tourist? A person not here long enough to get any real cultural insights—that was me. Bangkok... nothing but foreign.

I wasn't expecting any kind of relief in Bangkok. Especially because my dream... my dream still had me wrapped up. It was every part of the last couple decades of my life. Disappointments, uncertainties, instabilities and shocks.

I had all but forgotten about Morocco... Morocco? *Djellabas?* Where did that come from? I was already off balance. And that dream? That weird dream pushed me into a hazy fog... do-gooder? A joke? My career? Do-gooder fallacy? Me? I sat up straight and wiped my face with the warm towel.

In more ways than one, I was anxious when my flight touched down. My contractually required bachelor trips every six months over the past six years had always been to London or Amsterdam—trips to make sure my equipment was serviced and drained. I had no interest in going East. First time in the Orient. First time in Bangkok. But I was on a mission. I was on a quest.

After my friend and colleague Gordie's suicide, the information, the clues I had uncovered were meagre—a thin strip of a map of Thailand with a red circle around Bangkok, and the names Kaytee Cheng and Creed written in red. And the local gossip from the barber who shared that Gordon was planning to marry that girl. I was looking for her... why? Close the loop? Find out how she helped Gordie close his own loop on family disasters? I didn't know for sure. Searching for Kaytee and searching for answers.

I had done some online research. I learned that Creed on the thin strip of map was likely The Creed, a bar in Patpong, a seething tourist hotspot. So, I reserved my room at the Peninsula Hotel, an established tourist sanctuary fairly close to Patpong. I controlled my entry to this strange new place by arranging the Peninsula Hotel greeter to meet me at airport arrivals just as I exited the first-class flight cabin.

I was taken to the first-class lounge, while my greeter completed the formalities necessary for passport, luggage and customs clearances. Within fifteen minutes, I was in the HeloTransfer, and in fifteen more minutes I was in my pre-checked-in room.

I opened the drapes. My room was on the 14th floor. I had given myself two nights in Bangkok to find Kaytee Cheng. There were still two hours of daylight left. I hoped to solve the business at The Creed that night and pick up my flight to Amsterdam in 36 hours.

I needed to be in Amsterdam, a place where I understood how it, the street culture, worked. It was a culture thing for me. I had been torn from my Yenbo work and design cocoons—my only remaining connection, my only thread to grasp was my quest for Kaytee. Finding Kaytee had become my purpose, my pilgrimage. I had to do it for Gordie, the Canuck.

From my hotel room window, which did not have an option for opening, I looked over the city. It sprawled. It stirred, it bristled. The streets were tight. They were crowded with all kinds of motor vehicles, trucks, busses, cars, all sizes and ages, nothing in disciplined lines, everything blended into a huge, stuttering flow and on the edges, even the pedestrians blended into the flow. It was all one.

I thought again about Morocco, its medinas. All pedestrian. And all jammed into a flow. Below me was the same flow—but to motor vehicle scale. It was all "outside my cocoon".

Even the sidewalks were jammed. From my 14th story hotel room, the Bangkok public realm looked like everything "East" I had imagined—oriental Asia, shoulder to shoulder, 24/7, with absolutely zero cultural cues I could understand.

Yeah, I had imagined it; but with the real thing boiling before my eyes, even from the 14th storey, waves of anxiety washed over me. I was looking at real life in a foreign culture. I didn't want to get any closer than my 14th storey room. Counting my time in Morocco, I had lived almost seven years in strange cultures. Multi-cultural? I didn't like it but I had some kind of unknown magnetism that made it intriguing while repulsive. My body shuddered.

Mentally, I grabbed onto my task, my aim, my organization, my quest for Kaytee. I steadied.

Before going out, I read through my in-room hotel brochures, found nothing more that could help me, except a map that had the label, Patpong. I freshened up and headed straight downstairs to inquire with the Concierge, someone who hopefully might be a fountain of local details.

***

Getting In

...CJ continues...

Do you mock cultures? Think they are playthings? Think they are Playdough? Cross-cultural? Multi-cultural? The only people who mock multitudinous cultural uncertainties are those who have never left their own basements.

Even tourists race to get back home. Expatriates may have a taste for cultural challenges—and believe me cross-cultural challenges are many. Cultural challenges do not have fixed definitions and they are always shifting. They grow in number and intensity the more a person digs into a foreign culture. I learned that a long time ago in Morocco; and my time in Saudi Arabia... the same. I knew my roots were solid in generic Western cultures.

During my six years in Saudi Arabia, I, while on vacations in strange countries even in Western countries, relied on hotel concierges to be my guardians, my doormen for safe passage into strange cultures. They translated their local cultures and served filtered information for my use. The Peninsula Hotel Concierge confirmed there was a place called The Creed. The game was on.

The Concierge described it as an old place, an established place, in Patpong. He circled the location on a more detailed map, gave it to me, and asked, "First time in the City of Angels, here, sir?"

The irony absorbed me. I had seen no one resembling an

196

angel...

Without waiting for an answer, the Concierge suggested, "The streets are aggressive, sir, especially as you get closer to Patpong. It might be more comfortable to take a taxi."

I thanked him and asked, "Tell me, do you know more about The Creed? What's it really like?"

"Yes, I know it, sir. The Creed Bar. It is not really a place for a first-time tourist; rather, it is a place filled with regulars who know what to expect."

"Hmmm, uh... what do you mean?"

"The traditional shyness of the Thai ladies, sir, is not so obvious there. I must say, it is an 'all-business' kind of place. May I be of any further assistance, sir?"

"So the taxi'll take me to the front door?"

"No, sir, it can only get you two blocks away. Let me show you exactly on your map. When you get out of the taxi, here, just go straight up this street, and take your first right. The place is on a small street. No cars, no trucks. It is loud, and it has a large sign, The Creed Bar. You cannot miss it. Will that be all, sir?"

I nodded and asked him to call a taxi.

As the taxi arrived, I stepped outside for the first time. Exiting the air-conditioned lobby and still under the porte cochere, I choked on my first breath of still Bangkok air. My lungs did not get the oxygen. What did I expect at 13°N latitude—good as the Equator—big time humid and tropical.

I could feel the sweat quickly forming on my forehead and back. I could hardly inhale, the humidity so thick—not salty like Red Sea air but... chemical and stinky. I guessed a mix of vehicular air pollution and not fully completed sewage treatment. But there was something more. The late afternoon air, so hot, so thick, so full, seemed to constipate my thoughts. The street noise oppressed me and disturbed my breath. What I could inhale were strangely aggressive odours. They wrenched my gut.

I climbed into the taxi. Showed the driver my mapped destination. He understood; and I sat back. I noticed the rear-view mirror stretched all the way across the top of the front windshield, continuous from pillar post to pillar post. It didn't take long for me to understand why. Three-hundred-sixty-degree vision was necessary. It was all moving in every direction. Entering the traffic flow was like diving into deep river rapids. The taxi driver just dove in and somehow the other cars just made way. Just.

The entire traffic flow was stuttering. Stuttering and fast. Moving and not moving. Flowing. Not flowing. Traffic stammering everywhere. Moving vehicles everywhere. Motorbikes, tuk-tuks, you name it. Too much moving. Too much to see. Each vehicle was tight against every other. All just slipping along one next to the next to the next. Higgledy-piggledy everywhere. Painted stripes on the road meant nothing.

This taxi ride stirred claustrophobia with dizziness into my high anxiety. The taxi AC was weak. Every vehicle released clouds of exhaust, hanging low in the air. For me, it was an Oriental cross-culture IMAX experience. My clothes became soaked with sweat, anxiety-laden sweat. Peering through the taxi window, I felt... I felt the city... prowling. This city prowled.

***

Patpong

...CJ continues...

I got out where the Concierge had marked on the map and began walking. At first I saw a mixture of small Bangkok mom and pop stores next to larger Western franchise outlets. Low budget modern architecture infiltrating old Bangkok. Then the new stopped, and I was in old Bangkok.

Noise, food hawkers, entertainment hawkers. Every door had noisy music flowing out to the street. My ears were confused by the overlapping music. In my face I had many aural and visual cacophonies, each underscored with the eardrum-crackling base thump of unmuffled motorbikes and the scratchy soprano squawking of tuk-tuks. The blending cacophonies intensified, congealed into a foul, sweet, rancid, sour... a something of a sickening sound—awkward sensual overlaps.

And the smells? They were all overcooked. Flowing over one another, they were underlain by a continuously changing, stomach-churning blend of stagnant canal, its decomposition, its rotting veg, and its human sewage. It all welled up larger than visceral. The public realm, a noisome, aggressive atmosphere.

And people. The smells of people, smells all foreign. Moroccan medinas had no strange smells except for mint. And Saudi? The crowded medina smell was often oud or cardamon. But here? I could only guess it had to do with what I had read about the wet markets—the strange odours of unusual land and water animals cooked into soups. People seemed to carry

199

those odours with them. Not pleasant. Not attractive. And trapped within a coating of heavy, hot humidity.

All these new sensations were in my face, in my nose, cloyingly coating my skin. I could not walk a step without bumping shoulders with other people. In Amsterdam, I could mingle among crowds and remain on the edge of everything. Here in Patpong, there were no edges. Everything surrounded, suffocated me.

I was being touched too many times—pickpocket artists, who knows? Girly boys. Teenage girls. Everywhere was sexy time. Everyone looked barely sixteen, sweetly smiling and sexually ambiguous. Ready to ambush, ready to seduce, ready to play. It was all happening!

In the shadows, older people sat on steps watching, just watching... detached and watching the public realm as if it was on the television screen at home. And I, my thoughts smothered, choked. I felt like... I felt... I felt the devil. It was all too much! I bucked myself up. Just get on with it, I told myself, sort it for the Canuck.

Days later, I had time to reflect on the street, the sidewalk, the entire Bangkok public realm and my visceral disgust for it. It had forced me to explore the cultural differences behind my innate dislike.

I concluded that my time on Bangkok streets had been so uncomfortable, so awkward that my own Western cultural roots did not accept this. I am from the West and will always be Western.

I had always been into searching, into discovery... but this place... way over the edge. It had shut down my nature to inquire. As if the oxygen supply to my lungs had been turned off and my brain, my mind, my intellect and my thoughts immediately red-lined to a condition of advanced atrophy. Not good.

I surmised that culture, as I defined it, cultural imprints on groups of humans might be indicators... indicators of many, many types of sub-species of humans. Not just one species, not just one race, not just homo sapiens... unless these cultural imprints were like decals—tattoo decals.

No, more likely they were deeply implanted, deeply rooted. They would not wash off next week. Rather, they might slowly and gradually wear away with time... with centuries.

Cultural imprints are not well understood by current science, and thus, they should not be treated lightly.

Like television, if you don't like what's on a channel, don't watch it. If you don't like what is cultural behaviour in another place, stay at home. That is respect. I needed a cocoon.

***

Kurt Says

Man, when I read this, I knew CJ was not where he wanted to be. The dude I knew at the office, at Trader Vic's. In Bangkok? Not his thing.

But he did have a thing for pedestrian districts. His description of the Bangkok streets? It made me think of a city that first was for pedestrians. Then motor vehicles moved in. Then pedestrians said no way.

So different from LA where it was all for the cars, forget it pedestrians. It took big government to declare pedestrian zones in LA. And Bangkok, pedestrians were the force. That kind of interested me.

And CJ, like he said, needed his cocoon. He was out of his realm, and he had to be there. I couldn't forget what got him there—death and job loss. The Bangkok street scene? More agitation.

**

The Creed

...CJ continues...

I had learned The Creed Bar had been in Bangkok since the late 60s. It was known then, and is still known today, for its loud music and rowdy behaviour. The ladies there had built their own reputation, having provided services to the American troops from Viet Nam.

Just in that thought, coming from somewhere around the next corner on the right, I heard the refrains of "Who'll Stop the Rain", a Creedence Clearwater Revival classic. Welcome to "old school" Bangkok.

I turned the corner, and the flashing sign almost blinded me. The Creed Bar. Twilight had darkened, and the flashing lights along with the blasting CCR music were the entire story. Creedence Clearwater Revival, CCR, The Creed Bar, it all fit together. Yep, this was the place.

Before I could settle myself though, a beautiful 5'2" Thai lady was in my face, with her sweet smile, her 36D boobs barely covered by her spandex halter. She cupped her boobs with her hands and with her thumbs began massaging the nipples, which, under the spandex, were already inviting my attention.

She said, "You like my big titties?" I couldn't miss them. Animal need erased my anxieties.

Before I could speak, she put one hand on my crotch and said, "You have nice cock."

She gave a little squeeze to the shaft, felt the virile engorgement. Licking her lips with a willing smile, she added eagerly, "You have hungry cock."

Without hesitation she led me by my arm. "Come to my room, I make happy cock, special deal, first guest today, twenyfi' dolla US, rouna-world." She was aggressive, and at the same time her eyes were warmly welcoming. I was willing.

I had my share of experience over the past six years in Amsterdam. This part was familiar. As she led the way upstairs to the short stay hotel, I regained my thoughts and remembered why I had come to Bangkok. I thought, first get hosed down with this lady, and then seek the information.

Upstairs I went. She was sweet, energetic yet softly pleasant, thorough and efficient. She was a worker. Her eyes, her hands, her arms... she had a caring method—for too short a moment I found a cocoon. I felt relief.

She gave what she said, and I paid $25US, plus a $5 tip. After washing, she was fitting her spandex halter. I opened my wallet again, immediately catching her eyes as I pulled out three $20 bills. She asked, "Can I give more pleasure, massage?"

I asked her if she knew Kaytee Cheng.

She paused, looked quizzically. I pulled out two more twenties, and, meeting her eyes with mine, said the name, Kaytee Cheng, two, three more times. She tried to repeat the name a couple times, then recognition crossed her face.

"... nong Kaytee... she my fren'."

I gave her the $100US as she explained this Kaytee had worked for about a year, then she met someone fancy from Geneba.

My jaw dropped. "What? Geneba... you mean Geneva? Switzerland? What?"

"Yes, Geneba. Farang offer deal," she said, "...make her rich one year. She took it. Go fi' mons befo'."

"She's not here?"

"She no here."

"She have family here?"

"Family no here. Malaysia."

"Where?"

"Don' know. No say."

Focussing on Geneva, I pushed more, hoping to find who

or where in Geneva. All I could find out was, five-star hotel, special club.

I was reeling. What I had just heard had hardly sunk in. Somehow I managed a smile, thanked the lady for all, said goodbye, and stumbled in shock back downstairs.

***

Let Down

...CJ continues...

What I had just learned started to sink in. Having not found Kaytee at The Creed, my trip to Amsterdam wasn't going to happen. These new complications, plus an unfamiliar Geneva path, were just what I had not wanted. Let down is an understatement.

I had come to a dead end, and until my scheduled flight out of there, I had 36 hours to kill in that Bangkok hell hole. I had to come up with a Plan B and get out as soon as possible.

I crossed through the Creed's main dance floor and bar. CCR was blasting. The bar stools were full of eager men, all ages. The girls were selling. I spiralled down with disappointment and more uncertainty. The anxiety of it all grew. I tried to find a taxi back to my hotel while shaking off the girls, the girlie boys, and the wordless invitations every time my eyes rested on the eyes of someone else.

My head was swimming. I desperately wanted a way out. I had lost my job. I had lost my friend. My pilgrimage had come to a dead end. Maybe I should just take that reserved seat out of here to Amsterdam.

Hell, I thought, why not just return to LA? I was going crazy trying to think this thing through. LA? That made little sense. But even that thought enlarged the anxiety knot in my solar plexus! Then I saw a taxi. I climbed in and this time it felt like shelter.

On the way back to my hotel, I tried to focus. I grasped for the remnants of my Kaytee quest, the task I had set myself in Yenbo, following the Canuck's suicide. Grabbing hold of the root of that original plan, I felt temporary stability. I thought... now... so close... so close to closing this hunt. Do I gamble and go look for her family in Malaysia? Naw, naw, that's a non-starter. I had no leads to her family's location.

Now what, I thought... cancel the Amsterdam flight, reschedule and head to Amsterdam via Geneva? But who knows if even Geneva will be the end? I knew I had just one answer, one conclusion. I had to follow this new path. I had to continue this quest for Kaytee. I'd do it as I had started for the Canuck. The pilgrimage continued.

Calming a little more, I looked at the positive side. A broad smile crossed my face as I remembered. I got a hose down, and a good one at that. And I got a solid lead on Kaytee's path. And, I would go to Europe, so maybe it wasn't so bad after all.

I had to rejig my flight plans. Back at the hotel, I spent the next four hours online and on the phone. I tried all combinations—via Amsterdam, via Istanbul, via Dubai. Even pulling all the strings I could, I could not get a seat out of Bangkok to Geneva for four days. Four days!!!

I thought for a moment and concluded, bird in the hand. I took it. I booked my flight to Geneva, then I booked a room at the Hotel des Burkas, an established five star in downtown Geneva.

Now, I just needed to get some breathing room. I needed to get free of this hectic Bangkok scene. I could not do another day in this town. Murray Head was right about Bangkok when he sang "not much between despair and ecstasy". I was on the wrong side of that. That's all.

8-Ban Muang

Marty and Vinny

...CJ continues...

Despite my satisfying release via physical interlude with the lady from The Creed Bar, I was mentally wound up—tight. My first twelve hours in Bangkok had amplified my original Yenbo suicide and RIF shocks. It was edging toward midnight. I was trapped in Bangkok. Four days until my flight to Geneva. Bangkok's suffocating squeeze made me wretch, twisted me inside-out! I was lost.

Then I remembered Marty, an Australian colleague—a Southeast Asia landscape specialist. Marty, a certain Martin Foster, his work was to source plants from Thailand and other countries in this region. That was funny—back in SoCal good-looking large trees could always be found in the local nurseries—but they were often long-lead items. For my work in the KSA, good looking large trees had to be sourced from other countries—thousands of kilometres away. They were without a doubt hugely complex, long-lead items. That was Marty's business.

Marty supplied them to very large development projects, primarily in the oil-rich Gulf Region countries of the Middle East. Marty had always told me, if ever in Southeast Asia, call him, he could sort anything.

Born in the 1960s, Marty, without a university degree, had cut his business teeth as a middleman in Thailand, Malaysia, Indonesia, Vietnam, Singapore and China. He provided large numbers of higher-grade mature palms, trees, plants of any

211

type for my special projects in Yenbo. Marty was one of those guys whose phone was on 24/7/365. I called. Marty picked up.

"Hey Marty, what's up?"

"CJ! How ya keeping?"

"Guess what, Marty? I'm in Bangkok. Are you about?"

"Nah, I'm down south of KL, in Johor Bahru, on my way to Singapore. Glad to hear from you—hey, I'm makin' a contact in Singapore to go to Saigon. Somebody, some chieftain in the Nine Dragons of the Mekong Delta wants to sell all the plants growing on two square kilometres—lock, stock and barrel—a whole mess of mature palms. Ya' interested?"

"Whoa, hang on a minute Marty—slow down, first things first. I need some help."

"What's up, mate?"

"I just got into Bangkok earlier this afternoon and I'm dying to get out! Not my place; I've gotta get out; but I've gotta wait for four days for the next flight..."

Marty interrupted, "One night in Bangkok and you gotta get out! Shit, CJ, you're getting to be a real All-American pussy!" Marty laughed through every word in his sentence—and was still laughing.

"Wait, let me finish, Marty... I need to get some place quiet, some place where I can have some room to breathe. Say, a while back... didn't I turn you on to a special project—out in the middle of nowhere—up in Northern Thailand? A couple years ago? How did it pan out? Did it happen?"

"Hell yes it happened! That's another project my mate Vinny did."

"So Marty—is it open? Is it quiet? I need some Thai shelter!"

"Yeah it's open. It was the first big time project Vinny and I did together—a five-star boutique place for people not interested in seeing other people, or not interested in being found. Ban Muang Guest House, that's it. Have I ever told you about Vinny... he's the one that's making this connection for the big trees in the Mekong Delta?"

"Marty, tell me something more about the Ban Muang project first. You sure it's quiet, peaceful? I can't take the Bangkok street scene... it's a public realm too far!"

"No worries, CJ, I travelled up there a couple times. It's fine—a tiny footprint, great craftsmanship, an ecological respect for the landscape, and definitely, definitely off the beaten track. Quiet? It's a beauty. You'll get your Thai shelter for sure. But I've got to tell you about Vinny. He was the man who made it happen."

"Alright, go ahead. I'm listening."

"I met Vinny—long time back, when I first started this trading bit here in SE Asia. He's about fifteen years older than me—grew up in these parts—always looking for the big one. You know, the one special find—the one that solves all his spiritual, social and financial needs—all in one?!"

"Hey, isn't that what we all dream of—what's so special?"

"Listen mate, dreaming versus doing... then doing it out here, where the greatest ancient civilizations have washed over this landscape for millennia, millennia—think about it—millennia before the Westerners came to re-write history. Did you ever think of that, CJ? Did you? If you did like me and Vinny, you might just feel the magic attraction of this region yourself."

Marty continued, "CJ, for Vinny, it's all about stones. This part of the world is special because governments just don't get in the way—you know what I mean—no regs at all—suits him fine. He did development and operations work both with Kerzner and Four Seasons. Then he used his contacts to set up this five-star-plus kip—a sustainable luxury place—that's his Ban Muang Guest House—all regional architecture, art and culture. He calls it a boutique guest house. He linked it with adjacent National Park forest regeneration and protection programs.

"He got what he wanted—a quiet off-the-grid place where he could bring anyone anytime for anything—a hidden place where he could quietly move out in any direction—searching for the big one!"

"Sounds good; but tell me, Marty, boutique means small, right? Will there be any room for me?"

"Right, CJ, fifty suites, thirty-five huts, room for another fifty temporary—very Buddhist, very ethnic, very elegant, very practical. They have service that puts the Four Seasons to shame... really sweet. And Vinny always has room. So, ya interested?"

"Yeah, definitely! Sounds like just what I need. How do I get there? I've got to get out of Bangkok."

"Vinny runs G5s every other day out of Bangkok Don Muang to Chiang Rai with stuff for the project—sometimes guests. He runs an H1 Hummer from Chiang Rai, oh, about half an hour to the guest house. There's a flight tomorrow morning. Look, CJ, I'll give you my personal line to Vinny; and I'll let him know you'll be around—I'll set it up for you just like I set up all your special mature plant procurements—make it smooth as silk!"

"I want to be there now, actually tomorrow! That's just what I need. Give me Vinny's number... or better yet, can you make that happen? Can you call him tonight and confirm by text to me that all is okay for tomorrow? I'll need that flight up and back three days later, okay?"

"No worries. But now, my friend, you're gonna owe me!"

"Bullshit Marty! What are you talking about? How many hundreds of thousands of dollars in purchase orders for plants have I approved for you in Yenbo, huh?"

"Cool down, mate... cool down, I'm just helping, not to worry."

I stopped joking, and continued, "Seriously, Marty, any chance of you meeting up with me, up there at Vinny's, what's that name again?"

"Ban Muang Guest House. Nah, when I get to Saigon, I've got to rent a couple barges, cranes—and people—to move big trees like yesterday—it's one of those projects that's on the edge if you know what I mean—anyhow, if you need big stuff... hey, what are you doing out here in Bangkok anyhow, not looking for another supplier, are you?"

"Nah, long story. Tell you over a drink next time—don't forget to call Vinny and text me back, okay?"

"Yeah, okay, okay, no worries. How many nights, tomorrow and how many?"

"The flight up tomorrow, three nights and the flight back. Thanks, Marty, you're a life saver."

"Sure thing, no worries, I'll text you all the details and confirmation—I know you'll like it—see you later, mate."

***

Deep In

...CJ continues...

Marty set me up as promised and I flew out of Bangkok the next morning for a couple days in the north of Thailand. I was the only passenger on the G5.

As I settled back into my seat, I thought—am I chasing some kind of elusive mirage, or what? Here I am heading deep into Thailand... and I never wanted to be anywhere near this part of the world. When I tried to add it all up, suicide, RIF, now chasing my tail throughout Thailand... next off to Geneva... no guarantees. I am effing beat!

I hoped I could buck up my strength by resting and recovering during my guest house stay in Ban Muang. As the G5 taxied to a halt and the engines shut down at the private hangar in Chiang Rai, I saw the H1 Hummer and its uniformed driver waiting for me. Just what I needed, cosseting in privacy and comfort.

I exited the plane. When I stepped off the G5, I left behind my last connection with the dirty, modern Disneyland of Bangkok. I found the airport quiet, no crowds, a good start. The driver put my bag in the covered rear storage. It looked like an old H1, hard top military model, that had been tricked out, a pearl white satin finish paint job, and upgraded pearlescent tinted windows. As I climbed in, I found a dark blue leather interior, accented by red hand-stitching, all instruments in dark blue on white, and personal controls for silent six-fan air conditioning.

My driver told me there was a forty-five-minute drive to the guest house. Settling into the rear seat, I was relieved to be out of the intensity of the Bangkok street scene. I needed to get to grips on what really happened there, and how I was going to handle the task in Geneva.

The Hummer wound its way along a river's edge, and then slowly up some switchbacks into the low mountains. Everything was forested. The upgraded tinted windows kept out the solar glare and increased the clarity of the greens—a real pleasure. I compared these water-filled vegetative greens to the waterless sand and rock minerals of the Yenbo Hijaz landscape—water equals richesse equals life.

The driver told me that this was a national park. He said, "The guest house is at the edge of Khun Chao between two national parks."

At a switchback, I could see far down to a narrow valley floor. At the very bottom, I saw a river from which a faint, thin curling line of light bluish mist had just begun to rise. At other times, down the valley sides, I could see, well off the road, circular thatched huts.

These huts sat in small, graceful clusters—villages, it appeared. The village clusters had not a planned, but a natural grace that comes when humans develop in harmony with their understanding and stewardship of the landscape in which they live.

The driver was excellent, not too fast, and not too slow. He knew the route; and he knew how to give me the space, the confident feel of quiet privacy. I enjoyed this comfortable, casual ride through the Northern Thailand landscape. Thankfully, landscape started working its magic. I felt an inspired relaxation.

***

Kurt Says

As I read about the relief CJ felt getting out of Bangkok into the Northern Thailand countryside, I easily recalled my own relief each time I hit the surf at Manhattan Beach after a hard day at the office. He knew when he needed relaxation. He knew when to resolve the tensions of his life. CJ and I did have some deep things in common.

And his international landscape connections in SE Asia, well, far out! I have to admit I felt some envy. Made my specifying and securing plants in SoCal an exercise in paper-pushing. Man! Marty, Vinny! Those were some real dudes!

I had to search CJ's diary to see if he had any other references to Marty and Vinny. Sure enough, CJ had made plant procurement trips to Indonesia and Malaysia for palm trees. That's a romantic take on landscape architecture! Beats the hell out of a freeway trip to Orange County. Just far out!

***

Entry

...CJ continues...

The Hummer arrived at an archway, a substantial, rough-hewn teak construction. My driver paused in front of the archway and said, "This is the entry to Ban Muang Guest House. This archway has been sanctified with offerings. The offerings may look like decorations, but they give spiritual protection for all who pass through."

The archway was just wide enough to accommodate one Hummer. Passing through the arch, the Hummer entered a forest clearing, amid a natural grove of mature and juvenile teak trees. At the edges of the clearing were three buildings. Organized on what looked to be a square grid, the archway and three buildings fit comfortably in this clearing. The buildings subtly belonged to the sheltering forest. Two huge mature teak trees of ancient character had been protected and stood prominently in the clearing.

The entire setting and atmosphere looked refreshing. I opened my window. I was surprised that the temperature and humidity were utterly amenable. We were in the mountains. What were we, 1,500 metres higher than Bangkok? I turned the AC off. Back in Yenbo, KSA, AC was never off. I inhaled deeply the clean, cool outdoor air. I kept the window open. First time I had enjoyed an open window in... I don't know how long. What a pleasure.

Each of the three buildings had its own smaller scale archway with smaller teak members and bamboo offerings. These pedestrian archways were at the top of short sets of stairs and led to wide covered verandas. Everything had a rural, a naïve, a homemade feel, but with delicate craftsmanship.

Looking around the Ban Muang Guest House courtyard, I felt its trees, its shade, its architecture, its grid paths off to somewhere. I felt they all... just... beckoned me. Between the buildings in front of me, I could see down the paths to additional buildings laid out in the same grid. I was beguiled; I was charmed. I was relieved. This could be a place where I might refill, recharge my depleted energy, wipe the sweat off my brow, breathe some air. And it was quiet, peaceful.

The clearing was large, large enough to park eight to ten Hummers. So, the driver had enough room to parallel park in front of what he called the Greeting Sala. There were two formally dressed Thai ladies on the covered veranda of the Greeting Sala, each holding garlands of yellow frangipanis and bright orange marigolds. There were no other people about.

The driver opened the Hummer door for me.

As I climbed out, the two ladies stepped down the stairs from the veranda, through the archway to greet me. They each graciously placed the fragrant flower garlands around my neck. Then they each offered respectful humility via folding their hands and slightly bowing their heads, in what I was learning to be typical Thai fashion. *Wei*, they called it.

The two lady hostesses would show me around. Another gentleman arrived. The ladies introduced him as my Servant, available 24/7, for as long as I was their guest. He took my suitcase.

I paused at the Greeting Sala teak archway, admiring its carvings and its attractive bamboo craftwork decorations. One hostess explained, in soft, humble tones, but clear international academic second language English, that this was Lanna architecture, traditional architecture developed through an intimate understanding of local climate, topography and materials. Every building, every shelter had an entry blessed to protect the inhabitants. She continued to explain how the grid layout of the buildings was important. It assured that each building entry respected the East. The private inner rooms were located on the auspicious North side of the building.

The ladies led me into the Greeting Sala, which was not at all like a hotel lobby. It had three outer walls and the fourth, instead of a wall, was an open series of columns that led to an internal covered veranda on the edge of a central courtyard open to the sky. On all four sides of that courtyard were covered verandas leading to attached buildings.

The hostesses explained that the Greeting Sala was rather a place of ablution, a place where the guest could find varieties of spiritual inspirations to set the tone of the visit, thus the different rooms off the internal veranda.

I absorbed the setting. I was deep into a certain personal metamorphosis. Some kind of dam, some kind of blockage, burst. Thoughts flooded my head. I was now in a place with rain, topsoil, rivers, creeks, lakes, grasses, wild flowers, shrubs and trees all in vast numbers. It was like organic fertilizer for a part of my soul that had withered in Arabia and had been stepped all over in Bangkok. Everything green caused a tingle. Everything was new and fresh; and most of all, everything invited discovery.

The landscape of Arabia with no water, no topsoil, no green, with its gritty breezes, raspy winds, intense brightness and relentless heat drove me away... anywhere... but away. In KSA, I needed a cocoon for shelter. Here I wanted to emerge from my confining cocoon. I wanted to discover.

"Sir?"

"Sir?"

**

Tour

...CJ continues...

I broke out of my thoughts as the two hostesses introduced me to the central courtyard. In that courtyard, I saw a ground-level circular pond, large enough to display, to support the growth of what looked like maybe a half-dozen sacred lotus plants, pink petals, yellow stamens, *Nelumbo nucifera*.

I stepped down into the courtyard. Some lotus were in bloom, some were just budding, and others proudly displayed seed heads. All had healthy, serving-platter-sized leaves. The flowers, sitting with dignity above the water, had a friendly glow and a soft fragrance. At the edge of the pond, I stopped. I inhaled. Ethereal... pure. My only thoughts... the fragrance. And the colours... I thought, who said yellow and pink didn't go together?

On the other side of the pond, I noticed an engraving upon a raised stone base. It was a plinth, upon which sat a delicate bamboo water feature. The bamboo water feature, dripping slowly, made light, musical tingles, gentle ripples on the water's surface. I found myself immediately attracted by the soft sounds, sights and fragrance. I liked these simple pleasures. There was no mechanical noise. No rock'n'roll music. No cacophony of human screeches. Was I still in Thailand?

I examined the plinth engraving. It appeared to be in two languages. One must have been Thai or Sanskrit and the other, in English read:

"As the beautiful lotus is untouched by water, so is one who performs his duty, untouched by attachment". Bhagavad Gita 5:10

I guessed, and my lady hostesses confirmed, the quote to be spiritual and from Eastern culture... a brief memory of my departed wife, Sachy and her Eastern interests brushed over me. This was a different far Eastern culture compared to Bangkok. Here I felt some unusually deep comfort. What it was, I didn't know.

Then I thought, meditative, spiritual content on top of these garden sensual pleasures, how intriguing. I hardly had time to link my current professional realm of plants and landscape with the spiritual—maybe I had once upon a time—but the practical issues of growing plants in the Arabian sands had gradually hardened me.

I stopped and asked, "Before we go in, please, I have a question about hotel registration. When and where do I register?"

"After you settle into your room, your servant will come to you and complete the details, okay?"

I nodded my head and thanked her. Then we entered the Meditation Sala.

On a low table just inside the entry, the ladies pointed to a canister of fortune sticks. I looked more carefully. There were two tubular bamboo containers—each sized to be held in one hand. The first tube contained a lot of flat, long, thin pieces of bamboo—reminded me of a childhood game—pickup sticks or Mikado. But these sticks had red painted tips sticking out of the tube. The second tube contained two large pieces of bamboo.

Then my attention was refocussed. Between the two tubes sat a meditating Buddha, an incense burner, small, but delicately well carved out of stone, the incense smoke silkily turning around, about, and up through it. I took in the fragrance, a light overtone of jasmine. The happy fragrance left me smiling. It was almost musical... to my eyes. Underneath, I detected a forest scent, solid, refreshing. An incense cedar, *Calocedrus*, I remembered.

The ladies explained how I could have my fortune told by

the throwing of the red tip painted thin bamboo sticks.

"Not for me now, thank you," I said.

Beyond the Meditation Sala, the ladies showed me a broad set of stairs down to a lower terrace. They paused for the landscape view from the top of the stairs. I absorbed the large landscape of Northern Thailand. Enjoying that fine view to the distant northwest, I drew in a deep breath. My lungs were happy. The moisture and the temperature were soothing.

At fifteen hundred metres above sea level, I could see, down to the right, all the way to the river I had seen earlier. Still rising, the lightest snaking line of blue mist. To the left were row after row of forested foothills, then forested mountains. According to the hostesses, I was looking at Myanmar—old school, Burma.

In the foreground, I looked down the hill and saw terrace after terrace, descending almost like rice paddies, but with the grid of Lanna suites, each as individual houses. On each terrace sat one, two or three of the suites. Below these, the forest started to close in; but beyond, I could see a couple clusters of circular thatched huts, looking like the small villages I had seen earlier on my way here.

The hostesses explained the thatched huts permitted a true ethnic experience, a hair-shirt experience in my jargon, no mechanical HVAC, no electricity, no plumbing. An austere, monk-like experience.

**

Lanna Suite

...CJ continues...

The hostesses then led me to my more modern accommodation, a self-contained, free-standing Lanna suite.

On Marty's suggestion, Vinny had set me up in this Lanna suite with all the mod cons, wireless Internet, the whole bit. It was modern, but every detail built and decorated traditionally. My Servant had already arrived and placed my suitcase.

On the table next to my bed, I saw two noteworthy things— first, a bronze bell to summon my Servant. My Servant showed its use. What a deep and softly resonating tone. The ring refreshed the peacefulness. Second was a small, ornately carved teak bookstand. The bookstand held three books.

I looked at them. Jorge Luis Borges' *Short Story Collection*. I reached for it, and opened it to the table of contents: Aleph, Book of Sand, Garden of Forking Paths, interesting titles, some that long ago I had already read. I liked his work. The other two books, *Borderlines* by Charles Nicholl, a novel set in northern Thailand, and last, a classic by Thomas De Quincey, *Confessions of an Opium Eater.*

The Guest House was in the heart of the Golden Triangle, at the confluence of two major rivers, the Ruak and the Mekong. And the Golden Triangle, where the borders of Laos, Burma and Thailand meet, has been forever the historical center of world opium production. I turned to my Servant and the ladies to ask. But before I could speak, they told me that the books were welcome gifts, courtesy of the Big Boss, Mr. Vinny.

Then they showed me around the suite, including sitting room, bedroom with walk-in closet, bathroom with jacuzzi and rain shower. They showed me how the controls worked. From anywhere in the suite, I had fully automated control of windows, doors, screens and nets. The outdoor and indoor temperature at this elevation, this time of year, this time of day was 25°C, pleasant, relaxing. Indoors and outdoors were one.

On the walls were well-crafted woven hangings, I was told, in the regionally based, Akha style. The interior, in pastel ambers and umbers, offered me an immediate welcoming comfort. Home spun cottons dyed in various tones of indigo accented by white beads on the edges.

I saw a good blend of handcraft roughness, softened by elegant display. Observing the quality and the character in these new surroundings, I felt restful. Marty had done me well.

The ladies finished their orientation and asked me if I needed anything. I thanked them for their introductions, and they, along with my Servant, quietly excused themselves.

My night in the Bangkok public realm might just as well have been a nightmare—a bad dream. Because ever since I've arrived here in Northern Thailand, I've been in some kind of landscape heaven—a place ripe with plants, gardens and landscapes of special beauty.

I felt a deep, almost visceral cultural resonance—everything where it should be—villages next to a five-star tourist destination within a managed landscape—a landscape of legacy teak trees, a landscape of Golden Triangle dreams, a landscape of 21st century digital connectivity. Nobody was invading my space here. This was another world—clean air, plentiful water, ecologically rich, green and relaxing.

***

Relax, Discover

...CJ continues...

Alone in my sitting room, no hostesses, no servant. Finally, I had my desperately sought-after quiet. I put up my feet. I took a deep breath. I inhaled with a certain relief; but, rather than feeling relief, out came a deep sigh. Inside, I was still rumbled. Why was I rumbled? Gordie, Kaytee, my job.

When I was rumbled, I often took shelter in books. Books opened windows onto relief... windows, windows with views... views, always part of my design work.

Of the books provided in my room, I grabbed the Thomas De Quincey classic. I had heard of this well-known book, famous for its under-the-influence descriptions of opium use, but this was the first time I held it in my hands. Chance had brought me to the Golden Triangle. But not by chance I selected De Quincey.

Way back in my early college years, I had volunteered to take part in a Psychology Department experiment. A supervised experiment with mescaline and its cousins. The results horribly marked me. Under the influence, I saw the human life—all life—as meaningless. In fact, I had been overwhelmed by meaninglessness.

The meaninglessness—all my life I had been hiding from it—weaving a private world of cocoons to shelter me from that and other of life's misfortunes that have battered me. But Thomas De Quincey's opium descriptions tempted me. And this afternoon in Ban Muang, I felt I was in a safe place.

I read De Quincey at leisure. Time passed. I recalled the one positive from my university Psychology Department experiments. One day I had wandered into the university botanical garden and for the first time found, discovered... the plants, the trees, their bark, their leaves... each had become a world unto its own. Thus had begun my interest in horticulture, then landscape architecture.

The afternoon slipped away as I read. I looked outside, absorbed the open view over the veranda toward the direction Myanmar. The sun began setting. Shifting translucent blends... lilac mauves... lavender indigos... swept across the sky... brushed through the landscape. A softening chiaroscuro gradually eased all detail into the flat blacks of the tropical jungle night.

I liked this landscape. Especially I was enchanted by this setting here on the edge of the infamous Golden Triangle—nature without the roiling boil of modern human urban life.

De Quincey reminded and I decided. I found it easy to avail myself of the historical methods of regional relaxation. I hadn't foreseen this; but, that same evening as I settled into my room, my Servant came by and offered, "Might Sir be interested in regional tobacco?"

He showed me clay pots containing the dried tobacco leaves, and added, "We cut and wrap these dried tobacco leaves into cheroots, like these."

He then produced for my further inspection a carved bamboo container holding seven rolled cheroots. As attractive as these were to my eye, I declined and asked if they had any other local products for relaxing. My Servant explained the range of locally grown and processed natural products, with longstanding historical tradition. And so began my return to "the smoke", "the smoke" which once, long ago, had almost undone me in those Tangier gardens.

***

Frangipanis

...CJ continues...

Sometime later, my eyes opened. I had drifted off to a well-needed, long and deep sleep; but things were not the same. I looked up. I was outside. I saw the sun, in midday brightness, through a thin canopy of broad, large, green leaves, each with a silhouetted vein tracery... so pleasant... so beautiful... so calming. I was relaxed... in, maybe, 26-28°C... with a sweet fragrance in the air.

In due course, I recognized I was lying in a comfortable chaise lounge under a canopy of mature frangipani trees.

My eyes examined the trees. The frangipani trees, their slender yet sturdy and gracefully curving trunks were well pruned. We had frangipanis in Yenbo... but they struggled there—not reaching maturity like these. Around me, these frangipanis held up the roof, no, became the roof of my garden room. Dropping from those canopies on the well-mown grass all around me were the white, yellow, red, pink and orange frangipani flowers... each one, like a sparkling jewel, asking for my inspection.

Ahhh... ha, I thought... that was the sweet smell floating in the air. Light, delicate fragrance with just enough body to be pleasant. So many colours... must be *Plumeria obtusa, Plumeria rubra*... the more I looked, the more I saw unusual colourings, palish pink blended with twilight orange, soft buttery yellows, strong dark reds... they must have been hybrids.

My knees were stiff as I stood. I stretched. That felt better.

I must have slept in that chaise lounge all night. I vaguely recalled... this bit of disorientation might have had to do with the local tea and smoking, I enjoyed late last evening... or, was that a dream... it was not at all quite clear yet.

I noticed I had a loose top kadi kirta and yogi pants on— all natural cotton, neither bleached nor dyed, perfect for the weather. I saw no one else. I walked about. I was surprised to find I had been sitting just off the side veranda of my Lanna suite. That helped to stabilize my orientation. I turned my attention to the rather obvious garden room in which I stood. I wondered, amazed by the garden room, was this a dream?

I discovered a garden room? Discovery in the garden... that was old memories for me...way back in LA, maybe even as far back as Tangier gardens and the Hibiscus House. LA? Los Angeles, that was when I could conceptually design a garden for user's discovery. But real-world constraints had relegated "garden rooms" and control of "discoveries" to dreamland for me. Now here I was, in real life, in Ban Muang. In a garden room, making discoveries.

Hah! What pleasure. On with garden discoveries.

***

Teak Obelisks

Under the dappled sunlight beaming through the frangipani canopy, I saw, rising out of that flat lawn, a random scattering of rough-hewn, square teak columns—rather, miniature teak obelisks on teak plinths... but no.

As my attention to detail observation returned and grew clearer, my focus improved. Each obelisk on plinth was a collection of vertical teak columns, each column a different height, but each teak column had the same cross section, I guessed, thirty centimetres by thirty centimetres.

I looked closer still. The columns in clusters, depending on the feature, were as short as a metre, with others to three metres tall. They all sat on teak plinths about forty centimetres high, a good seat height, all on the flat, level grass.

I concluded these obelisk-like assemblages were actually teak display podiums. Each was unique by carved patterns on the faces of the teak vertical columns. When I looked more closely still, I found each assemblage comprising five, seven, or more teak columns.

So, in this mind-boggling garden room—no architectural walls, this wasn't Sissinghurst—all plants here, only plants. I discovered about a dozen obelisk-like groupings that were essentially a series of individual raised planters, all the teak parts uniquely carved.

As I walked and examined everything in this outdoor room,

I saw that each teak planter obelisk assemblage was a unique display... featuring plants... plants, like individual works of art displayed in an exhibition gallery.

The first obelisk assemblage I reached supported a beautiful bromeliad specimen; SW Florida native, I recalled, maybe Central America, I could not be sure. It was the beauty of the red and yellow centre that attracted me to inspect more closely. The colours harmonized with the frangipani flowers fallen at my feet. And in the bromeliad centre, upright lipstick fingers of yellow... they were alive with light!

Just breathtaking. It was *Guzmania sanguinea*, yes, a massive great specimen. But it wasn't just one specimen... there were two younger guzmanias, stepping down the assemblage of carved teak columns. The teak had been cut at varied heights, with the guzmanias pushing in against the raised members, and stretching over and down upon the lower members. The teak obelisks had been carved out to be filled with soil for the plants. The plants looked healthy, and at home... the "looking at home" that comes after years of establishment... a mature beauty.

I walked on, surveying six or seven different teak plinth and obelisk assemblages. In those teak planters, I saw world class arrays of begonias, bromeliads, orchids.... I noted the filtered sun canopy of frangipani, the bright tropical sun... the dark shade.

I, observing this sculptural—this horticultural display enclosed on three of its four sides by dense bamboo groves, had fallen under the influence of the garden room. I assessed the entire garden room as no larger than twenty metres by fifty metres. This was the real thing—no dream.

***

The Plants

...CJ continues...

This teak obelisk garden room was the best example of a built garden room I had ever experienced. Fine textured, closely cut green floor—suitable for lawn bowling. Fine textured and gracefully dense green walls—the bamboo. Coarse textured ceiling that let in sunbeams—rays to play on the artwork in the room. And the artwork? Plants. Remarkable plants.

I floated across and through diaphanous and fully absorbing layers of sensual attraction. Plinths offered comfortable places to sit and get close with the plants to observe their glorious details.

I walked over to another teak planter display. But along the way, the intense play of tropical light and shadow through the plumeria canopy became a random flashing, a staccato flashing in my peripheral vision. I lost track of walking... my balance slipped away... at the next teak plinth, I had to sit.

No sooner had I sat on the teak plinth when immediately... leaf growth details induced in me... a hallucinatory effect... wherein chaos eternally resolved itself into Julian and Mandelbrotian ecstasies... metaphors of richness carried me into the peaceful beauty of passages in literature... in music... swirlings of active... emergent... fractal patterns... along the edges. And in the centres... colours... electric light green... blindingly bright silver... iterative, jagged edge outlines in dark green engulfed me.

The play of the leaf patterns... rising off the leaves... emitted... a dynamic propulsion... a pulsating life of their own... the organically evolving patterns dissolved reference to dimension... three dimensions, four dimensions ceased to exist... and scale... neither human scale nor any scale entered my experience.

... and then... what... a breeze tickled my face.

My consciousness finally returned me from my absorbed frolic. I had been overwhelmed. By what? I looked around and found I was sitting next to a *Begonia rex*. It had to be a hybrid, a *Begonia rex hybrid*.

I looked again at the leaves and stems, gracefully rolling over and tumbling down. Then, I saw the teak columns, themselves only a metre tall. Cut level across their tops, lending support to this burgeoning begonia growth. The begonia leaves were in my face. That would explain my most recent dalliance... dalliance away from normal consciousness.

Before trying to stand up, I looked around, blinked my eyes a couple times, and took a deep breath or two.

Remarkable, I had never seen a display as entrancing, yet restrained. An absolutely elegant garden. And these plants transported me... where? I can't be sure. I had just experienced transportation through a window of ecstatic beauty.

***

Intoxication or Plants?

...CJ continues...

I forced myself to get up off the plinth. I found walking an unsteady exercise. Slowly, I returned to the chaise lounge and sat... and relaxed in a state of semi-bliss.

Time passed.

My eyes wandered back to the garden. My eyes relaxed to let the beauty enter. I felt my internal noise calm, my surface tension subside.

Then my Servant arrived, bowed, and asked if I would like the same order as last night.

I thought, last night? I still had no grasp of time. My Servant waited silently, patiently. I started to recollect. I had been in my room last night, and after discussing with my Servant, had concluded a certain historical therapy session.

My Servant recalled that I had ordered four custom-rolled cigarettes—*madaks*, a 100ml serving of laudanum tea, a bowl of fresh fruit, and a cognac.

I paused and thought. Better to clear my head and look at these gardens, without questioning if I was or wasn't in a dream.

I asked, "I am hungry for a meal. Is there a restaurant or..."

"Sir may partake of evening repas just off the lotus pond next to the Greeting Sala. The setting is relaxed and the ladies will provide everything. Tonight is an offering of North Indian cuisine. If you are interested, I can inform the lady in charge."

"Interested and hungry," I said.

"I will notify her of your interest. It would be best if you arrive just at sunset."

I thanked my servant; and he quietly disappeared. It looked to be about an hour till sunset, so I cleaned up.

Under the shower, I thought. I struggled still with my recent memories. Might it have been the intoxication that opened these magic windows to me? These fantastic, ecstatic experiences with plants—could they not be available to anyone, anytime?

Surely, as I've experienced in that teak obelisk garden room—it must not be required to take the intoxicating plant products to experience that glorious beauty of plants—their magic—through the magic garden windows?

In this garden I have sensed that plants have asked for my attention—experienced nothing like this—magic—magic? Or have I?

I asked myself, can plants ask for human attention? Hadn't I been here before—asked these questions once before—Hibiscus House, Tangier. It was happening again.

That got me thinking and writing. I thought about how far I had strayed from my original design intention—which had its root in Tangier—to share with people through my design the magic portals offered by plants to humans.

The practicalities of work had tamped, even hidden those hopes. I thought, after finding Kaytee, closing the loop for the Canuck and until I get a new job, I should attempt to blend my original design hopes with the practicality of real-life projects. I needed to set up some doable tasks along a path to implementation of inspirational plant portals in real projects. That was my thinking, that was my challenge. But the path was never obvious, never clear.

Oh, how limited is our means of understanding plants—yet they possess so many layers of beauty, so many opportunities to explore. How could I have forgotten my Tangier plant lessons?

And did I not go through a period of intense intoxication then? Did I not have to give that up before the secrets of the Oval Garden revealed themselves?

At that point I decided that in Ban Muang I should try

to approach those plants in the Obelisk Garden without being under the influence. I would try to learn if the ecstatic experience, that had just beguiled me, could be had without local intoxicants.

***

Kurt Says

CJ got fired up with his wild design concepts again. I read and re-read his description of the garden room and Obelisk Garden. It had some interesting design kernels. I was intrigued.

But... he still wasn't right—even though a green landscape and well-designed garden had enlivened him. Maybe it offered him some hope in his depressing condition—suicide, RIF, Kaytee gone.

9-Vrndadevi

Hide'n'Seek

...CJ continues...

Overall, my days at Ban Muang were too short but individually, each was languorous. And my day in the Obelisk Garden was especially long and enthralling. That same night, approaching dinnertime, I was famished.

Next to the Greeting Sala, I paused beside the open-to-the-sky courtyard garden and its pond. My eyes explored the large, open lotus blooms until taken away by crepuscule sky colours reflected as small dancing pieces on the pond surface wavelets. I forgot my hunger. I was mesmerized until I heard a female voice next to me.

"Beautiful, aren't they?"

The accent was North American. I turned and saw a lady of reticent beauty, maybe a few years younger than I. She had a Western look but a South East Asia aura. She appeared proper in a colourful silk sari.

That brought back memories. I knew about saris from back in a time long forgotten—Sachy, my best friend and wife. She had worn saris from time to time. Saris, so feminine they are. I had briefly pleasant thoughts of Sachy and her chaste saris. More recently on the TV at the Indo-Pak restaurant in Yenbo, saris and their cholis were worn lustily. Sachy was always chaste, and this lady was, too.

I agreed, "The sky, the pond and lotus... beautiful and with an aura of joyful peace."

"You must be Mr. Janus. My name is Vrndadevi and I'll be

241

your hostess. Your Servant told me to expect you for dinner this evening."

I said, "Pleased to meet you. I hear a tabla and sitar. Is that for our dinner?"

"Yes, you know about Indian music?"

"Not really. I've gone to an Indo-Pak restaurant over the last years in Saudi Arabia, where I work... ...worked."

"Well, here our dinners are quiet and the music is perfect. Most of our guests are hiding from something and they like the quiet discretion or... they are seeking—seeking inwardly for some kind of spiritual peace. They too appreciate the calm and soothing music during dining. Come with me. I'll take you to our dining sala. We are not expecting many tonight. Only four others have reserved. We have seating for twenty, so you will have a quiet dinner."

As we walked through an ablution sala into an adjacent room, I thought there was something about her voice... then it hit me... her North American accent and her vocabulary... very relaxed, not formal.

She asked me to leave my shoes at the door next to a pair of slippers that had my name on them. I obliged.

After I finished putting on the cloth slippers, she said, "Tonight we are serving North Indian specialties; and, Mr. Janus, if you don't mind, all the courses are vegetarian. But our chef can prepare meat or fish if you would like..."

"Vegetarian is fine and please call me CJ."

"I am glad to hear that. The vegetarian foodstuffs help clean the system and promote clarity of insight."

I responded quietly, "I need a little of that..."

"I beg your pardon?"

"What... oh... clarity of insight. I could use some of that. Never mind."

"Sorry if I misunderstood," she said.

Vrndadevi showed me to a low table where I sat down on an adjacent floor cushion. My table was in a cove of potted plants—combination of ferns and dwarf bananas. The music, the plants, the spiritual aura of the dining sala relaxed me. Gave me time to think. As peaceful as the setting was, my thoughts kept returning to Gordie, his suicide and the strange words we had had when he called me a do-gooder—the last thing I ever wanted to be.

Thai hostesses served me dinner... and every preparation pleasured my palate. At the end of the dinner, I was enjoying a sweet and some fruit. I was the last diner in the sala when Vrndadevi stopped and asked if I had been refreshed by the meal. She did not ask if I was full or had enough to eat, rather if I had been refreshed.

I asked, "Refreshed?"

She looked at me and smiled. I said, "Yes, indeed." As I stood up I said, "I'd like to see those lotus in the moonlight."

She led me to the lotus pond where we both shared the quiet amidst the moonlit glow of the lotus. I sat on a large boulder on the edge of the pond.

Vrndadevi asked, "Mind if I sit, too? It has been a long day."

"You're welcome, please do."

She respectfully asked, "Hiding or seeking? Does your visit to Ban Muang fit into either of those categories?"

***

Do-gooding Roots

...CJ continues...

Hiding or seeking? Her question didn't register. I thought, "What had been on my mind since dinner? Do-gooder. What is the do-gooder fallacy? Hubris? Megalomania? Naïve optimism? It had been hanging with me ever since Gordie called me that."

I said, "I'd like to ask you a question. A friend of mine called me a do-gooder and I felt offended by that." I paused as if I had asked a question.

"Offended? Why?"

"For me a do-gooder is a naïve idealist who is ignorant of real-world conditions; and I pride myself on my practical results-oriented professional activities."

"What do you do?"

"I'm a landscape architect."

Vrndadevi said, "And making gardens for people is doing good for them, no?"

"You're right there."

"I hope you don't mind; but I'd like to share a perspective on human nature that I have learned from Indian literature—the Vedas."

"Tell me. I'm all ears."

"I'll try to keep this short. Like sweetness is the nature of sugar, service is the nature of the soul, the nature of humans. Service means to help others. That does not mean to serve in ignorance. We use our intelligence to discriminate,

244

to analyze in perspective, to serve intelligently. Do the sensible, the intelligent thing. We investigate, we learn, and we serve. So according to that, doing good? You should not be offended unless you have been acting ignorantly. Do you follow?"

We were sitting quietly in the very last of the twilight appreciating the delicate fragrance, ethereal beauty and the intimacy of the peaceful lotus pond.

I thought, "Service, doing good. Making a difference—that would simply be helping others. Doing that without acting ignorantly. So I, as a landscape architect, investigate a site and its landscape, climate, geography and I learn from that investigation how to apply my skills to serve the people. And what was Gordie saying about do-gooding? That was about forgetting what the local people actually needed and wanted in their landscape—not a transplant from SoCal but something that merged smoothly with their local lifestyle." That made sense to me as the basis; but I had a question, or an uncertainty... do-gooder... making a difference?

"I'm curious," I asked, "as a landscape architect, I'm always thinking about the scale of different things—sidewalks, pergolas, water features in relation to the size of the site I'm working on. It seems that do-gooder and making a difference has a scale dimension too."

"How?"

"For example, I can try to make a difference for my friend, or my spouse, or family, or neighbourhood or community... or village, or country or world? Right? The difference I think is hubris. Who thinks they are powerful enough, knowledgeable enough to change a country, the world?"

"I see where you are going. That would make do-gooder motivation a mix of pride, greed, lust and envy. The Vedas call that kind of human behaviour action in the mode of ignorance."

"Then my work in Yenbo—where I used my technical experience to make a green town was..."

Without missing a beat, she answered. "It certainly wasn't ignorance; but not understanding the needs of the people you were helping or putting your own needs and desires first—that is different. There is a larger question—what is the ultimate good?"

"I'm just building gardens, I'm not saving souls. Making a difference was helping people to get by in an extremely harsh environment. I did good for them."

She asked again, "And so, CJ—seeker or hider?"

I took succour from her definition of doing good and now her question? Seemed like a fair question. I thought and said, "Probably both. I had to get out of Bangkok—couldn't stand the noise, the smell, the intensity—it was all too much. Ban Muang has been a pleasant cocoon for me—a place to rest."

"A cocoon?"

"A safe place—a place where I can collect my thoughts... and inspirational, too."

"Inspirational?"

"Definitely. The Obelisk Garden—at least that is what I call it. Gardens are my pleasure—and the Obelisk Garden and its plants took me to another world."

"Aside from greeting guests for evening meals, I have responsibility for all Ban Muang gardens. Would you like to see all of our gardens?"

"That would be fun." Many questions flooded my mind. She's in charge of the gardens? The Obelisk Garden?

"I have free time at 2 tomorrow afternoon," she said. "If you are free, I can show you around."

"I can make that. Where should I meet you?"

"I also teach yoga and have a Lanna suite called the Ashrama... ask your Servant, he can show you how to find it."

"Well, thank you—this evening has been refreshing. I look forward to tomorrow afternoon."

I said goodnight and she folded her hands and bowed her head before turning away. I returned to my Lanna suite.

After washing up, I rang the bell for my Servant.

I asked him about how to find the Yoga Ashram for my 2 o'clock appointment tomorrow. He said he would meet me at 1:45 and lead me to the Ashram—a short walk through the woods.

After he left, I prepared for sleep. I was looking forward to returning to the Obelisk Garden tomorrow—this time clean, neat—no additives.

***

Butterflies

...CJ continues...

I slept well. The tropical sun was high when I woke. I washed, shaved and dressed. When I finished, my Servant had already placed a fresh fruit plate and a mango lassi on my table.

After my breakfast, I headed out to the Obelisk Garden. First to command my attention was the largest obelisk assemblage of clustered teak columns. They looked as if they were covered by something, almost animated, delicately moving, gently frothing. That's what I saw. Only fruit and a lassi for breakfast—I was clean. Then stuff happened—this is the strange part—plants communicated with me—no language—just some kind of emotional "flow". Flow? Emotional or...?

Approaching the obelisk, I discovered a unique collection of multiple orchid specimens, *Oncidiums*. We couldn't use any orchids like these in the Yenbo climate. I recalled from my Los Angeles days, my visits at Santa Barbara Orchid Estate—maybe I was looking at *Psychopsis papilio*.

On top of the columns, just above my eye level, two metres above the ground, I saw a mass of fifteen to twenty arching spikes, bubbling with dancing orange and yellow blooms, by itself a superb specimen. But there was another layer—more happening, winding round and round. Spiralling up and down this teak column assemblage must have been six to eight more dwarf Twinkle orchids, each one with at least a dozen flowering spikes, with blooms, white, yellow, pink releasing the most mysterious floating weave of vanilla and citrus fragrances.

The visual interaction of these dwarfs with the *Psychopsis papilio* was animated... a swirling movement... blended with light... with fragrance... I was entranced by the multi-dimensional beauty... by a breathlessly elegant and graceful community of orchids... with faces... with faces that started communicating with me... they asked for my attention.

I looked closer, into one of the larger orchid flowers, inspecting its lip, its column... in a Georgia O'Keeffe moment... I tumbled inside that flower... I lost myself inside... still inspecting the luminous... the softly vibrating colours... until I was startled, startled by movement all around me... huge butterflies were fluttering around my head... so close, I felt, to affect my breathing... my forehead... my nose... my cheeks... my ears... my neck... beauty was fluttering all over me... it was a feeling... beauty was a feeling... fluttering out from my heart... all around me and back... I rode that beauty...

I was riding the internal essence of beautiful music... it was captivating... I was speechless... thoughtless... flowing... weak... my knees... I sat... I flowed with that feeling... until... a sunbeam touched my forehead, and spread across my face.

I had returned. I was sitting on the plinth.

I sat and sat... sat until I regained my breath. When I stood up, I recalled, from the hotel brochures in my room, that this region was known for its large butterflies, huge birdwing butterflies, as I remembered. There was no end to the breathtaking beauty in this garden. Was I living in a dream, or what? Gradually, I worked my way back to my room, had to prepare to meet Vrndadevi.

In that garden, I had just easily entered, softly entered in and out of multiple simultaneous sensual entrancements... that had just as softly crashed, or disconnected my linkages to time, to space, to reason. Yet, I had not been disoriented. I had been exhilarated! And all this happened with no intoxicants.

For so long, I knew there was something more to humans and plants. It started in Tangier, years ago.

Plant-dominated garden rooms weave magic via multi-sensual layers of attraction and somehow in that weave occur viewports or magic windows that have taken me somewhere free of time and space onto a ride, not unlike a great book, not unlike great music—a ride—but from where to where?

This reinforced realizations I had years ago in the Oval Garden and in my terrace garden in Tangier. But my career showed me that building such gardens was not as easy as I thought. People paid for my services. They had their own ideas; and governments had reams of regulations. In time, I gave up on what I called "my dreams".

Yet the Obelisk Garden rekindled my aspirations. I was a seeker. But a question, not a new question, bubbled up again... what was I seeking? I made copious notes in my design journal, concluding these garden experiences... they were like... Tchaikovsky's Nutcracker "Pas de Deux" but never reaching the conclusion... ecstatic build up... joyful beauty... but to what end?!

It made me think more about not only Tangier Hibiscus House but my last six years in KSA. What has happened to me here has been like Bertram described about the *mu'allaqaat*— stories that attach themselves to the heart. My experiences in the Obelisk Garden have been like a story attached to my heart—an incredibly deep experience. When I tried to measure these intimate private garden experiences against the Arabian Peninsula desert, I could not find a measuring stick. There was something in the landscape I still had to learn.

I realized that Thailand, Ban Muang and its beautiful obelisk garden rooms were actually a distraction. Distraction? From what? I was in the midst of experiencing great design and that special ride that plants can offer humans. But what was I after? Understanding the deep landscape? Finding Kaytee? This morning had been captivating. It had been transcendent fun.

***

Kurt Says

What did CJ want out of landscape architecture design? We had our heated disputes. He was in Neverland then and he was in Neverland in Ban Muang. But the more I thought about it... I recalled this was exactly how our best design ideas were formed for our SoCal award winners. Always a debate. Always an argument. Then an excellent result.

CJ wasn't into drugs in LA, maybe a little drinking at Trader Vic's but nothing else. Considering his stories from university times and his strange encounters in Tangier, I'm not surprised that he did what he did in Ban Muang. He was running away from emotional stress.

And the drugs? They aided him to recall his design hopes. His experiences in the gardens of Ban Muang? His experiences with plants there? Were they drug induced? They sounded like it.

But he tried to see if he could have the same results without drugs. For me, it was not clear that his system was totally clean when he, for the final time, visited the Obelisk Garden.

CJ was in the very heart of the Golden Triangle, the world-renowned drug landscape. There was nothing wrong with a little weed... but the Golden Triangle... it could be all downhill from here. I was amazed he could even write. But that dude wrote well. He was back in his realm of transcendent beauties.

His descriptions are seductive. However, the practicality of trying to design these kinds of experiences was, as was typical of CJ, a step too far. I had to step back for moment when reading these descriptions. Perhaps there was a design kernel that could be useful. Maybe if I twisted and turned CJ's ideas... CJ wanted to design something but even he couldn't find a way to do it.

I wonder, were his design frustrations what may have prompted a suicide? I can't give that a "thumbs up"—he was on an energetic quest for his colleague, Gordie. And he got into design with that same energy. Stressed, frustrated, disappointed perhaps, maybe even a bit depressed at times.

But the do-gooder thing—it bothered him. Though he did not know it, CJ had been spending his life trying to make a difference. And during his six years in the Kingdom of Saudi Arabia, he finally realized he had become what he always disliked. He was so caught up in his own design cocoon that he assumed the people of the Hijaz needed the same thing. He thought he knew what was best for anyone? For everyone? He was just... in his own words... just another do-gooder. Perhaps this was a seed of depression for CJ.

And frankly, religious stuff aside, I think that Canadian lady, Vrndadevi, had it right on—everyone tries to make life better. How you do it? That's freedom. Use your own tools and your own intelligence and get on with it—full speed—ride that wave!

But how did he close? Deep landscape? Where was he headed? Everything about his time in Thailand had him wound up.

***

Darshan

...CJ continues...

My Servant walked me downhill through the forest and, from a distance, pointed out the final path to Vrndadevi's office and place of teaching yoga. Vrndadevi met me on the lawn just in front of her Ashram. She welcomed me and, offering tea before we started our walk, suggested we sit for a minute. Sitting and talking, *darshan*, she called it.

She led me up the stairs onto the Ashram's veranda. On the covered veranda, up against the building, there was a low, half-round, metre-wide table and two chairs facing out with an aspect on the gardens. I paused because the half table and its contents were noteworthy. The table looked like... an altar. It had at the back, along the flat edge, a centrepiece. Three potted plants, good size clay pots, each, maybe fourteen-inch diameter, sitting on finely crushed gravel in individual saucers—all on an embroidered cloth.

Around the rim of each pot, I noticed a decorative bright garland of fresh, dwarf marigold double flowers, their strong, pungent fragrance setting a healthy mood. The focal plant in each pot, I observed what I thought looked like basil, one with green leaves and white flowers, two with red leaves and pink flowers. In fact, I was certain I had detected a faint earthy note of basil, a basil aroma. The basil and marigold pungencies worked well together, generating not just a healthy presence but in the air, an enlivening lightness.

"Basil?" I asked.

"Yes, they are *Ocimum sanctum.* We call them Tulsi. The red leaved are Krishna Tulsi, and the green leaved is Rama Tulsi."

She offered me a seat; and she sat down in the other chair. Our eyes did not meet. We both looked out on the peaceful yoga meditation area, a large, level, well-trimmed, green lawn, enclosed by forest. At the outset, we sat quietly without talking.

I surveyed the extents of the large garden. This was fun. I observed that, aside from the yoga area and grass path connection to other guest house gardens, there was a larger area to the right. These gardens included a substantial and regular layout of patterned grids. Raised beds, filled with flowers and herbs in variety, all healthy looking, and all well tended.

I said, "This garden setting for your yoga has an aura of beauty. It is peaceful and refreshing. The plants, the flowers, the herbs, their health, well, I must say, metaphorically, they all seem to speak to me."

"That is quite special," Vrndadevi said. "Thank you for your comments on the garden. But, please, tell me, do you have an interest in the Ban Muang Guest House Yoga Programs?"

"I am really not seeking in that sense; but since I've been here, the plants, gardens and landscape have had a... a healing effect on me."

"The peace comes from the devotion, the true devotion— the loving service that humans, through their daily work, are imbuing on these gardens," she said.

"I have to ask you about the Obelisk Garden. Are you responsible for it, too?" I reviewed with her the multiple transcendent experiences I had in the Obelisk Garden.

She said she was maintaining it; but an American expatriate established the original design concept years ago. I noted how successful maintenance had made the design inspirationally fulfilling. No sooner had that thought crossed my mind when the words of the Tangier Hibiscus House guys, Tolly and Fyodor, on plant maintenance, "respect and serve the plants, make it 50/50", seemed as fresh as yesterday.

Vrndadevi interrupted my thoughts when she asked, "Shall

we go on a garden walk now?" And off we went. In pleasant temperatures and clear skies, we walked and talked.

I said, "I have also noticed a personal thing, if you don't mind. You have a North American accent while appearing quite at home here in Northern Thailand. I wonder, how did you ever get here?"

"I'd be glad to tell you, if in return you tell me the story of how you got here... deal?"

I paused, thinking that I might get in deeper than I wanted, then said, "Deal." I concluded that this conversation just might be fun.

But I didn't let her answer. Instead, I continued on about how I had been mesmerized by the gardens of Ban Muang—these had been magic for me. I had no discomfort in exploring them. I felt that my Ban Muang garden experiences were the very core of what I had long ago theorized back in Tangier—about the magic salve a garden could be for a human. I shared that with Vrndadevi, calling it plant magic.

She said, "Cultural and geographic landscapes hold these magic gardens."

I tried to understand how the large scale and small scale fit together. We paused in the shade on the edge of a shrub nursery.

She continued, "The contemporary political borders in the Northern Thailand landscape have had little lasting significance. Why? Consider the millennial timescale movements of the human civilizations in this region. History shows that peoples of both India and China have washed over this landscape like cultural waves. And like waves on a shoreline, they receded, leaving remnants. The best of these peoples have left the internal insights of tolerance and peacefulness with the natives. Others have left external remnants of cruelty, intolerance, wickedness."

I said, "That is a rich context. I would have never guessed that on the streets of Bangkok. Tell me more about yourself and how you got interested in this region and its age-old culture."

"Working here I am part of the modern wave of Western cultural influence," she said, "a wave respecting authentic local culture, while bringing international commercial development. Before arriving in Ban Muang, I worked the last couple years in Ayodhya, the Ayodhya of Uttar Pradesh, India. This was the Ayodhya of ancient Sanskrit literature, associated with Lord Rama. Rama rajya, the rule of Lord Rama. The same Lord Rama so much a part of Thai historical and cultural linkages."

I respected the breadth of her regional landscape understanding. I was attracted to her presentation of the deep culture.

She said, "My name? I adopted it after reading a story that took place in Satya Yuga, the age of goodness. In that story, Vrndadevi was a lady of resplendent beauty, something I always strive to achieve. She rendered spectacular service to plants. And doing that, she had a spiritual goal of attaining pure bhakti, unconditional service to God, to the Godhead, the energy of God."

She was so clear and humble in her presentation.

"I was born Dana Stein," she said. "You detected my accent correctly. I'm a Canadian from Montreal. My father, now deceased, was a professor, in the Faculty of Divinity at McGill University. He was a major force in my upbringing. He taught me that religion was nothing if not an existential anchor and a pragmatic asset in daily life."

Her openness made me feel... unafraid... relaxed.

"In my birth my mother died after a difficult labour," she continued. "I remained an only child. My father was dedicated to only two things: my life, and his studies. He never remarried. He took me to the university every day. So, I grew up quietly in the Divinity School library. I played in the gardens and around the Herbarium—the roots of my natural attraction to plants. At university, while always dabbling in horticulture electives, I double majored in Cultural Anthropology and Business Management. I was only twenty-one when I graduated. But I felt something was missing."

She looked no older than thirty and had an inner glow that in my eyes was a chaste beauty... I thought of Sachy. Both had an inner warmth.

She continued, "So, I learned the personal form of Vedic philosophy from the books of A.C. Bhaktivedanta Swami. He was an Indian Swami who, in the 1960s and 1970s, had translated many of the fundamental Vedic primary references from Sanskrit into English. His translations were well respected both in the Western university divinity schools and among significant numbers of Indian followers. His Indian followers were both from the West and from the subcontinent—India as we know it today—Bharatvarsa according to ancient Vedic history.

"I use my knowledge of the Vedas, through the various systems of yoga while working with, protecting and serving plants. I do this by managing the yoga programs at five-star hotels in places that have a local or regional aura authentic to its practice and sympathetic to the philosophy. I have been working between Northern Thailand and Northern India for the past five years."

She said, "Let's walk further."

***

Permaculture

...CJ continues...

Vrndadevi continued the tour in the propagation and annual flower area. Then she showed me the tree nursery, which she described their focus, including the shrubs, on practical plants for economic stability and cultural longevity.

She said the entire process was a permaculture exercise. She explained how attitude toward the plants was key to success. That reminded me of the guys at Hibiscus House when they talked about a certain energy deriving from a service attitude toward plants.

I came to learn that in her management responsibility for all Guest House gardens, she oversaw ornamental and productive uses, including fragrances—patchouli and oud. These were large and included extensive support areas. Her gardens were part of Vinny's "green" reforestation agreement with the Thai government to propagate, grow and distribute traditional plants and trees of significant value. All gardening techniques were organic, local and small footprint. And according to the agreement, they recycled all green waste through composting programs.

I was interested in her application of permaculture principles to these gardens and forests; but when her descriptions tipped into philosophy, I numbed out. She saw it, and in her soft way summarized. "It really is simple. It's about innate human freedom and world control. I understand how you have defined permaculture as a challenge to your landscape architecture ethic; but kindly listen to what it means to me."

"How can I refuse? Tell me."

"Permaculture is a local and regional system for allowing people to have individual freedom to live and subsidise themselves—no big banks, no big pharma, no big food, no big tech (digital or manufacturing), no centralized control. It's a low-level system for people to live simple, happy lives. That's why I am here."

Something deep inside responded positively; but I preferred to remember dreamily my morning with the orchids in the Obelisk Garden.

I was getting more from this Ban Muang cocoon than I hoped for. But I had something to do in Geneva for Gordie. I was bushed. I knew I had to prepare soon for my trip to Geneva via Bangkok. But Vrndadevi was not through yet... in her own gentle yet authoritative manner.

Our conversation began easily enough after we had finished our tour and returned to her ashram to refresh ourselves with *sandesh* (white curd sweets) and tea.

Vrndadevi said, "I told you my story—how I ended up in Northern Thailand on the Mekong River. Now, it's your turn. How did you get here and what had you been saying about cocoons?"

I paused. My thoughts about cocoons took me way too deep—Sachy and the kids—I did not want to open that door.

I deferred, asking, "Cocoons? What were you saying about hide'n'seek or was it hide or seek?"

"Well, you don't have to tell me your life story; but you told me Ban Muang was a fine cocoon for you; and the need for a cocoon implies a fear of something... please tell me your story."

"Bangkok! Couldn't take the street scene, the smells, the noise."

"I understand that, but you talk of cocoons like they are a regular part of your life. And you still haven't said how you got here."

I took a deep breath. I felt relaxed talking with Vrndadevi. I wasn't being cross-examined. I found a safe path and opened up.

**

Cocoons

...CJ continues...

"Cocoons?" I said. "You're right, they have been a regular part of my life. In Saudi Arabia, my work was my cocoon because, as a non-Muslim and a Westerner, I was not welcome into their culture. I've been there six years and even though I have trained young Saudis and made presentations to high-ranking Saudis, I've never been invited to their homes or even to go for coffee out in public. My cocoon is my work... or I should say my cocoon has been my work."

She was surprised. "Has been? What?"

"Has been—my work—how did I come here—it is all the same story. About a month ago in my Saudi job strange things overtook me. My colleague, also my best friend on the job, committed suicide. Huge shock. Then shortly thereafter my job was ended. Details not so important except for the clue I uncovered in my friend's desk drawer. I learned he was engaged to a Thai girl from Bangkok. So after my job was terminated, I took it upon myself to find her and let her know. That's how I got to Bangkok; but she has left—moved to Geneva. That's my next stop—leaving tomorrow for there—to close the loop on my friend's untimely death. So here I am."

"Wow... such commitment to your friend."

I said nothing. The whole thing with Gordie the Canuck was becoming too unsettling for me. I was glad when she changed the subject... at first. But it turned around.

"Tell me about other cocoons in your life. I sense that you have an innate understanding of good and bad, higher and lower, gross and subtle, material and spiritual. Even with the gardens and maybe with the cocoons you are seeking something special... something out of the ordinary... something not normal to everyday material life."

I didn't really have a grasp on the difference between the higher and lower self and the spiritual side. Despite my conversations with my friend Bo years ago about Jacob's Ladder and the "stairway to heaven", I, personally had never come to grips with portals as some kind of definitive interface between material and spiritual, though I had in the past tinkered with the idea of transcendent beauty. Funny how she brought up this subject because my experience with the orchids that morning was definitely what I used to call a portal experience.

I said, "Do we have to talk about cocoons? I was more into the plants, gardens and landscape stuff."

"OK, let's talk about your experience this morning in the Obelisk Garden. You are wondering about the effulgent, multi-sensual beauty you briefly experienced with plants in the garden this morning, right? What I suggest might have been a brief experience of the Godhead..."

I said, "Yes, maybe... possibly... something like that."

**

Seeking Transcendental

...CJ continues...

"And you wonder how to access that same feeling logically for longer periods, yes?" Vrndadevi asked.

"Exactly!"

"Well, if we agree that the wonderful effulgence experience is spiritual... okay?

"Okay."

"Then, in order to reach any spiritual understanding in these days, which are called in the Vedas the Kali Yuga, the most difficult for quality of life, CJ, one needs to take on disciplined, regulative principles, what you might call... hard work. Following these principles facilitates success for any of the eight forms of yoga."

I was wavering... wandering... as if some internal noise had impaired my hearing, limited my concentration, my comprehension... maybe I should have stuck with the cocoons.

Vrndadevi continued, "This can be difficult to understand, so let me use some quotes from the Bhagavad Gita..."

I interrupted, "Excuse me, but this Bhagavad Gita, I know it is an Indian book. You refer to it regularly. What is it, really?"

"Bhagavad Gita translates into English as Song of God. It is a Vedic book of instruction for humans in the Kali Yuga wherein two friends, Krsna and Arjuna, have a question-and-answer session about the purpose of life, our existential condition, and how to proceed with the appropriate activities. Krsna identifies the restless mind as a major obstacle to understanding when he tells Arjuna:

"'For the mind is restless, turbulent, obstinate and very strong. To subdue it is, it seems, more difficult than controlling the wind.' BG 6:34.

"'My dear Arjuna, because you are never envious of Me, I shall impart to you this most secret wisdom, knowing which you shall be relieved of the miseries of material existence.' BG 9:1."

And again, she quoted Krsna telling Arjuna about the ultimate result of understanding the difference between the observer and the observed.

"'This knowledge is the king of education, the most secret of all secrets. It is the purest knowledge, and because it gives a direct perception of the self by realization, it is the perfection of religion. It is everlasting, and it is joyfully performed.' BG 9:2."

I inquired, "Wait a minute, I used to think I could design a garden to give these portals, these transcendent experiences to the garden visitors. Are you telling me there is another way to achieve the same thing?"

Vrndadevi said, "Exactly. Human life is a gift to develop this yoga—this linking with the spiritual; and we benefit from acting upon that realization."

"But does that mean that all my efforts with plants, gardens and landscapes are useless?"

"No, not at all. Think of them as crutches, assistants, portals in your quest for information, for relief of anxiety. In the quest for the metaphysical, the quest for that which transcends the lower sensual self, many have already been on that same path. But the question is what to seek and how to seek it. You are a seeker. That is good."

She continued, "This verse from the Bhagavad Gita tells how fortunate you are as a seeker, where Krsna says to Arjuna, himself a seeker, like you—seekers of the transcendental, the absolute knowledge, 'O best amongst the Bharatas, Arjuna, four kinds of pious people engage in my devotion, the path to transcendental knowledge—the distressed, the seekers after knowledge, the seekers of worldly possessions, and those who are situated in knowledge.' BG7:16."

She added, "Go to Switzerland armed knowing that your internal quest is doable. You will find a path, well worn by others."

***

Magic Garden

...CJ continues...

I wasn't sure what we were talking about, so I asked, "Many already on the same path?"

Vrndadevi said, "Yes, the path of the plants, the gardens, the landscape as inspiration to search for the higher self. So, you are on your way to Switzerland, right? To do your duty regarding your friend, right? Have you ever read any of Carl Gustav Jung's writings?"

Surprised, I said, "Oho, that's an interesting turn. Yes, I have; but I was looking at his descriptions of archetypes, trying to find common roots, you know, shared landscape experiences from which some kind of landscape architecture design theory might emerge."

Vrndadevi continued, "Well, Jung was quite intrigued on how East and West addressed the issues of spiritual life, the outer versus the inner landscape, the lower versus the higher self and its impact on the perceived purpose of life. You knew he was Swiss?"

"Well, I'd never really thought about it."

"Your trip to Switzerland might be an eye opener for you. There are solid traditions of great thinkers and writers inspired by the landscape in Switzerland. One such line stretches back to the famous alchemist, Paracelsus, followed by the botanist Haller, and can be traced through the last century with Jung, Hermann Hesse and Thomas Mann. And these people were all inspired by the landscape, particularly the Swiss landscape.

266

Hesse and Mann both wrote entertaining and instructive landscape fiction with existential themes."

I listened. Vrndadevi was a fountain of knowledge. In the back of my mind, I formulated the beginnings of a plan. I thought my trip to Geneva might just be shaping up into multiple opportunities: hopefully to close out my obligation to Gordon, and as a bonus, take a step toward resolving professional design and personal issues that had kept me off-balance.

Vrndadevi got up and walked inside. She returned with a couple well-worn paperbacks.

"I keep this lending library for people with interest in human dilemmas—the fundamental questions of life. Perhaps these might interest you?"

***

Magic Mountain

...CJ continues...

She described, "*Peter Camenzind* was Hesse's first book."

Handing me the book, she continued, "It is about a Swiss mountain man who gets a chance for an urban education, and then returns to the mountains in the later years of his life. This is a fine portrayal of a man influenced by the landscape, and how that man comes to grips with purpose in his life."

I flipped through the book, and asked, "This Hermann Hesse, I've read *The Glass Bead Game*. Didn't he also write about culture from India?"

"Yes, he did, in *Siddhartha*. He takes the reader through an entire range of traditional Indian approaches to religion. His other books also deal with human preoccupation with some kind of knowledge or experience that transcends those things in life that our senses can easily comprehend. And what, you might ask, is that area of those things beyond our senses? That is the realm often described as transcendental. That is the same realm for exploring, as is inherent in the questions and realizations of the observer versus the observed, the field of activities—it is life's puzzle for humans. And landscape and gardens—how humans interact with them can be an important part of preparing to solve, even solving that puzzle."

It was getting a bit too heavy but I listened. I heard.

Vrndadevi opened the second book. "This one is *The Magic Mountain* by Thomas Mann. It focusses on a young professional, perhaps not unlike yourself, who goes to the Swiss Alps to visit his cousin, an army man his same age, who was in a sanatorium, recovering his health from major tubercular problems. The main character likes the setting so much, he checks himself into the sanatorium and spends seven years there, examining life, death, health and people, in the Swiss Alps, all seasons, all landscapes, all weather."

She continued in summary, "This is a book about humans, the landscape and their existential relationships, relationships between the higher and lower self."

I flipped through *The Magic Mountain* and, intrigued, said, "Books are special for me. They have become more so during my six years in Saudi Arabia. You have handed me two books rich in landscape. I appreciate them. They will probably become part of my magic garden, the explorable place to which good books always take me. Thank you... but, I have nothing to offer in return."

Vrndadevi said, "Just read them in your free time, and what do you have, ten or twelve hours' flying time to Switzerland? Promise me in return, after you finish your duty in Geneva, you will go to Zurich and stop at the Hare Krishna Temple there. Leave the books there. They are good bhakti yoga people."

"Okay," I said, "and thank you again. I'll be happy to take them with me. Hasn't it been fun this afternoon? Talking about the North Thailand gardens, plants, landscapes? Tomorrow, I'll be on my way to Geneva. But, before I go thank you again for your regional landscape context... your words... your suggestions... but, I must say that I still do not have any interest in doing yoga exercises or postures. I have made a commitment to close the relationships of my good friend and his untimely death, which remains my priority. After that, I may need to revisit what you have shared with me. Indeed, there may be a way to link my personal 'purpose of life' with my professional goals. That interests me. And, that may require some meditation, some yoga; but now is not the time."

As I returned to my Lanna suite, I thought about the books Vrndadevi lent. I remembered another book with a major landscape theme, one of my all-time favourites, Voltaire's

269

Candide. I speculated, maybe I should be as Candide, on the road, and just cultivate my own garden... but... I have no land... and, except for books, I have no garden.

***

Kurt Says

CJ continues to describe his intense landscape experiences in Ban Muang when he meets the Canadian lady who gives him more reasons to visit Switzerland. He was not on a path to suicide, for sure! Life had mysteries to solve, and CJ was deep into that.

Permaculture? And CJ? That's new altogether. That blew me away. But... as I recall... getting blown away by CJ was the beginning of a useful "edge of design" solution. I had to give him some latitude.

Weird, he used to bad-talk permaculture as some kind of Marxist political gimmick. But when I read all his diary entries around this time, I understand he had both an unusual Faeryland vision and a very practical maintenance vision of how plants and humans interact.

Outside his landscape architecture maintenance understanding, he had a large, almost other-worldly input of the importance of maintenance when he was at the Hibiscus House in Tangier. Maintenance and permaculture together seem to have been a part of CJ's design utopia, his Cloud Nine.

I just can't see how his maintenance/permaculture blend can be applied to my SoCal urban projects. In our pop-art landscape architecture design, it is a thing, a fleeting fashion. It is not, to use CJ's words, an existential essential. Never a transcendent pleasure. More a "wham-bam-thank-you-mam" design. Maybe I am missing something. Maybe he is onto something I just cannot see.

Now CJ is off to Switzerland. Even I know how much different is that Alpine landscape from his tropical jungles in Thailand—from his lifeless deserts in Arabia. Those are big changes in short periods of time. I don't understand how CJ can do it.

I feel at this point that suicide was not for CJ. What's left—murder? Kidnapping? No clues for either, at least in the official docs that I read. Or going off the grid? That's my guess—I'm down with off the grid. But how does he ever get on the path to Cairo? And why?

I tried to get inside track info from my friend in Cairo; but haven't heard back.

10-La Feuille Verte

Quest On

...CJ continues...

The next morning, after calling Marty and thanking him for the Ban Muang set up, I left the Guest House, flew out of Chiang Rai and made my connection via Bangkok, direct to Geneva.

On my flight to Geneva, I had hours to myself. I wrote about my garden experiences in Thailand—frankly, all my time in Thailand felt like a dream—bad in Bangkok—good in Ban Muang. I looked at the books from Vrndadevi.

I had enough time to start *Peter Camenzind*, and *The Magic Mountain*. My flying time was well spent.

But the books, though interesting, were a distraction. I really owed Gordie. He had been my portal to clear thinking. I wondered what clarity he lacked to take his own life. As I thought about this, I saw how important was this quest for Kaytee. I had seen my friend pass away; and I had lost my job. I had... only... the quest.

As the jet began its long descent and glide to land at Cointrin, I reviewed once more my plans for Geneva.

Geneva, part of French-speaking Switzerland, is the home of the World Health Organization, the administrative heart of the United Nations and the centre for the most powerful of international non-governmental organizations (NGOs). Geneva is a large city in the southwest corner of Switzerland, on the border with France.

Foremost, I had to find Kaytee. I had to close out that

unfinished communication for the Canuck. I had to unravel the mystery of their relationship. On one hand it appeared the Canuck had gotten beyond his own family disaster; but then why did he commit suicide if he had a glorious future with Kaytee?

I knew I had to find a special VVIP adult entertainment venue. How and where were still a puzzle; but I had a plan. I had learned over time that well-heeled, alternative culture aficionados frequented certain urban cultural nodes, like art and architecture bookstores and botanical gardens. And of course, there were the hotel concierges.

I had done some online research, and for my starting points, I had chosen two prime cultural nodes in Geneva: a renowned international bookstore, and a historically significant botanical garden. For easy access to those destinations, I had booked a room at the Hotel des Burkas along the Quai du Mont Blanc. The hotel was on the Rive Droite waterfront in Geneva city centre—the very busy heart of town.

I checked in, cleaned up, ordered a room service sandwich, and reviewed my map of Geneva. My room was on the third floor and had a semi balcony. This was my first time in Geneva, in Switzerland. It was early afternoon. I went to the window and opened it.

Looking out, I noted the four-lane road in front of the hotel was busy with cars but no klaxons, no horns. The traffic moved orderly in lanes. Stopped at traffic lights. Let the intersections clear. Let pedestrians cross the streets. I saw discipline. I was enlivened. Ban Muang had been biding time—interesting, pleasant in the gardens but a distraction—now I was in the game.

I closed the window and prepared to go out. I stopped at the Concierge station and asked, "I'm looking for a certain VVIP adult entertainment, associated with a five-star hotel. Please, do you have any idea about where I can find it?"

The Concierge replied, "The best source for the adult entertainment, sir, is the list in the city guide our hotel provides on the desk in each guest room."

I continued, "I have seen that; but, what about something

276

more than escorts and nude dancers?"

The Concierge suggested, "If you walk two or three blocks out the hotel front door and to the left, and just one block in, off the Quai de Mont Blanc, you will find, sir, a full range of adult entertainment, just there in the Paquis District."

I persisted, "Can you give me some help? I need to find a special place—in particular I am looking for high class, VVIP special shows. Is there anyplace known for these?"

"I'm sorry, sir; but I have not heard of any."

"Thank you," I said as I headed out to the waterfront promenade, thinking this guy was almost useless. I had read about the strong Calvinistic past in Switzerland; but... I wondered about the concierge's response. Am I seeing the cultural remnants of Calvinism, alive and well today in Geneva? Or, is it just the general decline in truly knowledgeable concierges?

Fortunately, this was not my only plan. I headed out to the botanical garden—looked to be an easy walk on the map. I walked with vigour. I was hungry for a result.

I observed the urban landscape by nature. It was my landscape architecture work. The waterfront promenade, just across the street from my hotel, appeared to stretch around both sides of Lake Geneva. I was on the Rive Droite side, the west shore of Lake Geneva, as I headed north on foot to the botanical garden. Walking along the waterfront, I saw many small marinas, filled with 15-25-foot smallish sailboats.

Lake Geneva filled the horizon. Large and expansive, this lake had frontages in both France and Switzerland. As I had read, Geneva was an international fashion and style city with a world-famous waterfront and water jet—definitely a place to see and be seen. I was surprised there were none of the huge yachts, or even the cigar boats common to other similar world-class destination waterfronts, like Monaco, or Miami Beach.

Even though the season by calendar, early May, was well into spring, the weather made it more like winter. It was just how I remembered this temperate, maritime, European climate, at times modified by continental influences. Sometimes it was spring in March, other times spring did not come until May.

Today, Lake Geneva was choppy, cold. The clouds were very low, racing with dark grey bandings, running with the brusque north wind. The hotel brochures had shown glorious snowcapped mountains against a backdrop of beautiful blue, sunshiny skies. I could only see scurrying bands of low clouds and overcast. I saw nothing but grey.

I zipped up my coat and enjoyed having almost to myself the broad pedestrian promenade along the water's edge. I relished having my face buffeted by blustery, fresh, almost too cool March-like winds—nothing like it ever in Yenbo. To my pleasure, I had the open space to walk. Such a relief from Bangkok's suffocating street crowds, and their pushy, seeking obsessions. But nobody on the promenade? I hoped that emptiness wasn't a foreboding.

I walked up the coast, toward the United Nations complex. The botanical garden was just before the UN. Along the way, besides the marinas, I passed a series of parks and restaurants. In less than thirty minutes, I had walked to the Geneva Conservatory and Botanical Garden. At last. I entered with renewed hope. I needed a contact. Entry was free.

I always looked forward to first-class, European botanical gardens. I felt comfort from their orderly and well-labelled presentation. I expected nothing less from my years of regular visits to Hortus Botanicus in Amsterdam, as well as Kew and Wisley in London. Upon entering a proper botanical garden, or arboretum, I always breathed a sigh of cultural relief.

***

Botanical Garden

...CJ continues...

Despite my focussed searching for a lead to find Kaytee, I could never shut down my landscape architecture analysis vision. And I was thirsty for this repository of landscape, garden and plant information.

I found the botanical garden to be physically small; but it had huge historical significance. A. P. Candolle founded the institution in 1817. He followed in the footsteps of the naturalists of his time, the Swiss von Haller and the French Cuvier and Lamarck. Plant classification systems were the original purpose of this institution. Its main feature has always been the Herbarium with six million specimens.

In less than an hour, I had walked the perimeter of the twenty-five hectares, seen the major greenhouse collections, and the library. The Geneva Conservatory and Botanical Garden was old school. Beds of annuals in lawns. Rock garden collections featuring perennials. Everything sitting under massive mature broadleaves and conifers. *Rustique.* This was a 19th century Édouard André design. I had seen similar in André's book, *Plans de Jardins et de Parcs Paysagers.*

But it had nice contemporary outdoor exhibits. They used interpretive signage to explain plant and human relationships as ethnobotanical items of cultural heritage. This small country had over 70% of its gross land area covered with steep mountain slopes. Arable land only 10%; a culture built on landscape management was absolutely critical. Without an applied stewardship over centuries, the arable land would have become infertile. To my interest, these management processes were interpreted in the botanical garden's outdoor collections.

One exhibit took me right back to my orchid effulgences in Ban Muang. The outdoor exhibit instructed children, sense by sense, how they could interact with the varied objects of the senses as provided by plants. Then, for each sense the descriptions and the adjacent plants were addressed with the intensity of an *Alice in Wonderland* experience. Great stuff for kids—get them on the road to plant appreciation and respect at a young age.

Even though I enjoyed these exhibits, I disappointedly found few people on the grounds. The weather didn't help. I headed for tea at the Buvet, a small buffet/snack café in the botanical garden. The Buvet terrace, sitting on a gentle slope down toward the lake shore, provided a pleasing perspective on Lake Geneva, 500 metres distant. The garden was peaceful. I liked that. But, for helpful clues, to solve my VVIP conundrum, the thinly visited garden was not the resource I had expected. I was disappointed. Kaytee—I needed to make this quest happen

The sun found an opening in the clouds, and, for the mid-afternoon, I enjoyed its warmth in my wind-sheltered corner at the Buvet.

The Buvet had none of the homemade, alternate culture character of the Orangery at the Hortus Botanicus in Amsterdam. I enjoyably passed the next couple hours trying to keep my anxiety at bay. Time passed slowly. I finished reading all of Hermann Hesse's *Peter Camenzind*.

I thought maybe I should have come earlier, maybe there had been a lunch crowd. It was just after 5PM when, finally, some visitors came in. I started a conversation with a couple of fashionably dressed young men who had sat down for espressos near me.

Walking over toward them, I said, "I'm a tourist, and have just come into Geneva for the first time."

Then, smiling, I asked, "I'm trying to find a certain type of adult entertainment. I just wonder, as a first-time visitor, about the Calvinistic history of Geneva. Has it reduced variety in the adult entertainment industry? Has it left Geneva only with escort services and nude dancing bars?"

They discussed a bit and one responded, "Depending on your preferences, there are several alternative places for consenting adults. Do you have something particular in mind?"

"I am looking for a very high-class club, for VVIPs. I have only heard about it; I have no name, no location. It's probably associated with a five-star hotel—any ideas?"

"Well, Geneva has its share of highly paid international bureaucrats and private sector lobbyists. So, I would not be surprised if such VVIP clubs existed, but we don't really run in that crowd."

They wished me success in my search, finished their espressos, and walked off into the garden.

That was as close as I got to sourcing my VVIP search. At half-past five, I quit the botanical garden and took a bus to the Librarie Genêve, a well-respected English and French bookstore near to Cornavin Station, close to my hotel.

**

Bookstore

The botanical garden had been a dead end. I pushed on to the bookstore. Bookstores always had customers who were seekers. I, too, was a seeker. My search for Kaytee drove me onward.

The bookstore looked recently renovated. Modern, clean, refreshing in appearance. Upon inspection of the stock though, I was disappointed by the less than significant size of the art and architecture collection, not even near matching the content or the character of my regular bookstore haunts in Amsterdam, like Architectura and Natura.

More disappointing, the so-called indoor café comprised only two tables, empty, squeezed into a corner. It had no ambience at all, and worse, no customers. Not only that, the store closed at 7PM; another Calvinistic remnant? I wondered.

I was missing the urban ambiance of the seemingly always open Amsterdam brown cafés—always next door to the bookshops. I flipped through a couple of architecture books. Then I looked at the rack of local entertainment papers.

I found nothing, either in books, papers, or people. But as I left, I paused outside the shop window. I saw some featured coffee-table books with historical images from central Switzerland of the Jungfrau Region in the Berner Oberland (the section of the Swiss Alps found in the Bern Canton).

I went back inside, found a most interesting book, and paged through this geographic history via primarily black and

282

white photographs, older brushwork and engravings. I mused over some landscape paintings by the Swiss artist Caspar Wolf. His use of light reminded me of one of my interests, the late eighteenth century, the German Sturm und Drang Movement, artists who made focussed examinations of light. I enjoyed their depictions of an almost visceral energy in light, a sunlight of action, a sunlight of vibrating strength. Light that dominated landscape. But the light in the Arabian Peninsula deserts had no romance. It was a killer. That was my landscape over the past six years.

Landscape, light and emotion in the mountains had sidetracked the lack of results in my search. But I was intrigued. Perhaps the light in these mountains would be similar to the Arabian desert light. Or, maybe something different?

Then I was fascinated by the amount of aggressive, almost super-scaled glacier tongues being shown in old 18th century works from Grindelwald in the Jungfrau Region. The old village photos of the region reminded me of Hesse's descriptions in *Peter Camenzind*; but interesting as these images were, they were another distraction. I was as devoid of knowledge as I had been in Bangkok. I had no Geneva leads on five-star VVIP adult entertainment venues—no clues on my quest for Kaytee Cheng—no path to close the loop for the Canuck.

I was not really sure what to do next. I had no Plan B. I had to re-think.

***

Paquis District

I went back to the hotel, reviewed again all the bumf, hotel advertising in my room, and searched online for some kind of clue, some kind of link to reveal where I might find Kaytee's adult entertainment venue. Nothing. I cleaned up and went down for dinner.

After dinner, about half-past nine, the Concierge shift had changed and another man, an older man, the Night Manager, was on duty. I went through the same drill as earlier. This time I got a step further; but only that the Night Manager had a personal contact, who could arrange what needed to be arranged.

The Night Manager dialled up his contact, Monsieur H., and handed the phone to me.

Monsieur H. spoke with a heavy French accent. I couldn't follow at first. After a couple repeats, my ears adjusted.

Now it started to get weird because this middleman, for a good price, was used to handling the strange sexual desires of every variety of foreigner who passed through the hotel. So he definitely protected his knowledge, his turf.

I had only nebulous information to offer of some activity occurring somewhere. The conversation was going nowhere because I did not know what the activities were at this supposed special VVIP venue; and the guy on the phone just wanted a lot of money to hook me up. I did not want to go down that rabbit hole.

I was running out of leads. I hit the streets, gave the Paquis District a go, just on a chance. On my way, I stopped at a couple other five-star hotels. From their concierges, I found no new direction. I walked on and made it to the Paquis District in less than 10 minutes.

I was smashed by what I found—what a scummy place—dog stool on the streets—vomit on the dark sidewalks—girls and boys on corners—most every place was slapdash low rent prostitutes—all flavours—not anywhere near VVIP standard—not even VIP cars cruising the neighbourhood—a total strike-out.

I asked a couple of obvious pimps about a special place—blah, blah, blah—and all I could get back was: what is your desire? I can find it for you. I might as well have been in the Petit Socco in Tangier. Wrong place.

I trudged back to the hotel, seeking shelter in the solitude and cleanliness of my room.

I showered off the entire Paquis nightlife experience. Then I ordered a room service cognac, relaxed and sat down to look at the history of Geneva as described in the hotel brochure. It had a list and map of "must see" places. A couple destinations caught my attention, both reasonably close. Isle Rousseau, just across the street, dedicated to Jean-Jacques Rousseau and Place Favre, dedicated to Mountain Engineer Louis Favre.

I looked up those places online. Particularly, Place Favre caught my attention. Favre, I had never imagined that Brett Favre, the quarterback of the Green Bay Packers could have had Swiss lineage. It had nothing to do with my search for Kaytee; but I needed to break the depressing pattern of losses.

I sampled the aroma and took another swallow of cognac, soft, warm, smooth, comforting, then thought, what the hell, tomorrow morning I'll take the tram to Place Favre and see if Brett and Louis have anything in common.

Then I picked up Thomas Mann's *The Magic Mountain*. I had gotten attracted to the book because it had great descriptions of mountain landscape weather, overlaid on seasonal change. But tonight, I started on the long passages of social commentary, and reading Mann's interminable philosophical discussions between secular idealists, atheists and theists. Sleeping came quickly. I needed it. I needed energy refreshment. I needed to find the right path. I slept deeply.

***

Rousseau, Favre, Ashenden

...CJ continues...

I rose early the next morning with good energy. Sunlight was breaking in and out of low, partly cloudy skies. I had to change the air, so to speak. So, after breakfast, I took the short walk to Isle Rousseau, to think through, one more time, my search on behalf of Gordie, my deceased friend. He seemed to have gotten through the tragic death of his wife and baby, finally starting a new life with Kaytee. But the suicide?! Didn't make sense. I needed to find her to put my mind to rest; but alas no leads.

Only a five-minute walk from my hotel, Isle Rousseau was an island in the mouth of the Rhone, the centre point in Geneva, dividing Rive Gauche from Rive Droite. It was a small island, with a statue and an informational interpretative plaque, dedicated to the life and writing of idealist Jean Jacques Rousseau.

I leaned on the handrail and looked down at the Rhone River, its water racing out of Lake Geneva. Rushing water and sunlight reflections—white noise and flickering lights—hypnotize. And that was what happened as I was thinking about the words on the plaque, the words that described Rousseau's approach to human nature, "...the ultimate positive social value in the free flow of ideas from all people as the best form of government".

My eyes glazed over, and logic got carried away by the rush of water. In that moment, I experienced... free... free flow... free flow of ideas... free association. I found that same freedom that Rousseau talks about when unfettered by social constraints.

I concluded to relax my pressure on myself. Let off on my sole focus—the Kaytee quest. My new approach would be rather to flow with things instead of pushing things.

I walked on, found the correct tram, and went on my way to Place Favre, in the Rive Gauche. I started thinking about the successful career of Brett Favre in America in the National Football League. Brett Favre toughed it out, just like Gordon the Canuck. The Canuck's character memories quickly brought my thoughts back to my quest... this time sadness entered briefly. The tram took me directly to Place Favre, where, still in town, I got off.

Place Favre was a nicely shaped pedestrian public square, opening directly in front of the local city hall, *la Commune de Chêne-Bourg*. Louis Favre's full-size statue sat proudly. The text on an interpretive plaque explained his important part in building the Gotthard Tunnel—the safe passage connecting northern with southern Europe under the Swiss Alps.

As I was reading the details, a guy with a backpack... a backpack with a maple leaf red and white Canadian flag patch sewn on, stopped and struck up a conversation. He asked me, "Are you an engineer?"

"What?... no, my profession is landscape architecture. How about you?"

"I studied both civil and structural engineering at the University of Toronto. Louis Favre is one of those historic figures. He took chances that would embarrass today's engineers, even those of his day. In the 1870s he pushed the idea of a tunnel through Gotthard, the main pass through the Alps between northern and southern Europe, a death-defying pass to cross overland. Almost everyone nay-sayed him; but he persisted, and in the end it was built and successful, even though he passed away before it was completed. And he never gave up—died right in the tunnel. Anyhow, what brought you here?"

I chuckled and said, "Much more common for me. It was the

family name Favre that got me here. Favre as in Brett Favre, the quarterback of the Green Bay Packers. See, I have roots in Detroit, in the Midwest and..."

I was interrupted by the Canadian. "Hey, I follow you." He offered his hand to me and said, "I've always been a fan of four-down American football. My name's Alex, Alex Ashenden, born in Windsor, Ontario. We're as good as neighbours!"

I smiled and shook his hand, saying, "Pleased to meet you. My name's CJ. So, do you think these two Favres are related? They seemed to be very hard workers, you know, the never-give-up type!" We both laughed at the confluence of American football, engineering and Geneva, Switzerland.

Alex was friendly and talkative. In conversation, I learned he was not only a licensed multi-discipline civil and structural engineer, but he also had another side that he figured must have come from his English grandfather, John Ashenden. His grandfather had been a writer and, during the World War I era, had lived ten years of his life in Geneva. Alex had come to Geneva to pursue his career as a writer, a writer of fiction, stories having engineering and construction settings.

I speculated, "So, you're a Canadian from Windsor, into American football... let me guess... you or your dad must be a Detroit Red Wings hockey fan, too, right?"

"Yeah, Abel, Howe, Lindsay and then Delvecchio in the 60s, my dad brought me up on those legends."

I said, "Seems like another era now, doesn't it?"

"It was another era, alright—all Howe's scoring records are gone!"

"I see in Brett Favre the spirit of the hard work ethic of those times..." I said. "Have you been here in Switzerland for a while? Do you live here? Is a hard work ethic part of the Swiss national character?"

"Well, it is as a matter of fact—I'm surprised you didn't know that—it is one of those known Swiss traits. That same determination that Louis and Brett have shown is obvious in the fine technical achievements of the watch industry and all the incredible, high-altitude, narrow-gauge trains, bridges and tunnels built here."

I shared, "I've seen some photos of the narrow-gauge tunnel work done in the Jungfrau Region, but little more."

In the shade of plane trees, we sat down on a park bench beside Favre's statue and chatted about technology, and its impact on the incredibly steep landscape, the virtually impenetrable mountains known as the Swiss Alps.

Alex suggested, "Why don't we get some lunch. I know this part of town, and just across the street is a nice café, where we can get a sandwich and a draft beer."

One thing led to another over lunch, and Alex asked, "So, c'mon, tell me, what really brought you to Geneva?"

"Well, now that you've asked—you will not believe this, but it all has to do—it all started with an American, named... Gordon Howe... Gordie Howe."

"What? C'mon, what do you mean?!"

"Yeah, an American from Detroit. His dad named him Gordon after Gordie. And I nicknamed him, even though he was an American, the Canuck. We worked together in Saudi Arabia for the last three years."

I told my story about the suicide, the RIF, the thin strip map clue, this mysterious journey and how I felt an obligation to close out a relationship for Gordie, the Canuck.

I said, "I'm desperately trying to close this loop, and that brought me to Geneva... still no result. I'm really fried over this—striking out everywhere."

"I understand your confusion—confusion is the state of play in Geneva modern times—nothing is in reality as it seems on the surface. What's troubling you? What is it, CJ? What is it exactly that you are trying to find?"

I explained the details. "This girl was Gordie's fiancée. He knew her through his regular visits to Bangkok. Do you know the drill of Western expatriate bachelor life in Saudi Arabia?"

Alex nodded and said, "Yeah, a couple of my university friends worked for Bechtel in Jubail, the Eastern Region of Saudi Arabia. They told me all about it."

I continued, "Well, myself, I never went to the East on my leave, but Gordie the Canuck was so into this girl—that part of the world was new life for him. He was engaged to her. So,

I decided to find her, to let her know the circumstances of his 'disappearance'. I have followed her trail to Thailand, and then, was told that a 'fancy' guy from Geneva offered her work in some five-star, VVIP club. I have her name, but have had no luck finding any special adult entertainment club."

A look of surprise filled Alex's face. He said, "You won't believe this; but I have a friend, lives in my apartment building. He works at this five-star hotel in what they call, 'back-of-house'. He's an accountant, a fixer, for special hotel events, in an underground theatre. He tells me that about one night a month, at 3AM, they have some kind of adult entertainment, all very hush-hush, totally confidential, definitely VVIP."

He continued, "Maybe it is, maybe it isn't—let me call him, to see if it might be possible. If so, the three of us can meet this evening for drinks and dinner. I'd sure like to see you close out that obligation to your friend. It just might be easier than you think. Let me call him now. Just a moment." Alex stepped away for the call.

After the call, Alex brought back good news; but he confided to me, "My friend's name is Chandra Lal. This Chandra is a bit of a character. He rubs many people the wrong way; but, if he gives his word, you can count on it. He confirmed nothing during the call; but he agreed to listen to you over dinner."

We planned to meet for dinner at 8PM that night at an Indian Restaurant, there, in Chêne-Bourg. After all it had taken to get this far, I was hopeful, but not yet convinced.

***

Chandra Lal

...CJ continues...

Alex, his friend Chandra, and I were enjoying pakora and samosa appetizers at the Punjabi restaurant. But Alex's friend behaved exactly as Alex had advised, annoying, quite annoying. Chandra had done all his lessons on the British system in India, and by God, he was better than the Brits by a substantial measure.

It didn't take long for me to get a read on Chandra. He was in his early thirties; but with dark circles around his eyes, he looked ten years older. He was a short, stubby, loquacious, abrasive and, a tad too greasy, kind of guy. With a head full of slicked back, really long, ponytailed black hair, he was the kind that always had the answer. Before you finished asking—the best answer—the only answer. The even more annoying thing was that he was right. And more amazing, despite his irksome character, he was clearly successful at his work.

I went through the Canuck's story in more detail, including the trip to Bangkok.

"Bangkok!" Chandra laughed heartily. "Those girls are nothing but business there, looking for a free ride out. Every *farang* is a sucker, waiting to be had. Fresh meat!" He laughed until he was red in the face. I was getting red in the face, too—but not from laughing.

Alex intervened. "Okay, okay, back off, Chandra, let's work through this like gentlemen."

I needed to cool down. I slowly ate some cucumber and

yogurt raita—at least my tongue cooled down. I figured I'd give this guy one more chance.

I told Chandra her name, "Kaytee, Kaytee Cheng."

Chandra's eyes opened wide, his jaw dropped. "Did you say Kaytee?"

"Yes, Chandra, a great-looking Malaysian girl of Chinese descent."

"That's her, Kaytee Cheng; but she is known here as La Feuille Verte. Her eyes, her main costume theme, are both an amazing, luminous green, a spring leaf green, sparkling like emeralds."

Not taking long to regain his normal form, Chandra, in his dry arrogance, finishing with an almost audible snort, and turn of the head, continued, "But maybe it's a good thing your friend has passed away, he would not want to know what she's doing now."

"What do you mean?" I asked.

With a lascivious glance, Chandra spoke down his nose, as if addressing a British chav. "Let me simplify it for you, anything your girlfriend would do to your love truncheon, your meat and two veg, this girl does to a donkey, live, in front of a crowd, a crowd of so-called sophisticated, rich bastards."

"Look, I don't care what she is doing. Just tell me if I can see her. I need to close the loop." Inside, I was building up a stoked dislike for this Chandra character—a stoked dislike that quickly turns into a roundhouse knockout punch to the ingrate's jaw; but I controlled the building rage and focussed on the aim, as Chandra continued.

"Look, I had to sign ten pages of confidentiality clauses when I took this job and the last thing I am going to do is lose it because of loose lips. You, CJ, must swear not to share what we may discuss with anyone."

"Yeah, sure, definitely... whatever it takes."

"First, I cannot guarantee you will see her, talk to her, or even share a note with her. The security is incredibly tight. We all know what VVIP means in normal parlance, Very Very Important Person. In our operations, it means none of the guests know any of the other guests, and none of the guests know the performers. There is no public communication, and all private communications are double blind."

"...yup, uh-huh..." I drawled, trying to control my distaste for Chandra's pushy attitude.

Alex had been calmly listening to me and Chandra as we whipped up our own whirlwind. He added, "Listen you guys, I think I see some common ground here. Let's find a way forward."

Chandra, after being put off by the entire imposition for what he saw as a fancy street hooker, softened a bit when he heard the carefully chosen words from Alex and my plea for my deceased friend's sake. Chandra then asked, "All you need to do is to let her know that someone close has passed away; and that's all, right?"

"Yeah, but I'd like to get her recognition that she has received the message, so I know for sure that this loop has been closed. That's all. For me, the whole thing is complete, finished, and I'll move on with my life, having closed the last issue on my friend's suicide." I was thinking that no matter what Chandra says, when I see Kaytee, I am going to ask questions. There were things I needed to know.

Chandra said, "Okay, she's scheduled to perform this week, in the next four days. I am responsible for her movement to the show and after. I can send a note with your message, and arrange, on her arrival for work, that she acknowledge receipt of the message. I can give you a special lavaliere to wear that night, so she can easily see who you are when she moves from her transportation to the theatre."

Chandra, with his haughty, self-centred speech, continued, "These details are all mine, and non-negotiable, okay, clear?"

Constraining my impatience one more time, I thought... whatever.... I knew as long as I could get the message to her and receive her personal confirmation of receipt, I could take it from there. I bit my tongue.

Led by Alex, we all worked out the text of the message. I was finally feeling the relief of the storm being passed. I suggested the best wine all around on me. Chandra said, "This Punjabi place is not where we should drink wine. I know a fine wine bar two tram stops from here."

I looked over at Alex, who nodded, and then I said, "It's on! Let's go." I paid the dinner tab, and off we went.

At the wine bar, Alex selected a table toward the back where we could talk with a modicum of privacy. As we sat down, I, past my earlier anger and anxiety, said, "Chandra, this place is your recommendation and I am happy to have your cooperation to close this last chapter in my friend's death. You select the wine, I'll pay."

"Excellent," said Chandra, "I like this place because it features the best of Swiss wines, even though so-called wine connoisseurs like to belittle Swiss wines, because of their simple, raw, agricultural character—but that is what I like. These wines are not heavy; they are full. The character naturally flows from the people themselves, who have, for centuries, learned how to live with this mountainous landscape. They live with it, they do not try to dominate it!"

"I didn't figure you to be into the landscape," I said.

Chandra had his answer ready. "There's a lot you don't know about me." He paused then continued, "I was born in this country and everyone who has been brought up here knows and respects the Swiss landscape and the riches it provides." I, happy in the first real progress to find Kaytee, was in no mood to dispute anything.

Chandra guided us through two bottles of a Pinot Noir from, as he claimed, the highest vineyards in Europe—on the exceedingly steep slopes of Visperterminen in Valais—a vineyard longstanding heroic. I noted that its taste was just as Chandra described—raspberry and cherry notes and the fruity and velvety character. Very light, but full. Very enjoyable.

Chandra dominated the conversation, boasting about his business successes in Geneva. The wine had a gradual mellowing effect on Chandra. Still, he looked around before he answered my question on what Kaytee actually did in the performance. "I really can't tell you much. Making this show come off, roughly once a month, at 3AM, without a hitch, with no public knowledge, is part of why I am paid well for my work here."

He continued about the logistics of the monthly performance and some details which should not be part of this story. Chandra then summarised regarding her pay, "For her antics, she gets 50,000CHF a month, a furnished, catered and serviced flat in the best of the leafy suburbs, with 24/7 security. So she takes home 600,000CHF a year, if she can keep it up."

Chandra smiled as he added, "If I tell you any more, I'll either lose my job or have to kill both of you. The details are too much—100,000CHF per each of the fifty boxes, per event.

"So tomorrow," Chandra said, "I'll work it through and then I'll drop by your hotel after work and give you the date, time, place and lavaliere.

"The lavaliere," Chandra sniffed, "I'll let you keep as a souvenir."

***

Noise and Beauty

...CJ continues...

That same week, as I waited to hear from Chandra Lal, time passed slowly. I worked through some of Geneva's historical details. I thought there was something important in the thinking of the age of reason and the naturalists, like Rousseau, Candolle and others.

These were people who looked at humans and plants, exploring how human behaviour and plant life interrelated. Not on a measurable scientific level but on some kind of higher, altogether subtler level. The things I have been learning in my career about plants and humans—ethnobotany—were, already centuries ago, the focus of great people...

The next day, after final collaboration with Chandra, I was standing at the Paquis Mouette dock, with my flashing mini LED wrapped day-glo pink and white striped ribboned lavaliere around my neck. It was 2AM. The waterfront promenade and the tunnel through to the Rave Club were pulsating, alive with people. Their posing and posturing reminded me of West Hollywood or South Beach. It looked like a major Vogue magazine photo shoot, the beautiful people everywhere. Things were hopping.

A 40' Broadblue Catamaran, under engine power, quietly docked and off came four big, bald, tattooed, burly bodyguards, wearing black torso Ts, black sport coats, black trousers and army issue black boots.

Behind them came three ladies in flowing white burnooses,

two in cotton, one in fine silk. The burnoose hoods were up; it was virtually impossible to see any of the ladies' faces. Those seven were additionally escorted by six plain clothes security men who had quietly arrived dockside.

Those three white burnooses were A-list party mademoiselle features. I was living inside a ZZ-Top video. It was a multimedia procession with a "you'll never have this" worldly walk, fashion model, high heel, shapely leg strutting, and yet, with it all, a French Swiss bit of elegant understatement. I tried to stay focussed.

One burnoose, the white silk burnoose at the centre of the whole procession, stopped, and they all stopped. She looked at my lavaliere and motioned toward me. The security made an access and I walked over.

Her eyes were clear, a stunning iridescent green, and focussed. She looked directly into my eyes, performed a *wei* and said, "My name is Kaytee; and I have your note. I'm sorry to hear about our friend Gordon. Thank you. My career is short and this is business." I was shocked, stunned and speechless.

She performed another *wei*. Then she turned; and, with her entourage, disappeared.

I was left in their wake. It all had happened so fast.

I was numb... void... without... without what? Then I recovered... somewhat... I thought, I guess I've finished. But I hadn't. I hadn't asked any questions. Frustrated with nothingness, I threw my lavaliere into a waste bin.

But how she responded to me answered all my questions. I felt sad, sad for Gordie. A marriage would never have worked. Kaytee had her goals—larger than the Canuck ever imagined, I was sure.

I guess I achieved the aim. I guess I closed the loop. I guess I reached my quest. Maybe the Canuck thought he had a future with her; but it was clear she had other ideas about her future. My head was swimming.

On the water's edge, all around me, on this early summer's night, with sweet breezes in the air, beautiful people were striking poses. The weather had changed for the better—but my sadness for Gordie had taken root. My deeper hope that he had shown me an example of how I might get beyond my own deathly tragedies of Sachy and our kids. Not easy to take.

There, in my face, was another example of cross-cultural gaps. Where does multi-culture fit in? So many thoughts dizzied me. I could only see things from the roots of my own culture. I was hurting. Maybe Gordie was spared the hurt by his suicide. Maybe he knew what had gone on?

I walked slowly along the waterfront, back toward my hotel, thoughts piercing my mind, images burnt into my memories— the white burnoose, the green eyes, her business-like attitude, Gordie the Canuck, Vrndadevi, my lost job, all swirling into a mist of confusing and exhausting images.... I made it back to my room and crashed.

It was clear there were emotional times when I needed someone to talk with. I had no one. The emptiness I felt as I went to bed was larger than melancholy.

When Kaytee performed the *wei*, I felt my deep friendship for Gordie pluck my emotions ever so deeply. And Kaytee herself for that briefest moment, through her sparkling eyes, released in me more heartfelt sadness.

My emotions had been spent. I had run away from heart-aching sadness once, twice, three times before in my life. I didn't want to revisit it—a place rarely experienced and not understood. Sleep became my medicine—my cocoon... for the first five minutes. Or so I had hoped... before dreams set in.

***

The Next Morning

...CJ continues...

In my dream, ten years ago was now. I saw her eyes... Sachy's eyes as she read mine after she had asked with her last breath about our three kids. Rips my heart, hurts my mind, unleashes a flow of the worst heartbreak. Again and again. I was racing to get to the accident scene, I never got there. Three kids dead and it was all in the forlorn sadness coming from Sachy's eyes as she died. Eternity. Eternal sadness. Sickened. Profuse sweat.

I had, I don't know what I had—sleepless night or relentless nightmares.

Next thing I saw was daylight—the midday brightness. The room clock showed it was almost noon.

I rolled out of bed, hit the shower, shaved and ordered petit déjeuner room service. Fresh orange juice, coffee and croissant normally started my engine. But... today... nothing... all blahs... and worse.

Needing something, anything, I opened the balcony door, went out and looked carefully over the landscape, the distant landscape.

It was superb. Breathtaking. The weather had changed in the last days. The cloudless sky revealed a spectacular view I would not have guessed existed. Across Lac Leman in front of me, above the Geneva Rive Gauche urban texture, above the Salève, above the additional range after range of middle ground mountains, stood, gleaming in the midday sun, against a cobalt blue sky, the brilliant, snow-covered Mont Blanc massif.

On the balcony, the sun and warming air refreshed my lungs... but the sadness of my dreams and meeting with Kaytee kept me down. Sunshine wasn't doing the trick.

Room service delivered my petit déjeuner, but the tray just sat untouched as I troubled over how I felt and what was next—what to do.

I went online and emailed Alex and Chandra, writing, "Thanks to all. CJ."

This task rescued me from my disappointment, my damning thoughts of how Gordie, having tragically lost his family, put hope in this Thai lady. And she? For her Gordie was just another business venture. Those thoughts hurt. Deeper than I can describe.

I went out again on my balcony and looked carefully over the distant Mt. Blanc landscape. My thoughts were elsewhere. Here in Geneva, everything in the urban landscape was very dark, very noisy. I felt a quavering uncertainty, went back inside and slumped down on the sofa.

Struggling, I had to turn my day around. I reviewed all that had happened. My quest complete, I felt some relief... though broad veins of emptiness tore at my heart. Sighed... and sighed... then....

Standing up and walking out again to the balcony, I took a deep breath and up came previously suppressed thoughts and pictures... Swiss mountains... Hesse... Mann...Vrndadevi. They all revolved around the landscape—the Swiss landscape.

The only bright spot over this past month, the only hope, the only ray of light had come from Vrndadevi. But here, here in Geneva, things—the urban landscape and the sad yet business-look in Kaytee's eyes... I thought it's over now, right... right? I had to turn my back on this past week, on these past weeks. I had to turn the corner. I had to move forward. I was still homeless... and I was jobless.

Then I remembered, there was one more thing—one unfulfilled obligation. I had promised to return Vrndadevi's books to Zurich, a three-hour train ride north-north-east from Geneva.

With finality I concluded, right, I am out of here! I went online. Checked to see if I had anything about my old job in Yenbo. Nothing about my old job.

But I did find a new email, from my old friend in Los Angeles, Mark Hennessey of Hennessey and Ingalls, a world-renowned art and architecture bookstore. Mark, one of my few dangling connections with LA of the old days, had responded to my earlier Bangkok email, answering that if I was in Switzerland, I should get to Zurich to visit Krauthammer's Art and Architecture bookstore, and, by the way, he wrote, try to stay in the Dolder Waldhaus hotel, a convenient location, with beautiful views. That all was good news and fit right into place. I zipped off a quick thank you email to Mark, and then made a reservation at the Dolder Waldhaus. Sorted.

As I packed up my things to go, I stumbled. My brief excitement about going to Zurich fell into a depressed emotional recall of Gordie, Kaytee, Sachy and my uncertain future. I choked. I had no cocoon.

***

Kurt Says

So CJ achieved his quest for Kaytee, but with utter disappointment. CJ expected a lot from his meeting with Kaytee. He got nothing.

Then his memories of his own family tragedies overwhelmed him. And on top of that, CJ had no job. He was on edge. He was down. Beat up.

Beat up isn't strong enough. And he had nothing. Maybe this was the kind of depression that could have pushed him toward suicide. Seems out of character but... there was a lot of death in CJ's life.

And Kaytee? Perhaps she was his last hope that he could move beyond the disasters in his own life. If that was his hope, it was dashed when he met her.

Bad scene.

CJ, really down in the dumps.

Who wouldn't be? CJ—lost his family, lost his right-hand man, lost his job and found out that right-hand man's fiancée didn't give a damn.

I was surprised, still in the dark and now fearful after learning of CJ's dreadful experience in Geneva. This changed my take, my perspective, on CJ's death. Finding out this truth about Gordie's fiancée blew CJ away. And I was rethinking about his emotional condition. Fragile. For the first time I thought... maybe CJ was fragile.

I needed more info. What was he doing during his twelve months in Cairo? Early on in LA, after receiving the "Special D" about CJ, I, in a desperate search for more info, had sent an email to my old friend, a high school teacher in Cairo. He hadn't answered back. It's time to re-send that email.

But that was not my only hope. I still had to go through the diaries and design journals covering the time CJ spent in Switzerland after Geneva. He went to Zurich and then the Bernese Highlands. Did he recover from the Kaytee shock in Geneva? Or did his emotional bummer get worse?

Illustrations

1-CJ's Journey (also in front matter)

2-CJ's New Home (also in front matter)

3-CJ's New Landscape

4-CJ's Diaries (also in front matter)

5-Hijaz Oasis Qsar

6-Hijaz Bedouin Today

7-CJ in Al Nawa Village

8-CJ's Haii 3 Lifestyle

9-Arabian Sands Findings

10-Arabian Sands—The Dunes

11-Saudi Gold 22karat

12-Shaded Greenways in New Yenbo

13-Kaytee Quest

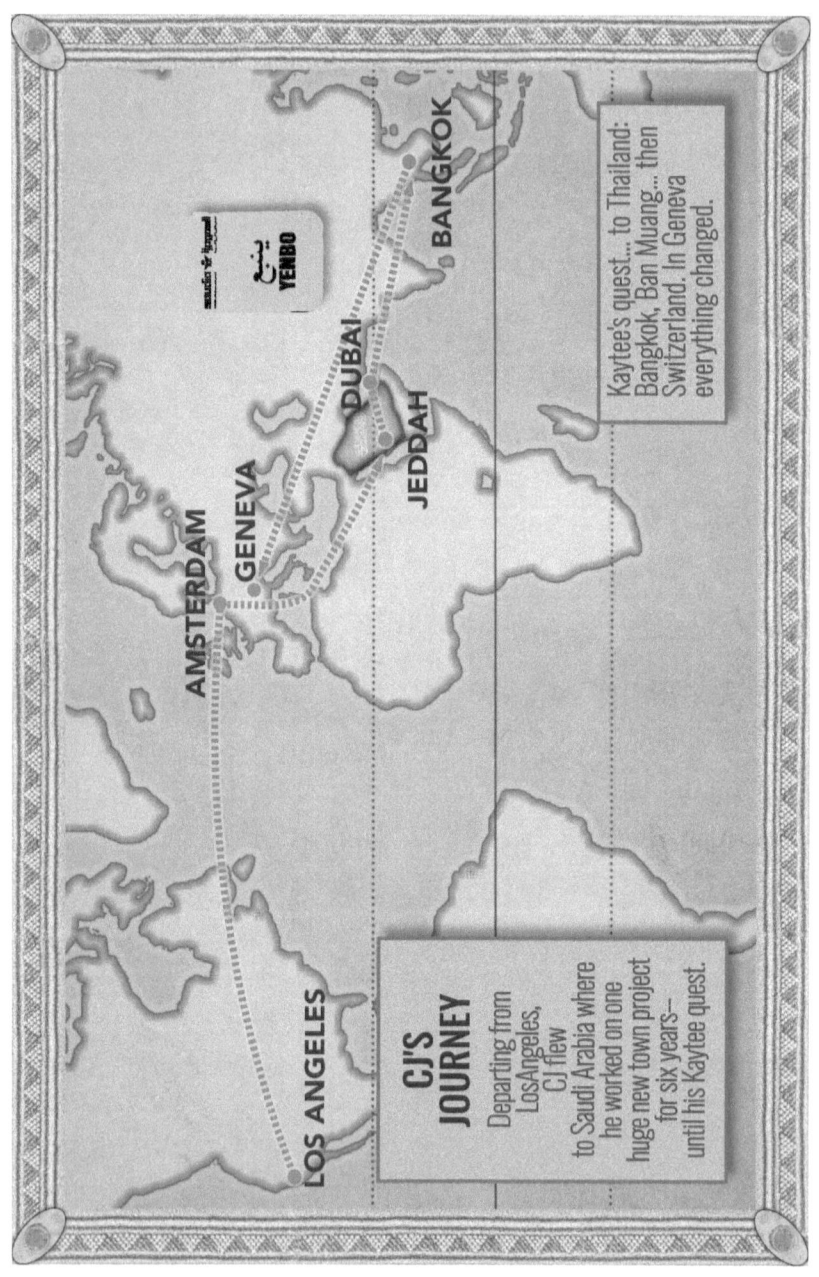

CJ'S JOURNEY

Departing from Los Angeles, CJ flew to Saudi Arabia where he worked on one huge new town project for six years— until his Kaytee quest.

Kaytee's quest... to Thailand: Bangkok, Ban Muang... then Switzerland. In Geneva everything changed.

LOS ANGELES

AMSTERDAM

GENEVA

DUBAI

JEDDAH

YENBO

BANGKOK

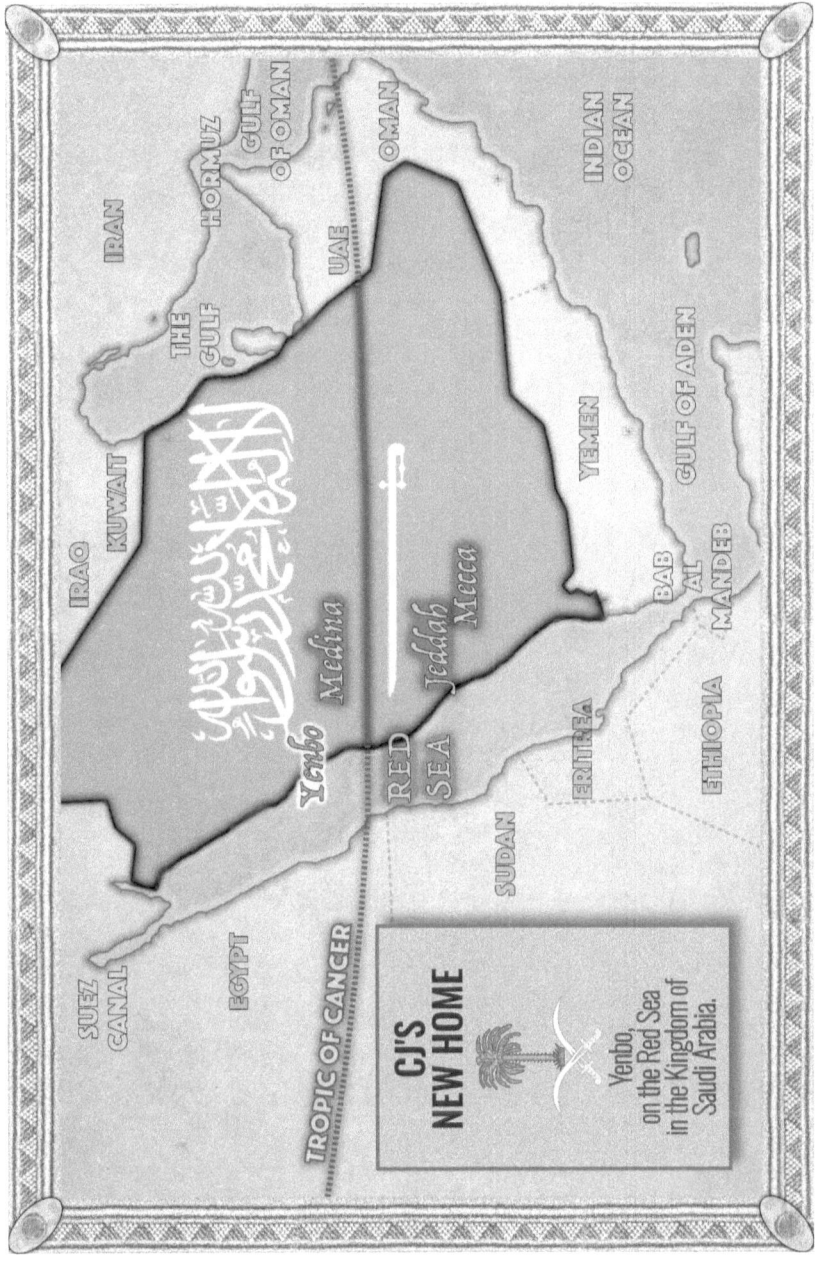

CJ'S NEW HOME

Yenbo, on the Red Sea in the Kingdom of Saudi Arabia.

HIJAZ
MOUNTAINS

TIHAMA
COASTAL
PLAIN

Yenbo
al Nakl

Old Yenbo

Yenbo New Town

Mangroves and
Coral reefs

**CJ'S NEW
LANDSCAPE**

Yenbo New Town:
40°Centigrade,
salty sea,
sandy plains and
red ochre mountains.
Plants?
...mangroves and
coral reefs.

RED SEA

15 kilometers

N

When Kurt, as CJ's executor, took possession of CJ's diaries and design journals, he found six years of diaries, a dozen of them, all handwritten; but the design journals, there were several in A4 size hardcover, looseleaf ring binders. They were filled with hard copy computer print-outs. Kurt found more--plastic sleeves holding memory cards and thumb drives with all of CJ's Saudi Arabian landscape photos.

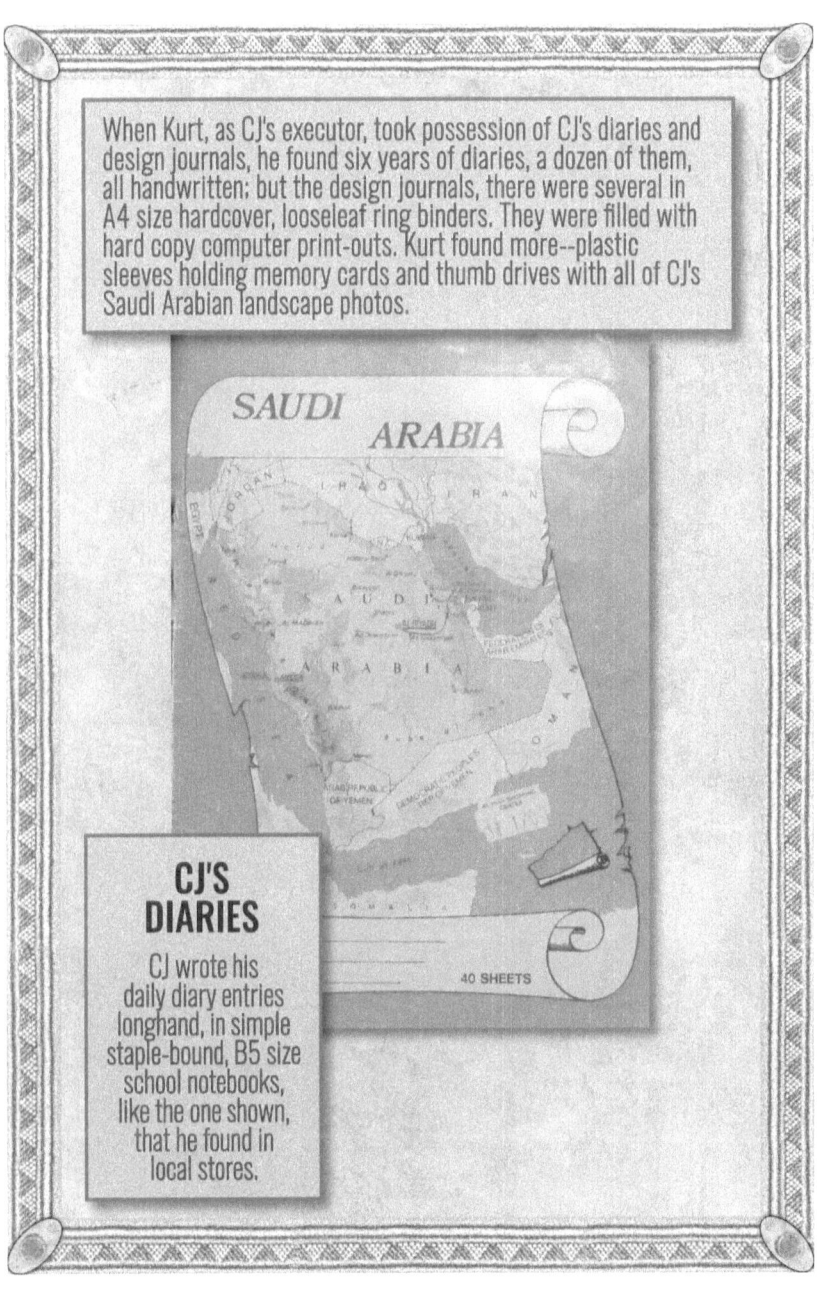

CJ'S DIARIES

CJ wrote his daily diary entries longhand, in simple staple-bound, B5 size school notebooks, like the one shown, that he found in local stores.

This qsar had a rare natural ground water source. It was an oasis that had to be defended. Date palms grew and prospered. So did people. Got it? Water, plants, food, people.

In the Western Region of Saudi Arabia, where CJ worked, there were very few oases.

Between his new home in Yenbo and Jeddah there was: Red Sea, Tihama coastal plain, Hijaz mountains and the Tropic of Cancer.

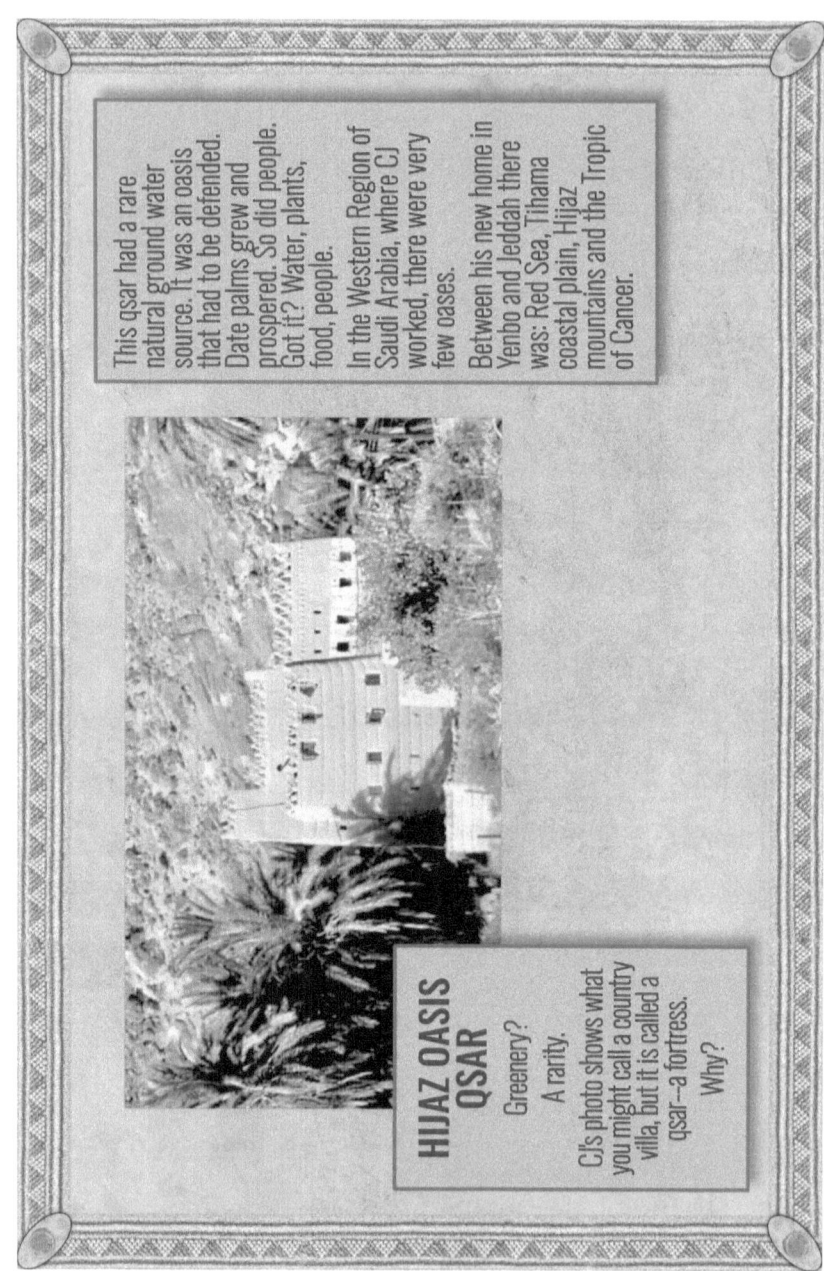

HIJAZ OASIS QSAR

Greenery?

A rarity.

CJ's photo shows what you might call a country villa, but it is called a qsar--a fortress.

Why?

...now it's 4WD Toyota pickups. Essential because unpredictable local and regional rains that produce a rush of annuals and other tender juicy plant ephemerals require relocation.

CJ noted that during 4 straight years in Yenbo there was not a drop of rain. Definitely unpredictable.

The Bedouin Toyotas chase the rain.

HIJAZ BEDOUIN TODAY

Between Yenbo & Jeddah, CJ found these 20th century Bedouin with their flocks of sheep, traveling no longer with camels...

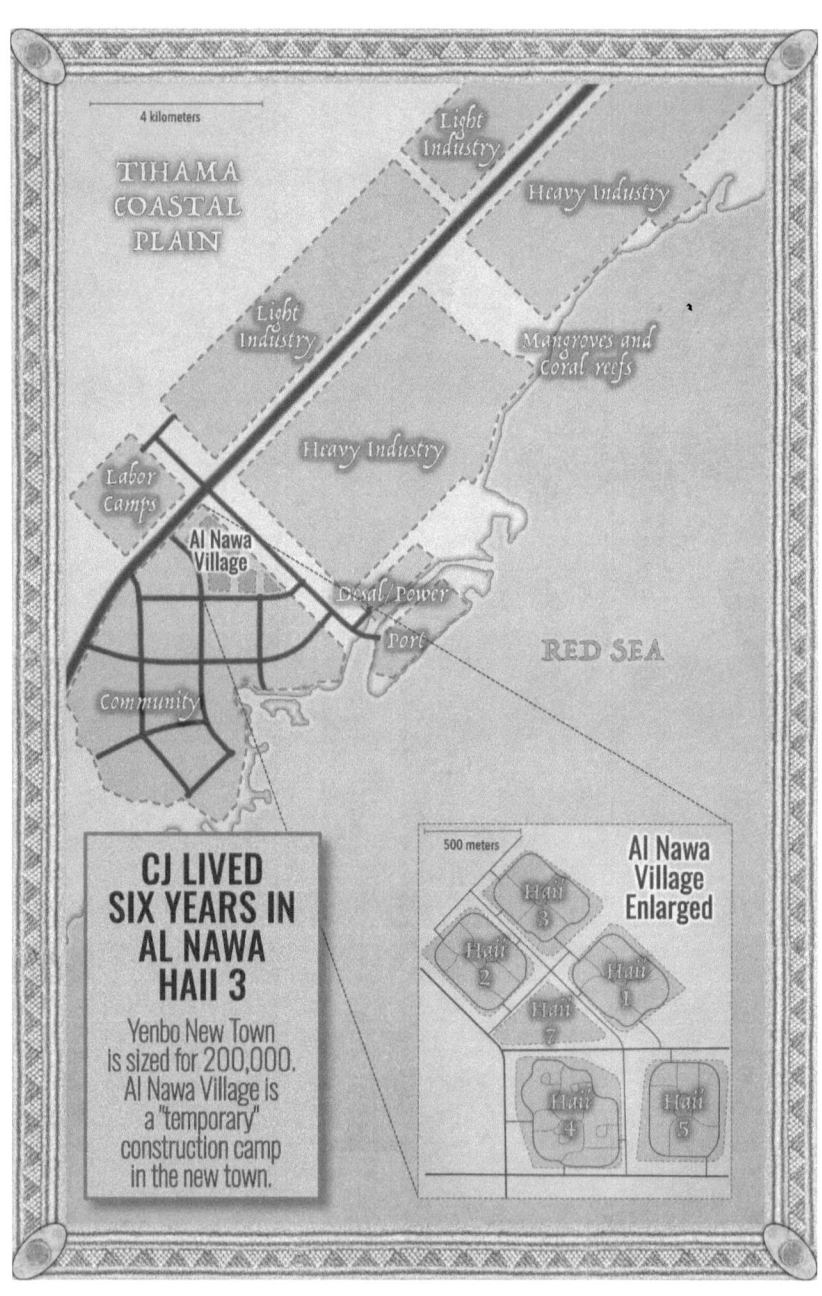

4 kilometers

TIHAMA
COASTAL
PLAIN

Light Industry

Heavy Industry

Light Industry

Mangroves and Coral reefs

Heavy Industry

Labor Camps

Al Nawa Village

Desal Power

Port

RED SEA

Community

CJ LIVED SIX YEARS IN AL NAWA HAII 3

Yenbo New Town is sized for 200,000. Al Nawa Village is a "temporary" construction camp in the new town.

500 meters

Al Nawa Village Enlarged

Haii 3

Haii 2

Haii 1

Haii 7

Haii 4

Haii 5

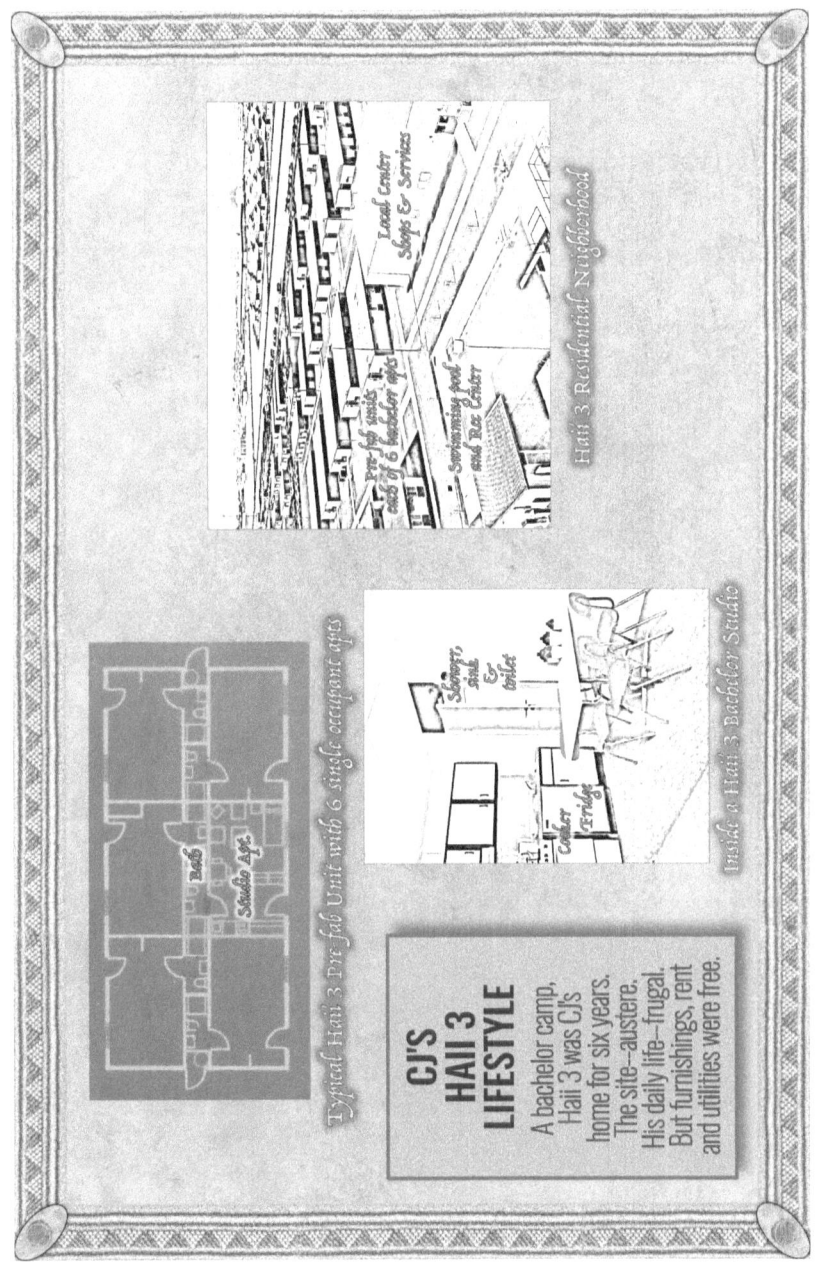

Haii 3 Residential Neighborhood

Land Center
Shops & Services

Pre fab units
each of 6 bachelor apts

swimming pool
and Rec Center

Typical Haii 3 Pre fab Unit with 6 single occupant apts

Bath

Studio Apts

Inside a Haii 3 Bachelor Studio

Shower, sink
& toilet

Cooker

Fridge

CJ'S
HAII 3
LIFESTYLE

A bachelor camp,
Haii 3 was CJ's
home for six years.
The site—austere,
His daily life—frugal.
But furnishings, rent
and utilities were free.

Bertram took CJ to the Madain Saleh sites; but it was JeanClaude who spoke to CJ of deeper pre-Islamic stories embedded in the sands—the Emerald Tablet, the Lazarus oases and the Djinns.

CJ weighed this desert sands info against what he had experienced years ago in north west Africa including Bree's tales of the Sahara.

CJ concludes the desert landscape hides ancient human civilization mysteries and that intrigued him.

Jordan

Kingdom of Saudi Arabia

ARABIAN SANDS FINDINGS

Carved from stone, these are landscape-driven modifications. In the KSA, CJ visited Madain Saleh, very much like Petra in Jordan.

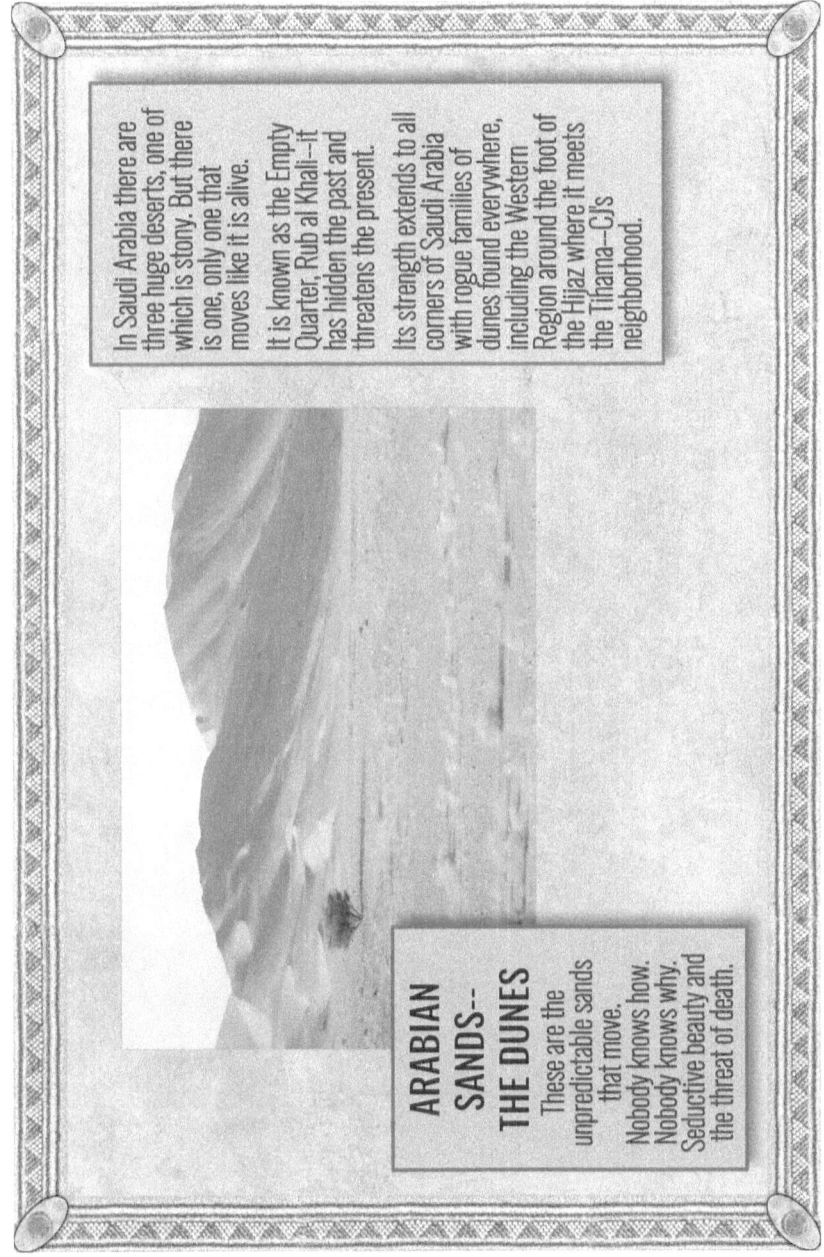

In Saudi Arabia there are three huge deserts, one of which is story. But there is one, only one that moves like it is alive.

It is known as the Empty Quarter, Rub al Khali--it has hidden the past and threatens the present.

Its strength extends to all corners of Saudi Arabia with rogue families of dunes found everywhere, including the Western Region around the foot of the Hijaz where it meets the Tihama--CJ's neighborhood.

ARABIAN SANDS-- THE DUNES

These are the unpredictable sands that move. Nobody knows how. Nobody knows why. Seductive beauty and the threat of death.

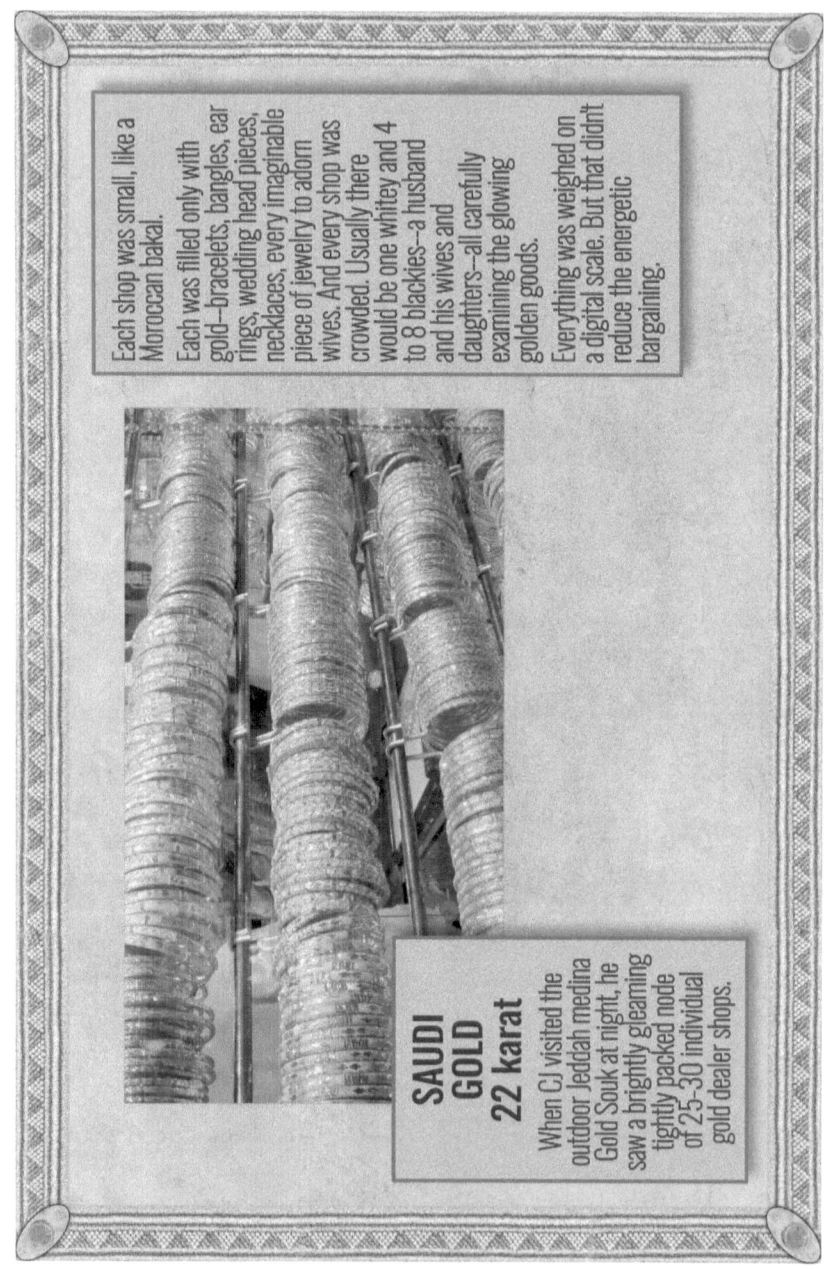

Each shop was small, like a Moroccan bakal.

Each was filled only with gold—bracelets, bangles, ear rings, wedding head pieces, necklaces, every imaginable piece of jewelry to adorn wives. And every shop was crowded. Usually there would be one whitey and 4 to 8 blackies—a husband and his wives and daughters—all carefully examining the glowing golden goods.

Everything was weighed on a digital scale. But that didn't reduce the energetic bargaining.

SAUDI GOLD 22 karat

When CJ visited the outdoor Jeddah medina Gold Souk at night, he saw a brightly gleaming tightly packed node of 25-30 individual gold dealer shops.

Unusual and shocking events caused CJ's departure from Saudi Arabia.

But in New Yenbo, he had achieved successes in the planning, design, construction and maintenance of a greenway network connecting to all community centers and the greenbelt.

The quick results were due to fast-track programs, sub-tropical growth rates for the plants and the richly fertile treated sewage effluent irrigation water.

SHADED GREENWAYS IN NEW YENBO

After 6 years of hard work, CJ saw results in the permanent community.

Vedic roots, Chinese roots, the Golden Triangle, indigenous hill tribes, Kung Sa, Papaver somniferum... there is nothing simple about Thailand. But it was more about CJ's long forgotten portals.

Ban Muang

Chiang Rai

LAOS

BURMA

THAILAND

KAYTEE QUEST

Bangkok undid CJ. He sought solace in Ban Muang, northern Thailand.

Bangkok

"The Landscape Architect" Series

In this Book 3, *Yenbo Palms*, we learn how CJ built his landscape architecture professional career first in a small office then, after becoming professionally licensed, in a design/build/ maintain firm. But his personal life exploded on him. He was devastated by the loss of his wife and three young kids in an horrendous automobile accident. It hurt so deeply. He tried to hide from it. His career path changed; but the personal hurt didn't.

The Landscape Architect series is about CJ, Christopher Janus. He wrote it all. The six stories are his collected memoirs. He was into asking questions, discovering and writing. And above all he was a landscape architect deeply intrigued by foreign cultures, landscape and design. The six stories track the arc of his beginning interest in landscape architecture followed by his growth in the profession.

Who is CJ? CJ is an American, born in the Midwest, raised in New Mexico—a hard worker who found his muse in the landscape. At university in the late 1990s, he grew to embrace landscape, literature and all the fine arts with humanitarian, environmental and spiritual sensibilities. He became a landscape architect and despite his heart-felt attraction to the New Mexico landscape—inspired by the works of Ansel Adams, Georgia O'Keeffe, and the writings of JB Jackson—he travelled the world because, like it or not, life had its own plan for him. CJ's personal life and professional landscape architecture career are woven through with drama in landscape, foreign culture and design—all presenting him with unrelenting dilemmas.

The series reveals the twists and turns in his professional

landscape architecture development. But the series explores further. CJ, drawing upon his fine arts history, becomes obsessed with experiences in nature and the landscape beyond the five senses. Beyond the five senses? The paranormal? He recognizes his limits yet always strives to achieve more.

CJ chases nature, its landscape and plants to their existential roots. He describes his interactions with cultures, landscapes, gardens and plants of the world—where the unexpected and downright strange become daily facts of life.

CJ, like his landscape architecture profession and its practitioners, obsesses over design. In one of the major themes in the series, he tries to get to the root of the gossamer, ever-evolving landscape design theory. Unique in this series, CJ, not a tourist, uses his expatriate life across the Middle East, North Africa and Europe, attempting to weave the threads of his foreign landscape and cultural experiences into a pragmatic design theory.

Throughout his adventures and to his surprise, he discovers, on the good days, not the normal landscape architecture world, rather an enlightening and exciting ethnobotanical world influenced by the likes of Lord Byron, HG Wells, Algernon Blackwood and Rod Serling. And then there are the "not-so-good" days... strange cultures and even stranger landscapes.

Previously in Book 2, *Curious Tales,* CJ, as a student in his term abroad design study final submission, responds to the unusual Moroccan landscape and culture he encountered in northwest Africa by writing a short story collection.

In Book 4, *Crystal Vision,* CJ is in Zurich, the Jungfrau Region of the Swiss Alps and on his way to Cairo. He has to make lemonade out of lemons—lost wife and three young children, lost friend, lost job, lost hope.

First edition 2025

Final illustrations and cover art by copyright owner.

Edited and formatted by Lin White, Coinlea Services,
http://www.coinlea.co.uk

ISBN: 979-8-9851600-5-5

Published by copyright owner
https://flahertylandscape.com

Acknowledgements

All illustrations prepared by the author. Base photos by the author.

Base maps from 2022 Google Earth: https://earth.google.

Illustration frame base images taken from *Traditional Crafts of Saudi Arabia*, John Topham, Stacey International, 1981, and post-processed by the author.

The following illustrations base images have been provided in 2024 as listed below:

Illustration: 9-Arabian Sands Findings Petra image from Quiltripping:

https://quiltripping.com/ancient-petra-pictures/ .

Illustration 9-Arabian Sands Findings Madain Saleh image from Alma de Luce:

https://www.almadeluce.com/memory/al-hijr-place-collection/ .

Illustration 10-Arabian Sands—The Dunes from One Earth:

https://www.oneearth.org/ecoregions/arabian-sand-desert/.

Colophon

Books are crafted. Colophons are the end credits of literature.

Books have a typographical tradition that to this author go nearly as deep into human culture as does the landscape.

Baskerville and Skia are the primary manuscript typefaces—cleanly bringing the Arabic heart to the West—that is how the author thinks of it. These typefaces are for simplicity, clarity and ease of reading—things that CJ could never find in his Arabian Peninsula landscape experiences.

Ends of chapters are indicated by the author's line drawings of a typical Tihama Red Sea dhow.

Cover Art

On this book cover you will find the following cultural clues as found by CJ in the Arabian Peninsula:

1. There is fruit from *Phoenix dactylifera*, the date palm—the dates, fronds and trunks of which form the ethnobotanical basis of the Arab desert lifestyle—their cultural bloodstream;

2. There are geometric design patterns often found in cloth (tents, carpets and bags) and jewellery (silver, white metal and semiprecious stones) all found throughout the Arabian landscape;

3. There is the unmistakable clarity in a public culture of black—the dress of women and white—the dress of men; and,

4. There are the two crossed scimitars and above them the date palm—justice, strength rooted in faith, vitality and growth—the Kingdom of Saudi Arabia's coat of arms.

All were daily influences in Christopher Janus' life while he was designing, building and maintaining the landscaping in Yenbo New Town, on the Red Sea coast in the Kingdom of Saudi Arabia.

Dedication

Dedicated first of all to my wife, her photographs, support and understanding. Then to everyone who has interest in landscape, culture or the profession of landscape architecture.

About the Author

An international award winner and frequently invited conference speaker, Edward Flaherty practiced landscape architecture over the past five decades on very large projects where he has lived as an expatriate in Africa, Europe and Asia.

In the Kingdom of Saudi Arabia, he made his home with his family for years in Madinat Yanbu Al Sinaiyah.

Professional details at LinkedIn, https://ch.linkedin.com/in/edflaherty1

Discussion Guide for Yenbo Palms

As I wrote this story, a couple big picture items kept me busy. I never fully resolved them, so I ask you, the readers, to discuss them and share your thoughts with me by commenting on my blog via this link: flahertylandscape.com.

1. Does human culture relate to the landscape? If so, then how?

2. What is the power in plants, gardens and landscape that induces peace in humans?

3. How do human cultures change? How do ecotypes in nature change? What happens at the edges of adjacent ecotypes and the edges of adjacent human cultures?

I look forward to hearing from you. Thank you.

Call to Action

Yenbo Palms is the third book in the fictional autobiographical series, "The Landscape Architect". In the series, CJ tracks the intriguing events he experienced in his personal and expatriate professional career in landscape architecture amid the strange cultures and even stranger landscapes of Europe, the Middle East and North Africa.

If you enjoyed reading about CJ's *Yenbo Palms* personal hardships, his landscape architecture career growth in the USA, his six years in the Kingdom of Saudi Arabia and his quest for Kaytee which took him to Thailand and Switzerland, then please write a short review and share it on my blog flahertylandscape.com.

You might also enjoy reading my first and second books, *Tangier Gardens* and *Curious Tales*, about CJ's peculiar personal and professional adventures in Morocco, the northwest Africa landscape.